ALSO BY KAMILLA BENKO

The Unicorn Quest
Secret in the Stone
Fire in the Star

∽o∽

Frozen II: Forest of Shadows

THE UNICORN LEGACY
Tangled Magic

KAMILLA BENKO

BLOOMSBURY
CHILDREN'S BOOKS
NEW YORK LONDON OXFORD NEW DELHI SYDNEY

BLOOMSBURY CHILDREN'S BOOKS
Bloomsbury Publishing Inc., part of Bloomsbury Publishing Plc
1385 Broadway, New York, NY 10018

BLOOMSBURY, BLOOMSBURY CHILDREN'S BOOKS, and the Diana logo
are trademarks of Bloomsbury Publishing Plc

First published in the United States of America in February 2024
by Bloomsbury Children's Books

Text copyright © 2024 by Kamilla Benko
Illustrations copyright © 2024 by Maxine Vee

All rights reserved. No part of this publication may be reproduced or transmitted in any form or by any means, electronic or mechanical, including photocopying, recording, or any information storage or retrieval system, without prior permission in writing from the publisher.

Bloomsbury books may be purchased for business or promotional use. For information on bulk purchases please contact Macmillan Corporate and Premium Sales Department at specialmarkets@macmillan.com

Library of Congress Cataloging-in-Publication Data
Names: Benko, Kamilla, author.
Title: The unicorn legacy : tangled magic / by Kamilla Benko.
Description: New York : Bloomsbury, 2024.
Summary: Olivia Hayes is excited to finally unlock her magic and attend the new Unicorn Academy, but quickly finds herself caught between embracing her magical abilities, clearing her sister's name of unicorn poaching, and unraveling dark secrets to protect the unicorns and Arden's future.
Identifiers: LCCN 2023037774 (print) | LCCN 2023037775 (e-book)
ISBN 978-1-5476-0882-9 (hardcover) • ISBN 978-1-5476-0883-6 (e-book)
Subjects: CYAC: Fantasy. | Siblings—Fiction. | Magic—Fiction. | Schools—Fiction. | Unicorns—Fiction. | LCGFT: Fantasy fiction. | Novels.
Classification: LCC PZ7.1.B4537 Um 2024 (print) | LCC PZ7.1.B4537 (e-book)
LC record available at https://lccn.loc.gov/2023037774

Book design by John Candell
Typeset by Westchester Publishing Services
Printed and bound in the U.S.A.
2 4 6 8 10 9 7 5 3 1

To find out more about our authors and books visit www.bloomsbury.com
and sign up for our newsletters.

For Jelena,

I've loved your story since the very first page.

THE UNICORN LEGACY
Tangled Magic

PROLOGUE

In the Valley of Wishes, a unicorn stood guard.

She arched her neck against the night, her eyes watchful as they settled on the sleeping herd below. Her kin slept in clusters, their luminous coats and radiant horns throwing silver shadows on the ground, enchanting everything in a hazy glow. A late-summer breeze whispered by, and a sneeze popped from somewhere in the dark: *Achoo!*

Amusement flickered through the unicorn. The wind had loosed dandelion puffs into the air, and one had landed on a sleeping foal, tickling its velvety nose. Closing her eyes, the unicorn breathed in the sweet smell of family, home, and moonlight.

All was calm in the land of Arden. All was right.

And yet.

The unicorn flicked an ear back.

She could make out the bubbling of the subterranean

rivers flowing miles beneath her hooves, the creaking of ships in a far-off sea, and a dragonfly's feet alighting upon a lily pad. Opening her eyes, the unicorn tilted her head up and strained her ears to hear the stars. For a few seconds more, nothing, but then, finally, faintly, there it was: starsong.

But it was so very, very quiet tonight. Usually, the stars sounded clear as a waterfall.

The unicorn shook her head, her white mane flying.

Closer. She needed to get closer if she were to have any chance of receiving the stars' message. With one last look at her slumbering herd, the unicorn turned and galloped up the mountain.

Her hooves nimbly threaded the hazardous trails. Root and rock were as much a part of her as the glimmer of gold or silk's softness. No matter where she went, the unicorn was always aware of the brimming potential—or magic, as some called it—that filled the world. And as a creature of *pure* magic, the unicorn leaned on the potential around her to orient herself, ensuring she could never slip. But then—

Her hoof caught.

Quick as lightning, the unicorn righted herself, but she paused in her gallop. Nothing could impede a unicorn, but *something* had. What had she missed?

Swinging around, the unicorn warily considered the path. It looked normal, but she knew the eye could be deceived.

Carefully, the unicorn lowered her spiraling horn to nudge

the rocky trail. She sensed Arden's magic swell in response. Snowdrops sprouted, leafed, and bloomed white petals within seconds. *Beautiful. Spectacular.* She shifted, her horn still touching the ground.

A mistake.

The unicorn reared back.

Where magic should have been, there was . . . nothing.

No, not nothing—an *absence*. A nothingness only noticeable by what was left behind, like a tear in a cloak. Only this was a tear in the fabric of the *earth*. A *rip* in the world.

The unicorn's hooves slammed back onto the ground, and she felt the sliver that had been wrung out, drained of all its potential and possibilities, and left empty.

Empty, like the space between stars. A place where not even sound could exist . . . which might have been why she almost missed the stomp of boots behind her.

The unicorn reared again as a rope whistled through the dark.

PART I

Tiller, Tiller, caterpillar
How does your garden grow?
With silver thorns and unicorns
And a snake in the grass below
And a snake in the grass below.

—Mother Spruce's Nursery Rhymes

CHAPTER ONE

Olivia Hayes didn't mean to turn the mayor into a mushroom.

It had happened the same way "just one more page" could turn into ten chapters or "five more minutes" into an extra hour of sleep. One second, she'd been standing behind the apothecary counter, watching Mayor Oakley sip from a vial labeled *Cap of Curls*, and in the next, there was a tinkle of glass hitting the floor and she was staring at the tallest, wrinkliest mushroom she'd ever seen.

And while the mushroom was very much a mushroom—complete with red cap, accordion gills, and a cream-colored stalk—it was also very clearly Mayor Oakley. The fungus hunched forward like the grumpy old man, and though there was no face, right at the level where Mayor Oakley's chin mole would have been was a small brown bump.

"Aphids!" Olivia swore as she darted around the table and

scanned the wooden floor. "Just a second, sir! I can fix this, but I need—there!" Under a shelf of potted ferns and between two dust bunnies, she'd spotted a dull sparkle. Flinging herself to the floor, she squeezed her hand under. The tips of her two auburn braids swept the dusty planks as she frantically felt around. Her fingers grazed something smooth and cold.

"Got it!" Pulling out the tiny glass bottle, she sat back on her knees. "Don't worry, Mayor Oakley," she told the mushroom as comfortingly as she could. "It must have been an expired bottle or something. The effect should wear off in sec—oh."

Olivia's stomach dropped as she smoothed the crumpled label. It did not, in fact, say *Cap of Curls*. Instead, it read *Cap of Mushrooms*. She bit her lip. How had she given him the wrong vial? But deep down, she already knew the answer. Her eyes flicked to the open book now lying abandoned on the shop counter.

Ten times that morning, Nan had gone over which package belonged to which customer, and ten times, Olivia had nodded, saying *yes, yes, she understood*.

And she had. Really.

Because Olivia knew she needed to take every chance to prove to Nan she could be useful, too, despite her . . . her *unusualness*.

Olivia looked like a perfectly average twelve-year-old. She was exactly four feet, seven inches tall, with two hazel eyes and hair that wasn't quite red or quite brown, and she had the expected number of fingers and toes. She could name the first king of Arden (Anders the Great), and if someone asked her what twelve times thirteen was, she could probably answer it correctly within two tries (answer: 156). She was as normal as normal could be—except she did not have magic.

And in Buddle, the northernmost hamlet in the land of Arden, that was *most* unusual.

Everyone who had ever been born in the tiny settlement squashed between the Endless Forest and Verglas Sea was a member of the Tiller Guild, a network of people who could coax magic from plants. In Buddle, it wasn't strange to see a thousand-foot-high beanstalk spring up overnight or to hear of someone inheriting a wooden spoon that could turn water into a hearty stew with a couple stirs. And if you visited a friend for lunch, you had to be extra careful when accepting a steaming cup, in case it contained Sinceri Tea, which would render the drinker uncomfortably truthful for the next hour.

There were other guilds in Arden, and though Olivia had never met anyone who wasn't a Tiller, she collected rumors about the others the same way a squirrel hoards acorns. Gemmers decorated their marble hallways with glowing jewels, while Spinners knotted nets that could catch both fish and good fortune. The fourth and final magical guild was the Forger Guild, whose members could spot the potential in a nugget of silver and hammer it into a mirror so smooth that it could reflect the future.

When she was younger, Olivia had dreamed of using a Forger's mirror to discover the exact moment when she would become a proper Tiller—that moment when she, too, would be able to call on plants' potential to create something magical. But as days turned into years, and as the other children in Buddle accidentally made chairs bloom or turned pumpkins into coaches, it was all Olivia could do to keep Nan's green beans alive.

Still, that didn't mean she was useless. Even though she couldn't help Nan and her older sister, Laurel, with anything magical—couldn't cultivate Rising Yeast that made heavy objects float; couldn't brew sap into Instant Bone Glue—she could use her slingshot to scare crows away from the garden, and she could heat up Nan's water bottle. And she could tell stories.

Olivia *loved* stories.

Which, unfortunately, was why Mayor Oakley was now a towering toadstool in Nan's shop.

Because while Olivia had told Nan she was paying attention, she was really only half paying attention. The other half was still somewhere in the pages of *The Wayward Wyvern*. Mayor Oakley had entered the shop at the exact moment when Sir Pod and Lady Sod were galloping into the Carnivorous Caverns. Olivia had been in such a hurry to return to the stalagmite fangs that she hadn't double-checked the bottle's tag before handing Mayor Oakley his order. And now . . .

Olivia shoved the empty vial into her dress pocket and scrambled to her feet. Pasting on what she hoped was a comforting smile, she turned to the mushroom. "Mayor Oakley, I'm afraid there's been a bit of a"—she waved her hand about—"complication."

It wasn't exactly the right word, because if she didn't fix this before Nan got home, there would be more than just a "complication." There would be a murder.

Her murder.

Marguerite Hayes, the most talented physician this side of the Rhona and renowned for her botanicals and cures, was not someone you *ever* wanted to disappoint.

"The good news," Olivia said, forcing cheer into her voice as she ran behind the counter and began to fling drawers open, "is that your spots are the *loveliest* ones I've ever seen on a mushroom. *Very* symmetrical."

The first drawer contained empty bottles and jars. The second held only seed packets. Olivia slammed both shut and reached for the third. It was locked. Luckily, Laurel had prepared her for just such an occasion. At the time, Olivia had been annoyed her older sister thought she would need the help, but now she was grateful for Laurel's foresight.

"The even better news," Olivia called as she grabbed a fern frond, "is that Nan keeps her Ambrosia right here."

And Nan's Ambrosia, Olivia didn't need to explain to Mayor Oakley, could cure anything. The secret recipe had been passed down through the Hayes family for centuries, and one day, Laurel and Olivia would learn it, too, but not before they became Master Tillers. Using the fern's leaf, Olivia tickled the drawer's joints. A moment later, there was a loud *creeeeeak* as the drawer fell open, and then Olivia's mouth fell open, too.

Treasure.

The locked drawer was filled with *treasure*.

Not jewels and coins, though there was some of that, but ordinary household objects that had been marked as extraordinary by a guild's mark.

Olivia shifted a garden boot with a Spinner's love knot embroidered on the heel, then picked up a clay chalice with a Gemmer's jewel stamped on the bottom.

When had Nan collected all these non-Tiller things?

She set the chalice down and examined a packet of nails with a Forger's hammer etched on the heads. Up until recently, it had been *illegal* to trade outside of one's own guild or mix magics at all—and for good reason.

For centuries, the guilds had lived together in the kingdom of Arden, but then war erupted. During the Guild War, each guild did terrible things—*crafted* terrible things. Gemmers transformed an entire forest into stone, while Tillers and Forgers exacted their revenge by jumbling green life and copper to create chimera, their brutal war mounts.

As the fighting dragged on, and mothers and fathers and sisters and brothers died on the battlefield, desperation rooted in Arden. Hoping to save themselves, citizens began to slaughter unicorns, wrongly believing that if they did, they would become immortal. By the time the war ended, the unicorns of Arden were no more—hunted to extinction all because of a lie. The only evidence that the once-glorious creatures had existed were the artifacts that had been hewn from their bones, their teeth, and their hides.

When the guilds finally gathered to sign the treaty and face a world without unicorns, the leaders agreed it was in the interest of all that the guilds stay apart. No communication meant no more bloody misunderstandings. No jumbling of magic meant no more monstrous creations. The great alchemist libraries of jumbled magic were burned to the ground, and laws were imposed, with harsh consequences for even the smallest infraction.

And it had worked—until four years ago, when word had come from the south: war loomed again. Nan and Laurel spent that winter doubling their healing botanicals, while an eight-year-old Olivia had practiced her sling and slingshot skills, just in case. But with that spring came warm weather and the news that a second guild war had been averted. The guilds reunited under the Prime Minister, and unicorns—*unicorns!*—had returned to Arden.

Since then, the Prime Minister had worked hard to rebuild the relationships between guilds, releasing alchemists who had been jailed for jumbling magics, and opening long-abandoned trade routes. So, while a drawer of magical craft from all the guilds was no longer illegal, it must have taken Nan much longer than four years to build such a collection.

Olivia wondered if Nan could have been the leader of an underground market, but as soon as she had the thought, she tossed it out. Nan would never break the rules—especially rules she fervently believed in. Just last night, Nan had grumped how her Moss-Aids had become practically unsellable now that most people preferred the fancy silk bandages the Spinners sold.

Olivia set the nails aside. She would have to ask Nan later, after she'd fixed her terrible, mushroom-y mistake.

Riffling through the drawer, she found bits of string, pewter scales, an alabaster box, and a scroll with brass handles, but no Ambrosia. Staring at the empty corners, Olivia's stomach flipped. There was nothing to do now but accept her tragic fate: she, Olivia Hayes, would have to get Nan.

"I'm going to town," Olivia informed the mayor as she threw everything back into the third drawer and pushed it shut. Or at least, she tried to. A scroll handle stuck out, and no matter how many times Olivia adjusted it, the scroll refused to fit, as though it had grown in the last few seconds. Fine. Olivia jammed the scroll through her belt loop and stood up.

She would deal with it later, too.

"Stay put!" she called to the mushroom, and then winced. "I mean, I know you don't really have a choice—you don't have any feet!—but . . . goodbye!" She bobbed a curtsy and raced out of the shop.

Olivia's braids thumped against her back as she jogged past the fishpond and Nan's prize beehives toward the dirt road that led to Buddle's center. Usually, she enjoyed walking through Nan's gardens, but today Olivia didn't need inspiration. She needed speed. Veering left, she headed toward the vegetable bed that would get her to the road in half the time. Reaching the fence, she hopped over and dropped into—

—a mess. No. A *massacre*.

Olivia gaped. Bits of cabbage leaves, tomato juice, and pumpkin pulp lay about like confetti. The basil had been completely devoured, and the sweet peas had been mashed into paste. But that's not what stopped Olivia in her tracks.

In the center of the mess was a single hoofprint.

It wasn't the smooth U of horseshoes so often stamped into the dirt road. This print looked more like quotation marks, with two little tips and teardrop bottoms. Too large to be a goat. A stag, maybe? Or . . .

Olivia took a deep breath as something prickled at the back of her neck. She straightened and scanned the fields, searching.

There! Where the garden brushed against the Endless Forest: a shiver of movement. She was too far away to see it clearly, but as Olivia stared at the spot, she thought she could see the outline of something with four long legs. Something that shimmered against the black velvet of the trees.

Something like a star.

Something like . . .

. . . a unicorn.

CHAPTER TWO

The unicorn was exactly what Olivia had imagined, but at the same time so much more. As white as a storybook page, and as perfect as a tale not yet told.

Regal.

Magnificent.

Glorious.

Gone.

"Wait!" Olivia shouted as her feet pounded across the garden. She wasn't sure when she'd started running. Her feet had made the decision for her while her mind whirled with possibilities. Tillers, Forgers, Gemmers, and Spinners could call magic from the material, but unicorns—they were *pure* magic. They made all guild magic stronger, shinier, and—some historians claimed—even to exist.

If unicorns could forge mountains from stars and spin diamonds into streams, they could *definitely* transform Mayor

Oakley from a grumpy-looking toadstool into an actually grumpy man . . .

. . . a unicorn could turn Nan's inevitable scolding into an *I'm so proud of you.*

. . . a unicorn could grant Olivia's most desperate wish.

Magic.

Olivia hiked her green skirts over her knees and pumped her legs. Her braids bounced down her back, urging her forward. Then she was at the edge of the Endless. Ribs heaving, heart racing, she skidded to a stop.

The Endless Forest was as its name said: its size was unknown, like the ocean, and like the ocean, mysteries lurked in its depths. She wasn't supposed to enter the forest by herself, not until her Tiller talents budded, but that rule had never mattered much before, because Laurel had always been willing to go whenever Olivia asked.

Olivia bit her lip. Not for the first time, she wished her older sister still lived in Buddle. But last year, Laurel had turned fifteen and left to continue her magical education as a journeyman, traveling across Arden and learning new healing methods in preparation for her trials two years from now, when she would become a Master physician and take over Nan's shop.

When Laurel first left, she'd sent letters every day, long chatty missives describing the villages she'd seen—Bloomsbury's libraries, the gold smithies of Overgilt, the bustling ports dotting the Sparkling Sea. Often she'd include a dried flower or two, which Olivia would carefully pin to the map hung on the underside of Laurel's upper bunk. The flowers made a whale-ish shape across Arden, and every night Olivia would fall asleep wondering where Laurel would be next.

But as the months passed, the letters slowed and the few that did arrive were brief.

Miss you! Remind me to tell you about Fyrton's gargoyles when I come back. Library's gorgeous! xL

Hand hurts from digging. Moss flower specimen from Foggy Bottom. xL

The last letter had been posted from Springmill, a tiny settlement at the foot of Constellation Range. That message had simply said, *Unicorns!!!!*

"She's focused," Nan would say when Olivia complained that Laurel had forgotten them. "The less time she spends writing, the more time she has to learn. Something that maybe you, Miss Chatty Chin, should take note of."

Olivia didn't think she talked *that* much. But since she lacked magic, she knew she had to be a little bit louder to be heard. Try a little bit harder to be seen. Take a few more risks.

Olivia plunged into the Endless.

The change from field to forest was immediate. Green shadows replaced orderly crops, and the thick curtain of trees muffled any outside sound. Olivia spun, trying to spot a bright white flank against bark or a flash of unicorn mane. But the closest thing she could see to flowing unicorn hair were the long-leafed ferns that hugged the ground.

"Hello?" she called. "Unicorn—are you there?"

The vast and hungry forest swallowed her question. It was as if the trees had eaten the unicorn—and might consume her next. If only she could see over the thick brush of late summer, she might be able to spot a unicorn.

Bending over, Olivia knotted her skirts into makeshift trousers, then swung herself up onto the lowest branch of a maple. ("When in doubt, trust the maple," Laurel had told her. "Their personalities are as sweet as their sap.") As she pulled herself up from branch to branch, Olivia tried to recall anything she'd read that might help her locate the unicorn.

Unicorn facts—there were only a few that every guild knew to be true: Unicorns were pure magic. They could open any door. Olivia also knew that snowdrops bloomed in their steps and that—

Olivia's boot slipped. Chunks of bark pattered as she scrambled. She regained her footing, but the sense of falling didn't go away.

Snowdrops.

How had she forgotten? Wherever a unicorn walked, the first flower of spring would appear . . . but there had been no snowdrops in the mess of Nan's garden.

Which meant that there had *never* been a unicorn in Nan's garden.

Olivia's imagination had oversprouted—again.

Groaning, Olivia leaned her forehead against the maple's trunk. The wind blew and twigs rasped against each other, a sound like secrets being whispered. Secrets she would never understand. For one second, Olivia had thought she'd been on the edge of something *big*, of her own *Story*, but no. Her future would forever only be on the edge of the Tiller hamlet, doomed to be the lackie who had turned the mayor temporarily into a mushroom.

At least, she hoped it was temporary.

Gripping the limb, Olivia tried to swing down, but something yanked her waist. Twisting to look, she saw that Nan's scroll, which she'd so hastily tucked through her belt, had shifted, both catching on the Y of a branch and anchoring Olivia in place.

"Aphiiiiiids," Olivia moaned. Reaching back, she tried to wiggle the scroll and herself free. Strangely, the scroll felt bulkier than it had earlier that afternoon, and longer. Much longer. She was pretty sure it had only been about ten inches long, but now it seemed to have doubled in length. With a final grunt, Olivia pulled the scroll free.

The scroll had *definitely* grown—it was now nearly as long as her forearm, and a label that had been tucked inside fluttered free:

THE UNICORN ACADEMY
OF ARTISTICAL AND MAGICAL LEARNING

Olivia frowned. She'd never heard of the Unicorn Academy. She flipped the tag over, and her heart stopped. Because on the other side of the label, someone had written a name. Not just any name. *Her* name.

Olivia Gladiola Hayes

Without thinking, Olivia cracked the seal.

After all, Olivia had never met a scroll she hadn't unrolled, and a scroll she'd found in a drawer of forbidden objects—a scroll with *her* name on it—was definitely *not* going to be the exception.

Unfurling the parchment a few inches revealed a gold-embossed unicorn, its spiraling horn pointing to four oddly shaped stars. Olivia squinted and realized they weren't stars at all, but tiny images of a hammer, a leaf, a gemstone, and a love knot. A few more inches of scroll revealed spiky handwriting in indigo ink:

THE UNICORN ACADEMY
OF ARTISTICAL AND MAGICAL LEARNING
Inspiration. Dedication. Courage.
1 Anders's Tear, Lumin City, Republic of Arden

The Right Honorable Prime Minister and Grand Council of Arden are pleased to announce the opening of the first all-guild school. The Unicorn Academy of Artistical and Magical Learning shall provide the highest quality of instruction led by the most talented and innovative artisans from across the land.

Olivia's eyebrows raised. An interguild school! No wonder Nan hadn't shown it to Olivia. She generally disapproved of the Prime Minister and her initiatives. But Olivia wondered why Nan had bothered to hide it from her in the first place. After all, Olivia couldn't go.

Not when she lacked magic.

Her heart pinched. Maybe that was the reason. Her grandmother had known it would hurt to see yet one more thing she could not do. Still, Olivia couldn't help herself. She read on:

Apprentices shall train in their respective crafts in addition to attending all-school assemblies with such topics including but not limited to:
- *Enchantment and Enchant-can't: The Magic of Positive Thinking*
- *First Aid for Accidents, Illness, and Magical Mishaps*
- *Craft or Crafty: How to Spot a Cursed Object*

On the back, please find eligibility requirements, rules,

and necessary supplies lists. Classes shall commence at noon on the first day of Ninthmonth. Be aware that apprentices are expected to arrive at 1 Anders's Tear by midnight. If not, they will forfeit their seat and their right to learn at the academy.

Yours most sincerely,
Aquila Malchain
Aquila Malchain, Gm. F
Provost of The Unicorn Academy

Olivia flipped the scroll over and blinked. She was pretty sure it had been blank a moment ago, but now indigo words ran across it in thin lines, glistening as though they had just been scrawled. Careful to touch only the edge of the parchment in case the message did smear, Olivia read on.

ELIGIBILITY: Any child twelve years of age is eligible to attend, provided they sign below. Please read on for specific guild instructions:
  TILLERS
  Enter through North Ivy Gate. Dean Holly Barry will host tea for apprentices and their guardians before a tour of the academy grounds. Tiller apprentices are asked to arrive with:
   • 1 pair of pruning shears
   • 1 hand trowel

- 3 pairs of gardening gloves
- 1 watering can
- 10 fast-growing beans
- 1 pouch of pumpkin seeds (carriage-sized)
- the core of a golden apple OR a root hair from the Tree of Youth

Olivia stopped reading. She already knew this list. She'd helped Nan fill orders with the same supplies every autumn for the other kids in Buddle. She skipped down to the other guilds, which were a little more interesting. Forgers were required to bring nuggets of gold, and Spinners were asked to bring five different kinds of silk. Most fascinating, however, was the Gemmer list, which consisted almost entirely of precious and semiprecious gemstones. Olivia read them all, from agate to zircon, which she thought would take her to the end of the scroll. But to her surprise, there were still a few inches left. Curious, she unrolled the final section, which contained not a list, but a single set of instructions:

DORMANT: Upon arrival, please knock once on the main door and inform the doorkeeper that you require assistance awakening your magic.

Olivia read the last three words again.
And again.
Awakening your magic.

Deep down, Olivia knew she was not the best shopkeeper's assistant. But she also knew that she was a *great* reader. Which meant that she must be reading the words on the scroll correctly: if she went to Unicorn Academy, she would find her magic.

She would become a proper Tiller.

Then a physician.

And then she would be in the workshop, stirring botanicals and crafting poultices alongside Nan and Laurel. She could already feel the crisp cotton of her physician's overcoat, could practically smell Olivia's All-Purpose Panacea simmering in a clay pot, smelling of all the best fragrances: old books, summer rain, and magic.

And all she had to do was sign.

But . . .

. . . Nan would never let her go.

The truth hooked into her like a burr, sticking more and more the harder she tugged at it. Marguerite Hayes believed in the *order* of things. Spices should be arranged alphabetically, spring should follow winter, and guilds should mind their own business. Olivia could practically hear her grandmother's response. *"You don't need an academy. You need patience."*

And Olivia knew that Nan needed her.

If Olivia left for this academy, Nan would be all alone. Nan's eyesight wasn't good enough to spot all the bits of broken glass when a jar broke. Of course, if Olivia *were* gone, there would probably be fewer broken jars to clean up, and mayors wouldn't turn into mushrooms—

The mayor!

Olivia looked up from the scroll at the darkening sky above her. How long had she been in the Endless? The shadows stretched out on the forest floor told her too long. There was no point in heading into town now. Nan would be on her way home, and Olivia *still* hadn't done anything to fix the mayoral mushroom. Jamming the scroll—which was suddenly palm-sized—into her pocket, she broke into a run.

The sun had just set over a distant hill by the time Olivia burst out of the Endless. Twilight draped over the field, and in the distance, she could just make out Bumblebee Apothecary nestled among the gardens. The shutters were open and light spilled from the round windows into the night.

Nan was already home.

The smell of frying onions and truffle hit Olivia as soon as she opened the cottage door. She wrinkled her nose. They only ever ate truffle if they had company over or if it was Laurel's birthday. But Laurel wasn't even here, and Nan knew how Olivia felt about truffle. ("It tastes like damp wood.") As she shrugged off her cloak and kicked off one boot, Olivia concluded that Nan must be making an apology dinner for the mayor, as the six-foot mushroom was nowhere to be found. It was either that or—

Panic spiked through her. What if Nan hadn't realized

who the mushroom was? What if she had turned Mayor Oakley into Mayor Risotto?

"Nan!" Olivia shouted, not bothering to kick off her second boot as she raced down the hall toward the clatter of pots and pans. "What are you cooking?!" she asked, bursting into the kitchen just in time to see Nan grind pepper into a steaming pan. "That mushroom is—"

"—delicious!" piped up a voice from behind her.

Olivia spun around. Nan wasn't alone. A girl sat at the round wooden table, peeling potatoes as her green eyes sparkled. She wore wide traveling trousers and a billowy undertunic of pine green beneath a crimson overcoat. Her overcoat matched Nan's, marking her as a physician and perfectly complementing the sprig of holly berries pinned to her sleek blonde bun.

"*Laurel!*" Olivia yelped as her sister scooted out from behind the table and enveloped her in a hug. "What are you doing here? You're not supposed to be back until winter!"

"I finished early," Laurel said. She squeezed Olivia tight, then took a step back and held out her arms. Three white rings wrapped around her sleeves like bands of snow. When Laurel had set out, there had only been two: the first to mark her status as an apprentice, and the second to proclaim her a journeyman. But a third one meant . . .

"You're a *Master* now?" Olivia gaped. "But you've been gone less than a year!"

"Your sister is the youngest Master physician in centuries," Nan said, lifting the pan off the stove and turning to greet Olivia. Pride softened the lines on Marguerite Hayes's face, making her seem younger than she had this morning. The amber beads she usually reserved for the winter holidays winked cheerfully around her neck. Like her granddaughters, she had hazel-green eyes and skin that turned pink in the sun. Her gray curls were cropped short, but they still wisped in the kitchen's heat.

"Can you get the glass goblets, please?" Nan asked, setting a steaming quiche on the table. "We're celebrating tonight!"

Olivia gulped. Nan wouldn't want to celebrate anything once she heard her confession. She took a deep breath. "Nan, the mushr—"

"I know where they are!" Laurel interrupted. Grabbing Olivia's hand, she dragged her out of the kitchen and into the dining room. As soon as they were out of Nan's hearing, she whispered, "You don't make it easy to keep you out of trouble." She shook her head, and the berries in her hair seemed to dance along. "I can't believe you turned Mayor Oakley into a fungus!"

"I didn't mean to," Olivia moaned. "Where is he?"

"Home, I think," Laurel said. She opened a cabinet and shifted some wooden platters as she reached for the back shelf. "I fixed him before Nan arrived and sent him on his way."

"He's still going to tell her," Olivia said as Laurel pulled out a goblet and inspected it. "And not just Nan—everyone!"

Laurel handed the goblet to Olivia. "I don't think Mayor Oakley is going to be telling anyone anything for a very long time," she said grimly. "You might have given him the wrong elixir, but it wouldn't have transformed him completely into a mushroom if he didn't have *this* on him."

She held out an amulet the size of a coin. It didn't look like anything special, but as Olivia stared at it, she saw a tiny crack in the middle of the stone. When she took a second look, she realized it wasn't a crack at all.

Olivia gasped. "Is that—?"

"A sliver of unicorn rib?" Laurel nodded, eyes grave. "Yes."

Revulsion puckered Olivia's insides, making her squirm. Unicorn artifacts—a bit of bone, a tooth, an inch of heartstring—while not as powerful as a living, breathing unicorn, still amplified magic. After the Guild War, these relics were all that remained of unicorns, and the guilds hoarded them to make their own craft more powerful. But with the return of unicorns, the guilds had agreed to relinquish all unicorn artifacts to the herds. It seemed, however, that Mayor Oakley had made an exception for himself.

"What are you going to do with it?" Olivia asked, voice hushed.

Laurel slipped the amulet back into her pocket and picked up two more goblets. "I told Mayor Oakley that as long as he didn't say anything about the mushroom mistake, I wouldn't say anything, either." She smirked. "You owe me, Olive Pit."

Olivia scowled as she trailed her sister back to the kitchen. Laurel was pretty good as big sisters went—but she was still a sister.

CHAPTER THREE

Evening wrapped around the Hayes family like candlelight, warm and cozy. The carrots had never been sweeter, the mashed potatoes had never been fluffier, and even the truffle quiche didn't taste too damp. Nan sat in her highbacked chair closest to the stove, while Olivia and Laurel sat knee to knee on the wooden bench, swapping stories and exchanging laughter. It was just like old times—but better.

Because now Olivia knew she wouldn't be here forever. The same way autumn leaves were most brilliant right before they fell, tonight the apothecary felt more like home than it ever had. With Laurel's journeyman trials over, she would be moving back to help Nan. Laurel would be able to do everything Olivia could do, as well as the millions of magical things Olivia couldn't . . . *yet*.

The Unicorn Academy would change everything.

She just needed Nan's permission—and the exact right moment to ask.

Sipping her raspberry cordial, Olivia plotted while Laurel described in excruciating detail the soil composition in Springmill and its ability to support medicinal herbs. If Nan was receptive, Olivia might even be able to ask about the other objects she'd found in the drawer. And why, exactly—

". . . Unicorn Academy sounds like nonsense," Nan's voice, suddenly sharp, sliced through Olivia's thoughts. "What is the Prime Minister thinking? She should know better!"

Olivia choked on her cordial and began to cough. When had Laurel and Nan stopped discussing the ratio of clay to mulch?! She had to steer this conversation down a more positive path, but all she could splutter out was, *"Snork coff snrt!"*

"Ew!" Laurel said, making a face as she wiped droplets of Olivia's raspberry cordial off her cheek. She tossed a napkin at Olivia before turning her attention back to Nan. "Physician Heliotrope was furious when the Grand Council agreed to it," she said, naming the head of the prestigious Healer Hall. "He voted against the school's opening."

Though her eyes were still teary, Olivia managed to wheeze out, "Why'd he do that? An interguild school sounds exciting! Better than exciting. It sounds *historical!*"

Nan snorted. "Nonsensical, you mean. The Forgers and Gemmers almost started a war four years ago, and now we're supposed to just trust them?" She shook her head. "The last time the guilds lived together led to the unicorns' extinction. The Prime Minister is just tickling a Flesh-Eating Fennel by founding this school."

"That's what Physician Heliotrope thinks, too," Laurel said. She reached out and patted the friendly philodendron that always liked to drape across shoulders during meals. "And he said that some of the other guilds aren't happy about the decision, either. There probably wouldn't be any apprentices enrolled at all if the Prime Minister hadn't *insisted* that each grandmaster send a relative."

Laurel shook her head. "The Forgers suspect that this is just the Prime Minister's ploy to spy on them, while the Gemmers can't even afford to send anyone, with their citadel in such disrepair." She shrugged. "But it's only for a year."

Olivia frowned. "What's only for a year?"

"The academy," Laurel said as she gave the philodendron a final pat, then stood to start clearing the table. "That's how the Prime Minister got the Grand Council to agree. They're allowing an all-guild school *now*, but at the end of the year, they'll take another vote to decide whether they should extend its charter."

One year.

Olivia's throat tightened. If she couldn't convince Nan to let her go now, she might never have another chance to awaken her magic. She would be dormant, magicless—a *lackie*—forever. "Nan," she said, trying to keep her voice calm. "I wanted to discuss—"

"No, leave that, Laurel," Nan interrupted, motioning Laurel to put the bowl of cucumber salad back on the table. "I'm packing a hamper up for your trip. Now, Olivia, what were you saying?"

But Olivia was staring at her sister. "Trip? You're leaving again?"

Infuriatingly, Laurel placed the plates in the sink and wiped her hands on a towel before turning to face Olivia with a small smile. On anyone else, Olivia would have called it a smirk, but on Laurel, it just made her look sweetly all-knowing.

"Didn't I mention it?" Laurel asked. "Not only am I the youngest Master physician in three hundred years, I'm also the youngest person *ever* to be asked to join Healer Hall!"

Of course Laurel would be invited to the elite physicians' society. Healer Hall, located in the capital, was the center of all Tiller medical knowledge. Only the most talented and powerful Tillers were allowed to study and work within its palace-sized greenhouses. Nan had been a member herself until she'd left to take care of her orphaned granddaughters. Membership was a huge honor at any age.

"That's great," Olivia said, and she meant it.

Mostly.

She tried to smile, but a splinter of something buried itself under her rib cage. It felt a little like disappointment and a lot like jealousy. Life was so easy for Laurel.

"When are you going?" Olivia asked, hoping she sounded interested and not utterly despairing.

"We leave tomorrow."

"Tomorrow?" Olivia protested. "But you just got—wait." She frowned at her sister. "What do you mean, *we*?"

Laurel was *definitely* smirking now. "Physician Heliotrope thinks I'm on to something *big*—a complete rethinking of how we look at potential in soil. He said I could select an apprentice to help take notes, and I chose you! If you want, that is."

Did she want.

Sometimes, Olivia thought that she was more *want* than girl, her skeleton not made of bones, but of dreams stacked upon wishes stacked upon hope. Except— "What about Nan?"

"What about me?" Nan sprinkled lavender petals into the sink, and fragrant purple bubbles began to fill the basin.

"You're—" Olivia was going to say *old*, but Nan's expression made her think better of it. "You're coming down with a cold! I heard you sneeze fifty times this morning!"

Nan arched an eyebrow. "Maybe that's because someone didn't put the goldenrod away properly." There was a clink of amber followed by the weight of Nan's hand on her shoulder. "That imagination of yours can spin tornados out of a sneeze," Nan said, kindness supporting her words like a trellis. "I spoke to the oldest son of the Millers, and he'll start his apprenticeship with me a week from tomorrow. I'll be just fine. Now go pack," she said, gently pushing Olivia in the direction of the hall. "Unless you'd prefer to stay here all winter and pickle the beets?"

But Olivia was already sprinting to her bedroom. As she flung herself to the floor and reached under her bed for her trunk, she thought she heard Nan say above the running water, "I think that's a 'no.'"

The rest of the evening was lost in a whirl of preparation. Name tags needed to be sewn into tunics, socks matched, and quills sharpened. It was well after midnight before Nan blew out the candles. Laurel fell asleep almost immediately, her breath in the bunk above as familiar as Olivia's own. Shortly after, Nan's snore mingled with the rustle of leaves in the drafty cottage. Only then did Olivia dare slip the scroll from under her pillow. She hadn't wanted to risk her sister or grandmother finding it and guessing The Plan.

Unrolling the parchment, Olivia held it under the splash of moonlight that trickled through the bedroom window:

THE UNICORN ACADEMY
OF ARTISTICAL AND MAGICAL LEARNING
Inspiration. Dedication. Courage.
1 Anders's Tear, Lumin City, Republic of Arden

She didn't know the exact location of 1 Anders's Tear, but it was somewhere in Lumin City, which meant it was somewhere near Healer Hall.

Reading through the scroll again, Olivia looked for anything she might have missed, anything that could disqualify her. But the instructions were clear: Be twelve years of age. Sign the scroll. Arrive at the academy by midnight on the first day of Ninthmonth, which was three days from now.

Sure, she'd be cutting it close, but there was just enough time to make it. And once they were in the city, she would tell Laurel that while she was very thankful for the opportunity at Healer Hall, she would be going to Unicorn Academy instead. That it was time for the youngest Hayes to do something impressive. Something first. Something without Laurel's help.

Olivia tugged the parchment and the final few inches unfurled. The brass handle came away in her hand, revealing itself to be a fountain pen. Without weight, the scroll's end fluttered, its final words waving like a banner:

I, _____, will attend Unicorn Academy and will abide by all rules and regulations as outlined upon this scroll, as well as accept responsibility for any injury, magical or otherwise, that might be attained during class.

Laurel coughed.

Olivia flung the quilt up and over her head, hiding both quill and scroll. One second passed, then two. The slats of the top bunk groaned as Laurel turned, but after a few more seconds, there was no sound at all except steady breathing.

Olivia shivered even though it was stuffy under the blanket.

She'd never kept a secret from Laurel before.

Laurel knew everything about Olivia—Mayor Oakley was only the tip of the root system. There was the time Olivia had spilled a bottle of peach fuzz and grown herself a delicate pink beard, and the several times she'd unknowingly weeded an endangered plant. But those were all instances where Laurel could help. This time, Olivia didn't need Laurel's help.

This time, she didn't *want* Laurel's help.

Pulling the quilt off her head, Olivia set her jaw, put pen to parchment, and in her fanciest, most grown-up handwriting, signed: Olivia Gladiola Hayes. The ink flowed easily, as permanent and certain as her decision. As soon as she lifted the nub away, new words appeared under her signature, welling up from the parchment:

> Welcome, Apprentice Hayes! We are delighted that you will be joining the inaugural class of the Unicorn Academy. Please be on time or risk expulsion. —Provost Malchain

Snap!

Olivia jerked back as the loose end of parchment flapped. There was a slight tug, and the remaining handle slipped from her grip. But instead of tumbling onto her mattress, the parchment stayed suspended in midair, folding in on itself once, then twice, then a third time. There was a second *snap* and a bird hovered before her nose, its paper wings beating as fast as Olivia's heart.

"What's happening?" Laurel mumbled sleepily from the top bunk. "What's that sound?"

"Snapdragons," Olivia whispered back. "Nan's cultivating them in the window box. Do you want me to close the shutters?"

No answer. Laurel appeared to have fallen back asleep. Just as well, as the window was very much still closed. The bird spiraled upward and tapped the glass. Moonlight illuminated the indigo text spiraling across its wings. Scooting to her knees, Olivia leaned forward and pushed the window open. With a sound like turning pages, the paper bird darted out and disappeared into the night.

CHAPTER FOUR

Olivia woke before dawn, but by the time she'd found a pair of socks, braided her hair, and pulled on her tunic, the sun had risen and Nan was already knotting the last tether to the Dandiloon. The dandelion puff had been coaxed to the size of a small moon and bobbed gently above the cottage roof, scattering lacy shadows onto the ground below, where Laurel was carrying out a final inspection of the vessel's rigging and gondola.

"Let's get going!" Laurel called as Olivia approached. Laurel's crimson overcoat had been packed away, and she wore a comfortable traveling outfit of fawn-colored leggings and a pine-green sweater that brought out the color in her eyes.

Olivia hugged Nan tightly, then hoisted herself up and over the gondola's woven wall—only to land with an ominous jingle.

"Careful!" Laurel warned as Olivia scrambled off a large woven hamper. "That's my tribute!"

"I'm sure it's fine," Olivia said airily, but she held her breath and whispered a prayer that she hadn't cracked or smashed or shattered anything as she lifted the lid. A nest of dried moss cradled three unbroken vials the size of her thumb. Inside each, a golden substance more air than liquid swirled.

Olivia's eyes widened. "Your tribute is Ambrosia?"

She knew members of Healer Hall were required to bring a tribute, a gift of sorts, to add to the hall's vast collection of magical remedies. It was a way to inspire creativity—and a chance to show off. It also explained why the Ambrosia hadn't been in the locked drawer. Nan had already packed these three precious vials for Laurel.

Laurel shrugged, not quite meeting Olivia's eye.

"Nan thought it would be best since . . ." She trailed off awkwardly, but Olivia understood what she did not say. Nan thought it would be best since Laurel was bringing a lackie to the hall.

Olivia flushed, but she couldn't tell if it was from anger or embarrassment. Either way, it didn't matter, because she didn't have any plan to stay at Healer Hall longer than necessary. She shoved the lid back on and snapped her goggles into place. "Let's go."

Nan blew a kiss to Laurel, but to Olivia's surprise, Laurel

didn't return it. Nan's smile slipped slightly, and Olivia wondered if they'd had an argument. Laurel wasn't one to hold a grudge, but the few times she did—look out, world. Glancing at Laurel and the set expression on her sister's face, Olivia had the squirmy feeling that their fight probably had something to do with her.

But there was no time to dwell on that now, for Laurel had turned her attention to the fluffy dome above them. Bringing a wooden whistle to her lips, she blew two short bursts. The notes spiraled up around the stalk, soaring into the fluff and setting the seedpods swaying. As the seeds brushed against each other, a soft rustle filled the air. The ground lurched. Olivia stumbled, catching herself against the basket's rim as they began to rise one, then five, then ten feet into the air. They were off!

"Goodbye!" Olivia shouted as Nan waved. Olivia kept waving even as they lifted over the apothecary's thatched roof, passed the tallest sycamore leaf, then soared even higher still. As her grandmother, her favorite willow tree, and the only home she'd ever known grew smaller, Arden grew bigger—as did Olivia's excitement.

"Lumin City, here we come!" The wind rushed over her, billowing her cloak out behind her like a princess's train. Leaning over the basket, Olivia flung her arms wide to hug the horizon. "I can't believe that in just three days, I'm going to be standing in front of the *actual* Clarissa's Arch! Seeing the

Silver Spires! And before that, we'll pass over the Foggy Bottom Swamp and Constellation Range!"

Leaning both elbows against the gondola's rim, Olivia rested her cheeks in her palms. "I've never seen mountains before," she said dreamily. "But I've imagined them. Tall silver peaks rising into the sky like points on a crown, the snow on top as dazzling as diamonds! And of course, that's where nearly all of the unicorns have chosen to live. Alice the Astute wrote that unicorns feel the most comfortable in 'thin places.'" She glanced back at her sister. "Isn't that poetic?"

"I guess." Laurel leaned over to adjust a tether, then rechecked the barometer. "But I have no idea what that means—the lack of nutrients in soil?"

A small wisp of a cloud floated by her nose, and Olivia gently blew it away. "I think it means that mountains are a place of transition, where nothing is really ever set and all things are possible. Alice the Astute said that in the mountains, opposites coexist. 'The tops sparkle with winter snow even at the height of midsummer, and it's where the earth becomes high and the sky becomes low, where hearts sing and—"

A set of binoculars suddenly appeared under Olivia's nose, interrupting her recitation.

"They're a place where killer storms sweep in with the blink of an eye," Laurel said as she knotted a rope. "Dandiloon navigation is no joke, and I'm going to need your help. If you see so much as a gray *dot* on any cloud, let me know. Got it?"

Olivia nodded and Laurel tugged a tether, turning them south.

For a few hours, Olivia concentrated on the sky, but being lookout was deeply dull. The chilly morning had turned into a warm summer's day, and the few clouds that did tumble by were small, fluffy, and white. No chance they would turn into storms anytime soon.

As carefully as she could, Olivia tugged a small compartment open. Laurel had said there would be plenty of books to read in Healer Hall, but Olivia couldn't leave without this one, *Actes des Ardenians: Tales from the Lost Age*. The Unicorn Academy would definitely have a copy—in fact, most households in Arden probably did—but on the inside of this particular cover was a note.

Rosemarie—all my love, Cypress

Olivia traced over her mother's name in her father's handwriting. She didn't remember them, as they had both died in a wraith attack shortly after she was born. But she knew they'd loved this book, and so she loved it, too, especially the sections about Lady Elaina, the first and only unicorn rider Arden had ever known. With the Golden Bridle, she'd tamed a unicorn and together, they accomplished many great deeds. It was their final act, however, that they were best remembered for, and that's where Olivia flipped to now. She'd read it countless times, which meant it would be easy to skim *and* keep an eye on the sky. Concealing the book behind a trunk, she began to read.

> Long ago, in that time before memory, something hungry stalked the land. At first, it only nibbled moon shadows and sipped willow tears, but as it grew larger, so, too, did its appetite. It began to gnaw on the dark edges of forests, slurp molten gold from the mines, munch mountaintops, and even chew through the seams of the world.
> Still, the Devourer craved more.

The story swept through Olivia. Her heart ached when Anders's army fell to the creature's great hunger. Her spine tightened as Lady Elaina and her unicorn stepped out to face the creature alone. Her eyes even blurred with tears as she read how, together, girl and unicorn provoked the Devourer, baiting it to follow them across the blue expanse:

> Lady Elaina crouched low across the unicorn's neck, whispering in his ear. One final promise. One final breath.
> They leaped into the sun, and the Devourer plunged in after, drowning in sun's fire.
> Monster gone. Rider gone. Unicorn gone. But the land of Arden remained.

Shutting her eyes as she closed the cover, Olivia tried to imagine what it would be like to gallop a unicorn into the sky, or how the sun's warmth, gentle at first, would grow stronger and stronger until it felt a million times hotter than the sand at noon, then a hundred million times hotter than all the Forgers' fires put together. Though as a cold wind bit at Olivia's skin, the fire of a hundred million forges didn't sound all that bad.

She frowned. When did the temperature drop? Usually, that only happened right before a—

Olivia's eyes snapped open just as Laurel shouted, "Olivia! Why didn't you say anything?!"

The book tumbled to the floor of the Dandiloon as Olivia fumbled with the binoculars. But there was no need. A black cloud loomed behind them, a great mouth ready to swallow them whole.

CHAPTER FIVE

"Can we outfly it?" Olivia asked, racing to join her sister at the front of the gondola as thunder rumbled.

Laurel consulted her flying instruments, then shook her head. "Too late! We have to land! Hold tight!" Olivia only had a moment to clutch at a rope before Laurel blew a low note and the Dandiloon plunged into the thick clouds below. Damp cold enveloped her and drizzle spattered across her goggles as the wind tossed them. In the cloud, there was no way to tell how high or how low they were. The only thing that existed was motion.

Up and down, left and right, right again, then down!

Olivia's stomach seemed to be everywhere except where it should be: in her throat one second, then somewhere below her navel the next.

Up, down, down, up!

Just when she thought it couldn't get any worse, that she

couldn't feel *more* sick even if she ate a barrel of poison ivy, a loud *rip* cut through the shrieking wind.

The Dandiloon plummeted!

They spun out of control, scattering giant dandelion puffs and luggage into the ether as they dropped through the last cloud layer—

—to see a mountain's peak suddenly emerge.

"OLIVIA!" Laurel yelled, yanking the ropes tight, her face fierce and her arms straining. Knowing this might be the last thing she ever did, Olivia reached out and pulled with her sister. The rough twine scraped her palms. Her muscles screamed. The Dandiloon slowed ever so slightly—but it was enough.

They thudded into the mountainside. The gondola skidded, throwing grass and dirt into the air. For one horrifying moment, Olivia thought they would never stop, that they would keep sliding until they careened off the mountain, falling forever. But then she heard Laurel sound a long, high whistle. Large roots burst from the woven gondola. They clutched at the sparse soil and sank into the ground. The gondola jerked, flinging Olivia against the sides, and then—everything stilled.

"Well," Laurel said after a moment of shocked silence, "that could have gone better. Are you all right?"

"Fine!" Olivia squeaked. Cold rain pelted her cheek, but she'd never been so grateful to feel things, because that meant she was alive.

"Are you sure? You look green."

"I'm *fine*," Olivia repeated, and to prove her point, she swung one leg over the basket and promptly toppled onto the wet ground. She moaned.

Laurel leaped over the gondola's edge and landed on the grass as gracefully as a dewdrop. "Here," she said, offering Olivia a hard candy. "You'll feel better in a moment."

Olivia popped the lozenge into her mouth. Ginger burst across her tongue, and its sharpness tickled her nose. Almost as quickly as the flavor had appeared, it was gone, along with her nausea. Her legs still shaky, Olivia took her goggles off and leaned on the gondola while Laurel walked over to the sad, wet pile of green and white that had accumulated a few yards away from them: all that remained of the once-glorious poof.

"Can you fix it?"

"I think so." Laurel shoved her goggles up on her forehead and knelt on the ground, poking at the soggy mess. "But that's not the problem. The problem is the Ambrosia." She blinked rapidly, and Olivia couldn't tell if a raindrop was rolling down her cheek or a tear. "I saw it fall out somewhere over that ridge." She gestured miserably to a ridge at least a mile away. "Bringing Ambrosia to the Hall was my first official task, and I blew it."

"We can go look for it," Olivia suggested, but her sister was already shaking her head.

"I have to fix the Dandiloon," Laurel said, already pulling on a pair of gardening gloves and laying out a small knife, a tin of wax, and a jar of quick-grow. "The sun sets in half an hour, and we don't want to be on this mountain when night falls."

Olivia shook her head. "You can't arrive without something extraordinary!"

"I'm not planning on it," Laurel said, reaching for the wax. She carefully began to dab it onto a nearby stalk. "Nan will give me something else. It might not be as special as Ambrosia, but we'll figure something out. Do you think she'll let me take a branch of sugar ash?"

The meaning behind Laurel's words slowly crystallized, like frost, chilling Olivia to her core: Laurel wanted to turn around. Laurel wanted to go back to Buddle.

"But we have to go to Lumin!" Olivia practically shouted. Laurel stared at her. "I mean," Olivia amended quickly, and much more quietly, "I'm fast—remember that time Azalea escaped her pen and I caught her? And I'm still the best slingshot in Buddle." Laurel opened her mouth, but Olivia pushed on. "Please, Laurel. I owe you—for the mayor, remember? Let me at least *try*."

Laurel stayed silent, but she tugged the tips of her gardening gloves, just as she always did when she was trying to decide which branch to prune next. Just a little nudge . . .

"Sugar ash is nice," Olivia said, "but it's not *Ambrosia*."

Laurel looked away, but not before Olivia caught a glimpse of her face. For a moment, Olivia thought she could see why people said the Hayes girls looked similar, because, despite their differences in age and coloring, the expression on Laurel's face was one Olivia knew only too well: longing.

"Fine," Laurel said, standing up and wiping her gloves on her trousers. "But you have to take this." She reached into a pocket and handed Olivia what looked like a single pistachio shell. When Olivia looked at her questioningly, she explained, "The Blastachio's stuffed with skunkweed and devil's breath. If you get in trouble, crack it. The smell will be so toxic that it will blind any creature's eyes with tears and make it impossible for them to track your scent. It'll also be really loud, so I will know where you are. Understand?"

Olivia accepted the Blastachio, as well as a pair of nose plugs. With one last promise to be back in thirty minutes, she set off into the mountains.

The storm had gusted away as swiftly as it had come, and the rain had turned into a light mist, scattering rainbows across the slope. The wet grass clung to her boots and thistles dragged at her skirt, but in the cool air, Olivia felt free. The mountains of Constellation Range stood snowy shoulder to snowy shoulder, just as dazzling as she always knew they would be. She took a deep, long breath, filling her lungs with pine-scented air, and lengthened her stride. Yesterday morning, it had been impossible to think that she would be here today. Who knew what tomorrow would bring? Tomorrows were wild and mysterious creatures, full of potential and promise. Like unicorns. Like her.

An unexpected anticipation fizzed through Olivia. A strange feeling of *rightness*. Of knowing that, for once, she was exactly where she should be. She was a knight about to face a wyvern. A queen ascending her throne. A Tiller just about to bloom.

Olivia tucked an escaped curl behind her ear as the wind tugged her braid. She *would* find the Ambrosia. She *would* pay back her debt to Laurel. She *would* get to the academy.

She would *be* magic.

Olivia sprinted the last few feet to the top to see—

More peaks. More grass. More sky.

From their crash site, the ridge had looked like it tapered into a single, searchable point. But it had been an illusion. The point wasn't a point at all, but the edge of a steep valley. A valley so wide that it looked like it could contain a *thousand* Endlesses.

"Aphids," Olivia swore as she bent over to catch her breath. Her long auburn braids fell over her shoulder, tangling in the grass. There was no way she'd find the missing Ambrosia in ten years, let alone the ten minutes she had. Not unless . . .

Her eyes strayed to the mountains that loomed higher still, their peaks lost in the clouds.

A place where sky meets earth; where impossibilities exist.

Maybe she didn't need to go to Unicorn Academy to wake her magic after all. Maybe she could enter Healer Hall on her own magical merit, instead of clinging to the strings of Laurel's physician coat.

Kneeling down, Olivia nestled her hand into the grass and closed her eyes.

A book she'd read once described magic as feeling like a hum in the bones. Laurel had always described it as an itch, while Nan had said it felt like song.

All Olivia felt was frustration.

The grass didn't whisper of how it'd cushioned the Ambrosia's fall. The roots beneath her hand didn't say anything about feeling the vibrations of a *thud*.

Olivia dug her fingers into the soil and tried harder. *Wished* harder. She ached for who she was not and who she wanted to be and who she knew—*knew* deep inside her—she *could* be, if only given the chance. If only—

A low, mournful note scraped across the mountainside.

Olivia's eyes snapped open.

It was probably just the wind rushing between the peaks, but she couldn't entirely rule out the possibility of prowling ghosts. Or maybe it was the voice of the mountain itself, inviting her to journey inside and find hidden treasure in its twisting caverns.

"I wish I could," she whispered to the peaks, and immediately felt silly. She wasn't a Gemmer; she couldn't talk to mountains. Still, she couldn't shake the feeling that someone—or something—was there, listening to her.

The sun was sinking fast now. She needed to turn back. But she wasn't ready to give up yet. Olivia lifted the binoculars to her eyes and swept the valley below, looking for any hint, no matter how small, that the Ambrosia had landed there. But all she could spot were two large boulders at the edge of the valley's forest. Except . . .

She blinked.

Now there was only one rock.

The hairs on the back of Olivia's neck rose. Maybe she really wasn't alone. After all, rocks didn't just get up and walk away—usually. Her heart did a double flip. Stories about stone queens and ravenous gargoyles were all fine and good in the safety of Nan's apothecary, but they were another thing entirely when she was alone in this wild expanse.

She fiddled with the binocular's knobs. The world turned into a foggy blur, and then the boulder snapped into focus. Now she could make out its details: the crystals that speckled its face, the fuzzy moss that clung to its sides, and—Olivia gasped, the binoculars almost slipping from her fingers—three faint streaks of light that shimmered in the gloom.

Not Ambrosia, but something equally enticing, equally rare, and equally—if not *more*—extraordinary.

Unicorn mane.

Olivia whooped and sprinted into the valley. She'd done

it! It was a tribute that would *dazzle* Healer Hall. This tribute would pay back *all* her debts. It would make Laurel *proud* to be her sister.

Darkness thickened as she pounded down the slope, the tall ridges of the valley blocking out the last of the sun's rays.

Maybe that was why Olivia didn't see the sinkhole.

Or maybe it was because she was distracted by that strange, mountainous howl that whipped up again, gathering in volume as she neared the boulder.

Or maybe it was because she was so focused on the three strands of unicorn mane that glowed brighter and brighter as she reached out a hand to grasp them.

But the reason didn't matter. Either way, she plummeted.

CHAPTER SIX

Olivia knew she must be screaming, but sound didn't seem to exist anymore.

Nothing existed anymore.

In this *non*place, as dark as the inside of a chimney and as deep as a bottomless well, she couldn't even be sure she was falling. In nothing, there can be no up or down, no beginning or end, no seconds or eternities.

Olivia just was, and then . . .

. . . she was naught.

CHAPTER SEVEN

Warmth curled against her cheek.

A perfume of sunlight and clover filled the space that had once been her lungs. Slowly, she became aware of feet and knees and chest. Of blood rushing, muscles straining, and skin feeling.

Velvet brushed against her shoulder. Then nudged her—hard.

She opened her eyes (she had eyes again) and met the unicorn's gaze.

This unicorn was no illusion. No trick of light between branches or subtle shimmer at the forest's edge.

This unicorn was as clear as a trumpet's fanfare, as solid as diamond, and as real as heartbreak. Her white coat shone with brilliant opalescence, a shifting tapestry of palest lavenders, icy blues, and faintest blush as her tail flowed down to her cloven hooves. From her forehead rose a slender spiral—the final exclamation point to the unicorn's existence.

The unicorn dipped her head.

In her sapphire-night eyes reflected a girl with auburn braids and a stubborn chin, dirt on her hem, and a slingshot at her waist.

At the sight, meaning flooded back to the girl, along with her name: *OLIVIA*.

Olivia *existed* again, and as the unicorn lowered her head, she knew what the creature wanted. Reaching up, her fingers caught in the frothy silk before wrapping around the unicorn's horn.

Heat seared her palms, but Olivia did not let go.

With a toss of her mane, the unicorn tugged Olivia upward, away and out of the strange hole and back into the world of Being. Olivia gripped the horn tighter, scared of slipping back into that chasm—into that void, into that space that was naught—and losing herself again.

A final tug, and she felt herself fly through the air.

CRACK!

I think that was my head, was Olivia's first thought as she felt solid ground against her back. Her second—*That can't be good*—was also her last thought before she passed out.

CHAPTER EIGHT

"Olivia! *Olivia!*"

From somewhere in the distance, Olivia heard her name, but she was so tired and achy that she doubted she could lift an eyelash, even if she wanted to. And she did *not* want to. Everything was sore and everything felt broken, except for her nose—which was unfortunate, as the world's most foul and revolting stench was assaulting her nostrils.

"Yelck!" Olivia jerked upright and slapped her hands over her nose. "What *is* that? It smells like rotten meat and burned hair and—is that damp celery?!"

"Olivia! You're alive!"

A moment later, her sister crushed her in a hug. Olivia let herself lean against Laurel, burying her nose into her mint-scented tunic. She breathed in deeply.

"What happened?" she mumbled. She felt like she'd skipped a page somewhere and was now lost in the story.

"I was going to ask *you* the same thing!" Laurel said, her voice strangely nasal. "I flew the Dandiloon to the ridge, but I didn't see you. Then I heard the Blastachio go off."

No wonder Laurel's voice sounded funny—she was wearing nose plugs. Wiggling out of Laurel's hug, Olivia pulled out her own pair and shoved them into her nose. Instant relief.

"I flew here as fast as I could," Laurel said as she began to dab an oily balm onto Olivia's cheek. An icy coolness rushed over her skin, sweeping away the aches. Over her sister's shoulder, Olivia glimpsed the gondola. Glass globes filled with glowing algae outlined the basket's lip and illuminated the dandelion floating above it. The dome fluffed out again, as magnificent as it ever was, the white expanse only occasionally interrupted by the yellow of newly bloomed petals. Roots still spiraled from the gondola, but it was sky-worthy once more.

Seemingly satisfied with the state of Olivia's face, Laurel began to check her arms, rubbing balm onto a few cuts and scrapes as she continued to explain, "When I got here, you were already passed out. Hey." Laurel frowned and stretched out Olivia's hand. "What's this?"

Olivia looked down to see three shimmering strands weaving between her fingers.

Here it was: her skipped page.

The evening's events snapped into focus, and she felt a

wide, slow grin stretch her cheeks. Unwinding the strands, she offered the unicorn mane to Laurel. "It's your tribute."

For the next ten minutes, Olivia tried to describe what had happened after she left the Dandiloon. Laurel hunched forward, listening intently while she stared at the strands cupped in her hand. They shone like seedling stars, casting a rippling light onto her face. Laurel's lips thinned as Olivia described the howl, and by the time she got to the unicorn's arrival, they had practically disappeared. When Olivia reached the end of the story, Laurel was looking at her with concern.

"How many fingers am I holding up?"

"Three," Olivia said. She stretched and was pleased to find the achy feeling she'd woken up with had all but disappeared under Laurel's quick ministrations. "Didn't you say we need to go? Onward to Lumin!"

But Laurel didn't move. "How many fingers am I holding up now?"

"Still three." Olivia rolled her eyes. "I feel great! Why do you keep checking?"

"Because," Laurel said, reaching behind her to unhook a fluorescent globe before shining it into Olivia's eyes, "there *is* no sinkhole."

"What do you mean?" Olivia scoffed. "Of course there's a . . ." She trailed off as she glanced at the boulder. Grabbing the fluorescence from Laurel, Olivia ran over and inspected the grass. There wasn't so much as a hoofprint, let alone never-ending nothingness.

"I don't understand!" Olivia turned to her sister. "It was right *here*! I *fell*."

"Or," Laurel said, walking up to her, "you had a bad reaction to the Blastachio. The fumes have been known to temporarily cloud the mind."

"Are you saying I'm lying?" Olivia snapped, feeling as stubborn as bindweed. "My slingshot isn't anywhere here—I dropped it in the sinkhole. And look at the mane in your hand! Proof!"

"All I'm saying," Laurel said, voice infuriatingly calm, "is that the mane was there before you 'fell.' I think you were probably so excited about finding the hairs that you tripped and smashed the Blastachio, which gave you some weird dreams."

Olivia opened her mouth to argue, to insist they stay and find the unicorn, thank the unicorn, but before she could, Laurel held up the strands of mane. They wove between her fingers, glowing brighter as the shadows deepened.

"They're beautiful," Laurel said quietly. She placed a hand on Olivia's shoulder. "Thank you."

Olivia's protest withered, then died as she soaked in Laurel's words. For once, Olivia had helped Laurel. She nodded and turned her back on the flawless grass to make her way to the gondola. A few minutes later, the illuminated Dandiloon soared into the night sky, trailing roots behind it.

Aside from an unlucky encounter with a flock of geese (and a half hour of scrubbing the splattered deck), the next day and a half were uneventful. Olivia's book stayed in the trunk, and her binoculars remained firmly fixed to her eyes. Without any distractions, she discovered she could read Arden like a page. She spotted the ruins of Hilltop Palace and a ring of rocks that had once been a well. She saw the red slopes of Mount Rouge and heard the chimes of Phlogiston Academy at its foot. There was history, *stories*, transcribed into the earth. And she wanted to read them all.

Laurel, on the other hand, was more interested in what lay underneath.

Specifically, *dirt*.

Her sister was *obsessed*. The ratio of air to water, sandy or chalky, color and consistency—Olivia hadn't known there were as many ways to describe soil as there were ways to describe a sunset . . . and she kind of wished she didn't.

"Are you listening?" Laurel called. "Read me the last thing you wrote."

During every lull, Laurel had been working hard to catch Olivia up on her research, which, as far as Olivia could tell, was something about some patches of soil lacking the potential of others. Olivia wasn't exactly sure how it connected to healing, except all the talk of "lacking potential" made her suspect that the dirt was just a stand-in for Laurel's *actual* project: Olivia and *her* lack of magic. Lumin City couldn't arrive soon enough.

"Right," Olivia said, quickly flipping to the previous page of her new journal. Laurel had gifted it to her just this morning, the emerald green cover specially embossed with *The Account of Olivia the Observant: Apprentice to Tiller Master Laurel Hayes*. She cleared her throat. "The last thing I have is . . . loam."

Exactly." Laurel nodded, then continued her lecture with no sign of stopping.

"How much farther?" Olivia asked later as the first star rose and twilight swirled around them like a violet cape. According to the sunflower seeds in the hourglass, there were only three hours until midnight.

Only three hours until the Unicorn Academy's doors would close to her forever.

Laurel shielded her eyes, and Olivia followed her gaze to where the sun glinted behind the horizon like half of a great golden coin. Except . . . the sun had *already* set. Which must mean—

"We're here!" Laurel grinned. "Brace yourself!" She blew her whistle, and Olivia's braids lifted as a sudden gust sped them through the air and toward the lights of Lumin City.

The capital of Arden was both new and ancient, like the unicorns themselves. For seven hundred years, it had been the heart of a prosperous kingdom shared by all craftsmen. Spinners strung long bridges while Gemmer masons and Tiller carpenters built majestic towers, sweeping buttresses, and lofty spires that Forgers then dipped into gold. But when the guilds had gone to war, the city, too, had fallen apart. Only recently, under the Prime Minister, had Arden worked to restore it to its former splendor.

Leaning over the gondola's edge, Olivia took in the tangle of lights beneath them: the red glow of Forger fires in Alloy Alley; the clear, steady beam of diamonds in Jewel Way; the fluorescent pinks and blues of glowing flowers in the Garden District, and the wafting green specks that swirled around Textile Mile, which Olivia knew must be luna moths, an insect valued by Spinners for both their silk and their ability to magnify moonlight.

Her stomach twisted. How in all the roots and twigs was she going to find 1 Anders's Tear before midnight? It could be anywhere! The only thing she recognized below was the Rhona. The black ribbon of water cut through the lights, splitting the city into east and west. Olivia focused on it as she raised her binoculars and tried to steady her nerves.

Boats of all kinds floated below them, but a Spinner's narrowboat with a lantern hung on its prow caught Olivia's attention. A woman wrapped in a white feathered shawl balanced on the needle-sharp point, her arms outstretched, and then—

The woman jumped.

Olivia gasped—but before she could tell Laurel to direct the Dandiloon down, that they had to help!—something white rose into the air. Wings beat and a swan glided over the boats. Olivia lowered her binoculars, wonder fizzing her veins. *Spinner magic.*

She followed the swan's path until its feathers disappeared into the shadow of the sister bridges, Sophronia's Necklace at the north and Clarissa's Arch at the south. And in between them . . .

"What's that?" she asked Laurel as they floated over a teardrop-shaped island in the middle of the river.

"That's Anders's Tear," Laurel said, following Olivia's finger. "It's where Anders built his first royal residence. You used to be able to tour the castle, but the Prime Minister claimed it for her academy—what's so funny?"

"Nothing," Olivia said, desperately trying to clamp down on the giddy relief that had burst out in very un apprentice-like giggles. "I'm just happy to be here with you."

"You're weird," Laurel said, and directed the Dandiloon toward the tallest hill outside the city, where a great glass house of domes and arches—more of a palace, really—glistened in the moonlight. As they neared the building, Laurel blew a low blast on her whistle, and the gondola sank gently until it landed on the roof with a soft rasp. Laurel smiled. "Welcome to Healer Hall."

Olivia marveled at the curved glass beneath them. Condensation smeared the glowing lights of the conservatory, making everything hazy, but she could still make out the shadows of plants and blooms.

"Grab anything you wouldn't want to lose," Laurel said as she slung her Tiller kit over her shoulder and started for the small door on the other side of the roof. "The apprentices on hospitality duty will unpack the rest of our stuff for us. I can't wait to show you everything! Singing sycamores, paradise fruit, bubble sap! I've even asked for a day pass for you so we can go inside the desert house and see the Thousand Year flower. We'll have so much fun together!" She paused as she reached the door and realized Olivia hadn't followed. Laurel frowned. "Is something wrong?"

Guilt yawned so widely within Olivia, she thought it might swallow her. Olivia was about to throw all of Laurel's kindness back in her face. Olivia was about to break her sister's heart.

Before she could gather her courage, the door behind Laurel opened and a short man with wide shoulders strode onto the roof. His face was smooth-shaven and had the weather-beaten look of someone who'd spent most of his life outside. Still, his gaze was sharp and there was no questioning his authority. Olivia would have guessed who he was even if Laurel hadn't greeted him.

"Physician Heliotrope!" Laurel said, delighted. "This is my sister, Olivia. I was just about to show her our apartment and then take her to meet you."

Olivia wasn't sure what she should do—shake his hand? Bow? *Curtsy?* After all, this was the current Tiller Grandmaster of Lumin City. Every community, large or small, Forger, Tiller, Gemmer, or Spinner, had a grandmaster to guide them. Grandmasters were typically older, with many years of magical expertise behind them. They sat on the Grand Council, selecting and advising Arden's Prime Minister. And while all grandmasters were technically equal, grandmasters of larger branches—like the Tillers of Lumin City—had stronger sway.

Olivia decided on a half bow, but as she dipped back up, she realized it hadn't mattered.

"Physician Hayes," Heliotrope said, ignoring both Laurel's introduction and Olivia's presence, "I need you to follow me to the council chamber. Immediately."

"The council chamber?" Laurel's eyes widened. "Yes, of course. We'll change and then Olivia and I will—"

"Hall members only," Physician Heliotrope said. He held the door open wider and stepped through. "Now, Physician Hayes."

Laurel shot an apologetic look at Olivia. "Our rooms are on the fifth floor—if you see anyone in an apprentice uniform, ask them to take you there." And then she was gone, leaving Olivia all alone on the roof with only her guilty secret and the speckling of stars above her that told her that even if she wanted to wait for Laurel, she couldn't. There was only an hour until midnight.

Ripping out a page from her apprentice account, Olivia scrawled over a list of valleys with the best topsoil. For once, she kept it short:

I'm going to Unicorn Academy. —O

As an afterthought, she added,

P.S. DON'T be a tale-tattle.
P.P.S. Please don't be mad.

She tucked the page between the lead tethers of the Dandiloon, then slung her book bag over her shoulder. After one last glance at the glass door and the life she might have had, Olivia made her way to the fire escape and fled Healer Hall.

CHAPTER NINE

It wasn't hard to find the river. All roads in Lumin eventually ended at its banks.

Under any other circumstance, Olivia would have spent hours—days, *weeks* even—exploring the Garden District. She would have soaked in the details of the elaborately carved wooden gates and tried all the pastry creams (even the ones that would have given her walrus whiskers for an hour) and basked in the smells of the spice markets.

But as it was, she'd hardly noticed any of it.

She'd run until the mansions became town houses, then storefronts and taverns, and finally the large wooden warehouses of Tiller goods ready to be sent up or downriver. She'd run until she thought her lungs might collapse and she couldn't remember a time her feet had ever been still. And then, just when she thought she would never get there, she heard the slap of water. With a final gasp, she rounded the last warehouse, passing by a man and his son lashing barrels together, and there they were: the Rhona River and the long, tear-shaped island that lay in its center.

1 Anders's Tear.

Her *destiny*.

But as she stood there, gasping for breath, Olivia couldn't spot much of the notorious school. All she could make of it was a solitary turret rising above a very large, very leafy hedge. Light shone from its single window, both illuminating an indigo flag and warning away any boats sailing past in the dark.

Triumph blazed through Olivia, and she would have let out a loud whoop if she weren't aware of the dockworkers. Still, she couldn't help a giddy clap. She'd done it!

She'd flown through Constellation Range, collected unicorn mane, arrived at Healer Hall, and run through Lumin City. Now all she had to do was get onto the island—

Now all she had to do was get onto the island.

"Aphids!" she swore. She hadn't thought that far ahead. There was the southern bridge, called Clarissa's Arch, that linked Jewel Way with Alloy Alley, and in the north, Sophronia's Necklace draped across the river to connect the Garden District to Textile Mile. But neither of them stopped at the island.

"Don't panic, don't panic," Olivia muttered as she whirled around. "Excuse me?" she called out to the dockworkers. The father had gone back inside the warehouse, but the boy, about her age, looked over as she asked, "Can you tell me how to get to the island?"

The boy finished tying a knot, then leaned against the pyramid of barrels. "There are tons of ways," he said. "There are flying cloaks for sale in the Textile Mile, and I heard there's a Forger in Alloy Alley who sells skates that will freeze the water with each glide. There's also the ferry—"

"I'll do that," Olivia cut in.

"—which will start up again at dawn," the boy finished.

Olivia stared at him in horror. "But that's too late! I need to get there by midnight!"

The boy shrugged. "No way you can do that, even if you already had a cloak. It's practically midnight already."

"Cooper!" a man called from the warehouse. "Come help!" And without another word to Olivia, the boy disappeared into the dark as the city bells began to toll the hourly hymn.

Olivia felt their vibrations roll across her skin. The sound stuck and caught, as though it were a net dragging and keeping her frozen in place. *Now* what?

The song ended, and then the bells struck *one*.

Olivia's thoughts scattered. If Laurel were here, she would probably coax river weed to grow into a bridge. Or perhaps she would convince river scum to solidify into a floating path. But why was she thinking of Tiller solutions? *Those* wouldn't help her! All she could do was tell stories.

Two.

And she could sling.

Olivia eyed the offshore turret. It wasn't *so* far away. Maybe she could write a note, a story of why she was late, and sling it to the Academy? Would the provost accept that as her arrival?

Three, the bells warned.

It was her best chance. She reached inside her book bag and pulled out the first book she could grab. It was *Actes des Ardenians*. With a flinch, she tore out the last page, the one that showed a sketch of Lady Elaina and her unicorn galloping into the sun. Grabbing her pen, she wrote her shortest story yet: Olivia arrived.

Four.

That would have to be enough. She plunged her hand into her pocket—and realized it was empty. Aphids! Of course it was! Her slingshot was somewhere in the mountains, lost and gone like the unicorn. But she knew how to make one—she just needed . . .

Her eyes fell on the barrels Cooper had abandoned.

Five.

In a few steps, Olivia was next to the barrel pyramid and pulling at its rubber cords. She was unimpressed by the city dweller's knots, as they practically melted under her fingers. With one tug the cord slithered free, and—

CRASH!

Barrels rolled in all directions. Still, she managed to keep hold of the rubber cord as she jumped out of their way and sprinted toward the nearest dock.

"Hey!"

Olivia glanced back to see Cooper and his father running toward her.

"Get back here!"

They sounded furious, but Olivia didn't have time to worry about them. Reaching the end of the long wooden dock, she looped the cords around its poles and knotted them into place. In less than a second, she'd created a massive, makeshift slingshot.

Wadding her note into a ball, she placed it in the center of the rope and pulled.

Six. (Or maybe seven?)

Olivia's lost slingshot had always felt friendly in her hand, like a cat pushing against her palm. She'd known exactly how far to pull the worn strap, smooth from use, and she'd known the exact tilt of the handle to get the perfect trajectory. The stolen cord, however, was stubborn. No matter how much Olivia tugged, it did not want to stretch, as if it knew its job was to contract and bind barrels together and did not approve of this new turn of events.

The bells chimed again—was *that* seven?

Olivia didn't know. But each strike of the bell felt like a strike to her heart. Her hands shook. From exhaustion or nerves or . . .

. . . something else.

Footsteps thundered onto the wooden dock.

"*Please*," Olivia whispered to the cord, and this time, when she tugged, she leaned the whole of herself into it. Not just the weight of her body, but the weight of Nan's disappointment; the weight of everyone's eyes in Buddle; the weight of Laurel's belief in her; the weight of her loneliness.

The cord pulled back easily.

It, too, understood tension and strain. It, too, understood wanting to tie itself to others.

. . . but how had *Olivia* understood the *cord*?

Eight.

"Got you!"

Olivia didn't need to turn around to recognize Cooper's voice. Before he could grab her, she pulled the cord up and over her head. Now she stood where she had held the story, where she would usually position an olive pit.

And then—she let go.

Nine.

Olivia catapulted high into the air. Her braids streamed out behind her like a comet's tail, gently tugging her scalp as she arced over the river and toward the island.

She could hardly process what *had* happened and what was *still* happening, but she was acutely aware that she *wasn't* flying. At some point very soon, she would reach the apex of her trajectory, and then she would begin to fall.

But before Olivia could completely panic, she caught her first glimpse of what lay beyond the academy's hedge: a large, manicured lawn, hedge mazes, a reflecting pool, all cushioning a rambling estate of diamond-paned windows, chimneys, and ivy. It looked like a very castle-y house, or house-y castle, with a wide, curved staircase that led up to three doors.

A marble staircase that loomed closer with each passing breath.

Ten.

Now, Olivia panicked. She was going too fast. She might be all right if she landed in the reflection pond, but she knew she was headed for the marble staircase and there was nothing she could do to stop it except scream.

"HEEEELLP!"

A strong jerk under her armpits suddenly yanked her, and a strange whir beat above her head. Looking up, she saw that her book bag had sprouted the papery wings of an Olivia-sized samara—or, as they were known to the children of Buddle, a whirler. After the storm in Constellation Range, Laurel had insisted on modifying Olivia's book bag in case they crashed again.

"How do I activate it?" Olivia had asked.

"Easy," Laurel had replied. "Just scream like your life depends on it."

Olivia clutched the straps of her book bag as the giant maple tree seed spun her down through the air like a corkscrew, depositing her gently onto the gravel in front of the staircase.

Eleven.

Stomach turning from the flight and head spinning with questions, Olivia staggered up the steps, the whirler's wings dragging behind her. She stretched, reaching for the door. Wood brushed her knuckles as the bells rang for a twelfth and final time.

Silence.

Was she too late? And then—

Light appeared under the door.

"Spinners are supposed to use the *South* Gate," a voice grumbled as the hinges squeaked. "But since you're here, come in."

PART II

One, two, magic your shoes,
Three, four, weave the door.
Five, six, cross your stitch,
Seven, eight, hang thread straight,
Nine, ten, Spin again.

—The Spinner's Book of Valor

CHAPTER TEN

Light engulfed Olivia as the door opened and the silhouette of a tall, thin man in scholar's robes beckoned her inside.

"Don't loiter," he said as he swung his lantern higher. "It's late enough as it is."

Half-blinded and still dizzy, Olivia stumbled across the threshold and into a grand foyer. She had the momentary impression of oak panels, thick tapestries, and soaring arches before the door thudded shut and the man swept in front of her. He set his lantern down with a *clank* and picked up a leather portfolio from a side table.

"Let's get this over with," he muttered as he began to riffle through the papers. His thick black hair swooped magnificently up and over his forehead like the crest of a tropical bird, and his wide sleeves only added to the avian effect. "Welcome-to-Unicorn-Academy," he rattled off. "A-place-where-magic-meets-history-and-apprentices-flourish. I-am-Scholar-Louis-Garmont-Dean-of-Spinners-and-you-are?"

"Olivia Hayes," she said, a beat too slow, dazed by both the speed of the dean's speech and the collar of his robe. Or, more specifically, the embroidered silver spider that she was sure hadn't been there a moment ago.

Garmont scowled and flipped the page. "I don't see an Olivia here." The spider dropped down to his breast pocket, leaving a thin silver line trailing behind it. "Did you register?"

"I—I think so?" she said, looking away from the spider and toward the page in the man's hand. Years spent behind the apothecary counter had made her an expert at reading upside down, and she could clearly make out its title: Spinner Apprentices.

"You're looking at the wrong list," she said, and because that sounded rude, she quickly added, "Maybe try looking at the Tiller list, sir?"

Garmont waved his hand impatiently. "Why in thread's end would I look for a Spinner on the Tiller roster?"

. . .

. . .

. . .

His question was a hook, and Olivia snagged on it. If she moved—if she so much as breathed or even *thought*—she would completely unravel. So she stood in the grand foyer of the Unicorn Academy, completely silent, completely still, and utterly confused.

"Well?" Garmont demanded, at last looking toward Olivia. His eyebrows (which swooped just as magnificently as his hair) raised as he took in the mud on her gardener's boots and the papery wings of the whirler that still dangled from her backpack.

Suddenly, he looked much more awake.

Flipping through the portfolio, Garmont stopped at another page, the word *Dormant* sprawled across its top. He glanced at her again. "Olivia Hayes?" When she nodded, Garmont produced a quill from his sleeve and made a quick mark. "Well," he said, snapping the portfolio shut and picking up the lantern. "I'd say you're dormant no more, Spinner Apprentice Hayes. Right this way."

Garmont was already halfway to the double staircase by the time Olivia could process what he had said, and his foot was on the first step before she managed to sputter out, "I don't understand— I don't have . . . I mean—" She threw her hands up, flailing. "My family are Tillers and . . . How can I be a— There must be some mistake!"

Garmont stopped and, with a sigh so big it practically whistled through the hall, turned. "If you follow, I'll do my best to explain. But it's been a very long day, and it's very, *very* late."

An explanation was all Olivia had ever wanted. Well, that and magic. And maybe, she thought as she sprinted across the foyer, she was about to get both.

"What do you know about the unicorns' return?" Garmont asked as they made their way up the staircase and underneath a chandelier of glowing jewels. Their light reflected off the polished floor, as though someone had scattered multicolored galaxies on the steps.

"Unicorns returned when the guilds reunited to face the wraiths," Olivia said, naming the monsters that had once infested Arden. "They joined with the Prime Minister as she led the troops to victory."

"Is that all you know?"

Olivia bristled. It was all she had been able to *collect*. Nan's customers had mentioned more—rumors about a broken crown, walking statues, visitors from another world—but living in the northernmost settlement made *dependable* information scarce. Besides . . .

"Nan's a Traditionalist," she explained.

"I see." Garmont glanced back at her. "Then I advise you to check *The Unicorn Quest* out from the library. Lyric the Lyrical covered the events extensively in three volumes. But yes, you know the most important part: unicorns returned when the guilds united. And with their return—"

"—magic flourished," Olivia said, repeating the often-used phrase and eager to show Garmont that she did actually know something, thank you very much.

But Garmont shook his head. "—came understanding. Magic isn't in *humans*, after all. It's in the material. As artisans, we help the thread be what it was always meant to be—a part of a moving tapestry, the fringe of a flying carpet, or a knot to catch luck. We don't *make* magic. We simply release it."

"But I've tried," Olivia said, the truth scraping her throat. "I've followed all of Nan's recipes exactly, but nothing magical has ever happened."

"You've tried Tilling," Garmont corrected. "But what about Spinning?"

Olivia shook her head. "No. Everyone in my family is a Tiller. They always have been."

"And are they all good at mathematics?" Garmont asked. "Do some of them run faster than others? Can you draw as well as your brother?"

Olivia frowned. "I don't have a brother."

Garmont waved a hand. "I'm making a point. Talents like running fast and having a good memory run in families—but not always. My brothers are terrible at singing, while I am an excellent tenor. The talent to release magic is the same."

He ushered her down a hall hung with portraits of people with severe eyes and questionable facial hair. "Think of it this way. You could be the best ice-skater in all of Arden, but if you've never been allowed on ice, how could you possibly know?"

Olivia didn't answer, but her stunned expression must

have told Garmont all he needed to know, because he continued. "Unicorns did not return magic to us," he explained as they turned down another hall. "Magic never left. But by not allowing guilds to intermingle—to share knowledge and *possibilities*—we weakened ourselves. Today, I'm guessing, is the first day you've ever seen someone Spin?"

White feathers against blackest water.

Eyes wide, Olivia nodded. Garmont smiled, unmasking his grumpiness for the act that it was.

"Then today is also the day you first heard the whisper of a new language—cotton's clamor to be spun into something stronger, wool's desire to protect against the elements, satin's promise to feel like candlelight against skin.

In these halls, we will teach you how to *listen*. You will learn how to cut silk so that it becomes a flying cloak instead of a dancing slipper. We will teach you where, *exactly*, a seam needs to be placed so that a pocket remains a secret to everyone but its wearer. Not only will you *hear* the language of thread, you will *speak* it."

Olivia expected Garmont's explanation to ground her, but now she felt adrift upon a strange sea of emotion. Joy churned there, of course, but there was also a current of grief. All her life she'd wanted to be like her family—magic like them. And now she was . . . but also not. What would Nan make of a Spinner granddaughter?

Garmont stopped in front of a tapestry of Honoria Sash,

the Spinner founder, immediately recognizable by her piles of shell-pink hair, and swept it aside. "Welcome to the Spinners' Wing. You are not allowed to venture into other guilds' wings without permission from myself or another one of the deans. Understood?"

"Yes," Olivia said, suddenly feeling nervous. "Are there any other rules?"

"Several thousand," he said, leading her to a door with a fish-tailed melusine carved into it. From behind it, Olivia heard a shriek of laughter followed by several loud shushes, which ended in even more giggles. Garmont raised an eyebrow and then his voice. "But there's only one rule you need to remember tonight."

The giggling stopped; then there was the padding of several feet, more whispers, and one loud yelp that sounded like someone had stubbed their toe against a nightstand. Garmont looked significantly at Olivia. "There is to be *no talking* once lights are out."

With that, he knocked once and opened the door to reveal a darkened room with four canopy beds. From three of them came the sound of suspiciously loud snoring. With a tilt of his head, Garmont indicated the empty bed, which was closest to them. Olivia guessed that one must be hers.

"Thank you," she whispered, and with a nod, Garmont clicked the door shut.

Olivia's eyes hadn't even begun to adjust before she heard the swish of curtains and the scrape of a match. Candlelight washed over the dormitory as three curious faces peered out from behind drapes.

"What are you wearing?"

Olivia flinched, suddenly acutely aware of the stains on her tunic, her frizzy braids, and the smidge of goose poop she hadn't managed to scrape off her boot, as the girl nearest her slipped out of bed and padded toward her in silk slippers. Her black hair was tied up in an army of lavender bows that matched the bows on her pajama set.

"Because that is the most *beautiful* cape I've ever seen!" The Spinner girl gazed at the whirler still trailing behind Olivia. "Look at the detail! The veins—it doesn't even look woven. It looks—" She gasped and looked up at Olivia, eyes wide. "Is it *Tiller* made?"

Olivia nodded and shrugged her backpack off. "It's more of a parachute than a cape," she said. "My sister made it for me after our Dandiloon crashed—"

"A Dandiloon?!" A second girl with chestnut waves appeared next to them.

"Crashed?!"

Olivia jumped as a third girl—who looked identical to the second, right down to the stray curl above her right ear—came up behind her.

"It was just a little crash," Olivia amended. "The real damage came when we almost skidded off the cliff—"

"Cliff?!" The first girl shook her head. "You have to tell us absolutely *everything*."

And before Olivia knew it, the girls had dragged blankets and pillows onto the rug in front of the fireplace, and suddenly she was in the middle of a cozy nest, with the others sprawled around her. As the girls leaned in, asking questions and demanding details, an unfamiliar feeling draped over Olivia.

A feeling that maybe—just maybe—she was finally where she belonged.

It was still dark out when something tickled Olivia's nose and woke her. Without opening her eyes, she rubbed her nose and turned her head. She never wanted to get up. Not when the pillow was so soft and deliciously (magically?) cool. Not when she was so, so, *so* tired. Still, she was tired for a good reason. The other apprentices in her suite—the bow-covered Paisley and the twins Camlet and Gabardine, or as they preferred to be called, Cami and Gabi—had listened late into the night, asking questions about Buddle and wanting to know everything about the unicorn in the mountains. Olivia was happy to share.

Mostly.

She had not told them about the strange chasm. Or how her sister had not seen the unicorn. Olivia's friendships were too new, too fragile, and she didn't want them to think she was weird. She already had all of Buddle for that.

Crinkle, crinkle—boop!

This time, Olivia's eyes flew open, and she found herself nose-to-beak with a paper bird. Upon seeing she was awake, the bird promptly unfolded, revealing a note in the same spiky handwriting as her original invitation. The indigo ink glowed slightly, allowing her to read even in the cocooned dark of her drapes.

Apprentice Hayes,
A ferry has been arranged to take you to Textile Mile to procure a Spinner kit. It departs from the academy dock at seven bells. Lessons begin at ten.
Don't be late.
—Provost Malchain

Excitement shot through Olivia. Suddenly, she was *very* awake.

"Thank you," she whispered as the paper refolded itself and darted out.

Pulling back the heavy drapes, Olivia slipped out into the chilly morning. She half tiptoed, half sprinted to the wooden dresser at the foot of her bed, where she'd found a set of pajamas the night before. The only other clothes she had were the ones she'd arrived in, and those she'd shoved in the bottom drawer.

Opening it now, she stared at the neatly folded fabric in front of her. In a way it looked like her tunic—it was the right shape, the same size, and the tag at the nape of the collar clearly spelled out Olivia's name in Nan's familiar round letters. But yesterday, her dress had been green, and today it was Spinner yellow, with a hint of green in the seams and hems, like a leaf not quite ready to let go of summer.

Awed, Olivia looked at the piece of furniture with new appreciation. So, not just a dresser, but a Dresser—a bit of Tiller and Spinner alchemy that combined thread with trees' ability to change for the season. She tugged the tunic over her head. It fit perfectly, down to the cream-colored ring that had bloomed on her right sleeve and the tiny unicorn embroidered over her heart.

Olivia's spine straightened. Her chin lifted. And for the first time in a long time, she didn't feel the need to imagine she was anything other than who she was: Spinner Apprentice Hayes.

Hurrying toward the door, she flung it open and barreled straight into something squishy.

"I'm so sorry!" Olivia gasped as Paisley stumbled back, almost knocking into a suit of copper armor before catching herself.

"No harm done," Paisley said, adjusting her bow. "I was just wondering if I should wake you. Hungry?" She handed Olivia a muffin that was hot to the touch and smelled incredible—but it would have to wait.

"Do you know how to get to the academy dock?" Olivia asked. "I need the ferry!"

"That's why I'm here," Paisley said, already starting down the hall. "We'll make it if we run."

CHAPTER ELEVEN

As Olivia tried to adjust her pace to slippery marble floors instead of good, sensible wooden planks, she caught tantalizing glimpses of classrooms filled with fabrics, courtyards with barrels of swords waiting to be swung, and a library with more books than trees in the Endless. She knew exactly where she would be after class. Paisley finally flung open a door that didn't lead to more corridors or alcoves, and they sprinted into the morning.

"There it is!" Paisley huffed. "Come on!"

Pebbles sprayed into the air as they crunched down the path toward an archway in the hedge. In the opening, Olivia could make out a simple wooden dock and, just beyond it, cutting through the mist, a small skiff. The girls thundered onto the dock just as the boat kissed the pier. It was empty except for the ferryman, who wore a wide straw hat and a glum expression. Paisley held out two purple tickets with familiar spikey handwriting. The man grunted, which must have been an invitation, because Paisley clambered into the prow and Olivia scooted in after.

Cool wind ruffled Olivia's neck as the ferryman pushed them out onto the river. Still trying to catch her breath, she looked back at the academy. It rose from the river like a water lily, its many gables as pointed as petals and its single, ivy-draped tower a bud about to burst into bloom. Rows of diamond-paned windows caught the rising sun, and the entire building sparkled.

Though it was still early, the outdoor markets of Textile Mile were already stirring as the ferryman floated them into port. Fishmongers wrote the catch of the day in chalk while vendors shook out bolts of shimmering fabric, yards of seed pearls, and spools of thread in every color imaginable, including highly specific ones like "the sky at sunrise Fourthmonth 27, year 366 G.E." and "seawater one fathom below on a snowy day," and much, much more.

"Where are the Spinner kits?" Olivia asked, rising to her tiptoes and straining to look over a stand labeled Thinking Caps.

"You don't want to buy those here." Paisley looked scandalized. "Provost Malchain made an appointment for you with the Mender. That's where I got mine." She patted the pink coin purse hanging from her belt. "She's *very* exclusive. We'll—oh, pins! There it is!"

But instead of pulling her into a shop, Paisley dashed to a nearby display of ribbons that fluttered in the morning breeze, the sign in front of them proclaiming this was Madam von Pleat's Rows of Bows. Paisley began to pull ribbons off, draping them across her shoulders and holding them up to her hair as she looked at herself in a full-length mirror.

"If you tell me where the Mender is," Olivia suggested as the ribbon seller walked over with an alarmingly large basket of spools, "I can find her myself."

"Are you sure?" Paisley asked, but it wasn't really a question, as she was already opening her coin purse. "Take my B.P.S.—Ball of Positioning String. Just drop it and don't let go. Ooh, look! Chambray!" And without a backward glance, Paisley hurried to the seller's tent next-door.

Olivia looked at the ball in her hand. It was an ordinary, if ugly, ball of mustard-colored yarn. If it were ever knitted into a sweater, Olivia knew it would be the itchiest, most uncomfortable sweater ever made. But Paisley hadn't said anything about knitting. Holding an end between her fingers and feeling more than a bit silly, Olivia dropped the yarn onto the cobblestones.

It rolled a few inches . . . then a foot . . . then it rolled out of the tent and disappeared under a cart at an impressive speed before shooting down a side street.

Olivia yelped and ran after it, trying to wind up the yellow thread before it could trip anyone. With her back to the river, she chased the yarn into the narrow, twisting alleys of Textile Mile. She was lucky it was still early; not many Spinners were up and about yet. As it was, however, she still saw several pairs of leather shoes, silk slippers, and sandals, as well as beautiful skirts sweeping the streets. She was just wondering if the ball would ever stop rolling when it bumped against a shop door and finally stilled.

"You stay with me," she ordered as she picked the yarn up and then looked to see herself in front of a large sign that read: The Mender.

It seemed to be the right place, though the shop could do with some mending itself. Paint flaked off the front, and instead of a fancy display, the single window held only a sun-bleached sign that said Closed. It didn't exactly match the *exclusive* label Paisley had bestowed upon it, but maybe after cleaning up other people's messes, the Mender was too tired to deal with one more repair.

Olivia knocked, but no one answered. She tried the knob, and the door opened.

"Hello?" Olivia called as she picked her way through piles of goods in need of repair. She spotted chairs with ripped upholstery and stringless guitars, and brushed past a set of bells that didn't jingle. "Is anyone here?"

"Go away!" a muffled shout came from somewhere to Olivia's left, and she peered around a wardrobe with a broken hinge to see she had reached the back of the shop, where a small counter stood in front of a closed door. "We're closed!" the voice said, and Olivia realized it was coming from behind the door. "Come back tomorrow!"

But Olivia didn't have tomorrow.

"Provost Malchain sent me?" she said. "I'm from—"

The door slammed open, and a woman with light brown skin wearing a magenta gown entirely covered in pockets surged out, waving a piece of parchment in her hand. Her black hair was pulled into a severe knot that looked like it might roll off her head but for the two knitting needles that pinned it in place.

"What don't you understand?" the Mender snapped. "We're closed. We're expecting—oh," she broke off as she peered down at Olivia, then looked at the creased note in her hand, whereon Olivia could just make out indigo ink. "I suppose we're expecting *you*. Olivia, is it?" Her floor-length sleeves swishing elegantly, she waved an arm toward a three-legged stool. "Have a seat."

The woman bustled away as Olivia sat on the stool she'd indicated. A moment later, she returned carrying a large basket on her hip. She dropped it in front of Olivia, who peered in, expecting to see shimmery satin purses or perhaps a backpack of embroidered brocade, but instead she found . . .

"Thank you," Olivia said politely, looking up at the Mender. "But I have plenty of socks."

"Good," the Mender said. "Then you'll know what they're

supposed to look like. Choose one that needs mending and ring when you're done." Before Olivia could say another word, the Mender had disappeared behind her door.

Olivia stared dubiously at the laundry in front of her. This was not the glorious beginning she'd been expecting on her first morning as a Spinner apprentice. But like in all her favorite tales, maybe it was a test? At least she wasn't a complete stranger to sewing. Olivia patched her family's clothes back at the apothecary. It'd always been one of her favorite chores, as she could let her mind wander while her fingers were busy. She could pretend to be the Forest Maiden, who used rose thorns for spindles, or the wise hermit who'd trapped a cloud and woven it into the very first sheep.

And maybe she liked it because she'd always been a Spinner, just as Garmont had said.

Picking up the needle and thread, Olivia selected a clean-looking sock with a hole at its heel and began. Soon, a thin line of yellow stitches replaced the hole. Holding the sock up, Olivia examined her work. Not bad, even if she thought so herself. The stitches were small and neat, and when she tapped the bell at the counter, she felt confident she had passed whatever test had been set.

Pretty confident.

The Mender bustled back. In the few minutes she'd been away, five more knitting needles had been added to her bun.

She also now wore thick leather gloves, and the hem of her long sleeve smoked slightly.

"What's this?"

Olivia pulled her attention away from the singed fabric and to the sock the Mender wriggled. She tossed it back to Olivia. "You mended it, but you didn't Mend it. You have to *walk* in the sock. You have to *listen*. Magic is in the material—" She broke off as a loud creak came from the front of the shop.

"Hello?" a man's voice called.

"Honestly." The Mender shook her head, and Olivia ducked as a knitting needle flew out. "Has everyone in this city forgotten how to read?" She disappeared behind a tower of embroidery hoops. "We are *closed*—oh. Thorn, welcome."

"There's been another," the newcomer said, keeping his voice low and immediately pricking Olivia's interest. She sensed a story.

"Another—" the Mender's breath caught. "Another missing unicorn?"

Olivia straightened, the words sending tingles through her. A missing unicorn! Or rather, unicorns. But how could a unicorn go missing? Unicorns were *pure* magic. They couldn't *get* lost. Nor could they die, unless they were killed. No one today, however, would ever slay a unicorn, not now that everyone knew the act would transform the murderer into a wraith, a monster cursed to hide from the sun. Once, wraiths had laid waste to Arden, but with the return of unicorns, wraiths had been defeated and none had been seen since. She had to hear more.

Scooting off her stool, Olivia peered around a tower of bobbins to see an older teenager, eighteen or so, with sandy hair and large ears standing beside the Mender. He wore simple traveler's clothes, but the signet ring on his hand marked him as a scribe of great importance.

The young man nodded. "I received a message from the herd leader that some of her more curious kin had vanished in recent weeks, and now I can't find *her* either. The only thing we did find was—" He cut off as his eyes landed on Olivia. He frowned. "Is there someplace we can speak privately?"

The Mender beckoned him to follow, and as they passed by, she handed the sock back to Olivia. "If you let anyone interrupt us," she said, "you forfeit your Spinner kit." With that, the door clicked shut—just as Nan's apothecary door had clicked shut every day of Olivia's life.

Olivia looked down at the sock in her hand, then back at the door. Her back straightened. Her chin lifted. She would *not* be locked out anymore.

With the same determination Alfred the Ambitious must have felt as he pulled the sword from the volcano, Olivia ripped out her neat, ordinary stitches and rethreaded her needle. She could do this. She *would* do this.

The front door slammed open a second time, and footsteps pounded through the labyrinth of broken things. A moment later, a dark-skinned girl with thick black hair, combat boots, and a wild expression burst into view.

"I need the Mender!" the girl said. "Where is she?!"

"She's busy," Olivia said, eyeing the saber slashed through the girl's belt loop. Between the weapon and the black leather tunic, there was no mistaking this girl for anything other than a Forger apprentice. "The Mender said no one can interrupt her—hey!" The girl had pushed by Olivia and slammed her hand on the counter.

Ding! Ding! Ding! Dingdingdingdingding!

"Stop that," Olivia said, worried the Mender had meant what she said about not giving her a Spinner kit. "She's closed."

"But it's an emergency!" The Forger whirled around, a panicked look in her dark brown eyes. "You're a Spinner—can you help?" She slammed a fraying bootlace onto the countertop. "It's about to snap, and I need it fixed, now! I have a bout in fifteen minutes!"

For Olivia, who had grown up in an apothecary, "emergency" usually meant blood or broken bones. A fraying shoelace was just a nuisance.

Olivia pasted on her most polite smile, the one she reserved for the most exacting customers. "The river market has many—" Olivia stopped as the girl shook her head wildly.

"No." Her black curls billowed around her like thickest smoke. "It has to be *this* lace. It's . . . *lucky*."

Oh. Olivia looked at the lace with new interest. She'd read stories about Spinners who could coax fortunes into laces. Some were made to protect the wearer from small mishaps, like stubbing a toe or stepping into a puddle, but more powerful craft was possible, too—like laces that made it impossible to lose a fight. They were banned from any kind of competition or exam. Olivia didn't know what kind of fortune had been twisted into these laces, but based on the Forger's choice of visiting the most out-of-the-way shop, Olivia suspected something more like the latter.

But the last time she'd tried to help in a shop, she'd turned a mayor into a mushroom.

Olivia shook her head. "I can't—"

"*Please*," the girl pleaded, and Olivia heard something familiar in her voice. A want. A wish . . .

Olivia prodded the shoelace. The frayed edge didn't look too different from a worn-out elastic from a slingshot, and she'd fixed those plenty of times. "I . . . I can try?"

The relief on the girl's face was so sharp, it cut Olivia to the core.

So, taking a deep breath, she laid the bootlace across her lap and picked up a tweezer. Everyone said magic was in the material, so she would start there.

At least that was easy. The lace was woven of jute, one of

Nan's favorite plants. Its leaves soothed stomachaches, while its stalks contained long, resilient fibers perfect for canvas bags and strong shoelaces. But it was its fruit—spindle-shaped, bitter, and served only during Starfell festivities—that Olivia liked best of all.

She'd gobble them up while Laurel played her recorder. At some point, Nan would grab Olivia's juice-stained hands and pull her into the Green Thumb Reel. They would whirl about the apothecary while Laurel laughed and played even faster. Olivia's heart squeezed. She missed her family, and the memory had come so swiftly and clearly that she could almost hear the music now.

No, not almost hear.

Olivia leaned forward, her nose only an inch away from the lace.

Could hear.

Not the Green Thumb Reel, but another tune tickled her palm. A song so quiet, she didn't hear it so much as feel it, but it was there, in the jute, in the bootlace, and Olivia wanted to hear more.

After all, the Mender had said to listen.

Using the tweezer, Olivia caught a filament and plucked, shaking out its note. Again and again, she pulled out a note and tucked it back in, until it built to a song while Olivia's fingers danced.

One knot, a twist to the right, then twist to the left, and tuck.

With each new knot, the melody sharpened and the fibers strengthened. They remembered the sound of wind rustling their leaves, remembered what it had been to grow tall and strong, remembered what it had been to be whole on the riverbed, roots catching water and nutrients the same way the bootlace now caught agility, speed, and . . .

Olivia frowned. There was something else in the lace; a song that did not want to be heard. She tried again.

One knot, a twist to the right, then twist to the left, and tuck.

The secretive filament slipped away again. Each time Olivia thought she found it, it would sneak away, only to reappear a few twists later. Her fingers flew, faster and faster, trying to catch up with the secret.

One knot, a twist to the right, then twist to the left—

Her fingers touched air.

Olivia blinked and looked down at her lap, where a bootlace—perfectly smooth, not a fiber out of place—rested, whole and complete.

"Thank you!" The Forger tugged the lace out of Olivia's hand, flung a silver guilder on the counter, and raced out of the shop, while Olivia stayed sitting, staring at her hands.

So *that's* what magic felt like.

No wonder Laurel had been so excited to leave their home to learn. No wonder Nan loved to putter in her apothecary from dawn to dusk. She would have understood better had they explained magic was like reading her favorite book for the first time—untethered from time and space, completely lost yet totally present.

Glancing toward the back room door, she saw it was still closed. Olivia grabbed the basket of socks and pulled it closer. She couldn't wait to Spin again.

"Call me an iron, but I am impressed," a voice said from behind Olivia minutes or maybe hours later. "May I?"

Olivia jumped, startled out of her quiet reverie, while the Mender, not waiting for a response, plucked the purple sock from Olivia's hand. Olivia glanced at the basket at her feet, now filled with socks that looked as though they'd never been worn, let alone mended. Unlike her first attempt, there was not a single seam to be seen on any of them.

"Well done," the Mender said, and Olivia looked up in time to see the woman reach into the sock and turn it inside out. Suddenly, it didn't look very socklike anymore, and looked much more like a small coin purse. In fact, it looked exactly like Paisley's pouch, though this one was indigo instead of pink, and its pull string tassel a bright, yellow gold.

Awed, Olivia watched as the Mender strolled through the store, plucking spools of all colors, needles of all sizes, hoops, pins, and many other Spinner-y things Olivia did not yet know the names of.

"Here you are," the Mender said, circling back to her. "One Spinner kit with everything a first-year apprentice might need." She held the coin purse out to Olivia. Despite the number and size of the items Olivia had seen her drop in, the little pouch remained palm-sized and light as a walnut.

"Thank you," Olivia said, looping the pouch onto her belt. "It's gorgeous." She reached for the B.P.S. she'd left on the counter, then stopped short at the sight of the Forger's guilder. Horrified, she faced the Mender. "I don't have any coins on me!"

"Your Mending more than covered the cost," the woman said. "In fact . . ." She made one last glance around the room, then walked over to a display of slings, and selected one. She handed it to Olivia, and Olivia marveled at its braided wool cord, so different from the rough hemp rope used to make slings in Buddle. Even though she missed the rough bark of the slingshot she'd lost in Constellation Range, she had a feeling that *this* sling would never miss its mark.

"That should make us even," the Mender said, sounding satisfied. "Now, shoo—I really am closed today."

Olivia tucked the sling next to her purse, then dropped the ball of yarn. Immediately, it began to roll, unraveling as it went. Breaking into a run, she chased it down the streets back toward the ferry, her new Spinner kit bouncing comfortably against her hip.

It was time for class.

CHAPTER TWELVE

Olivia and Paisley made it back to the academy in time for attendance, but only just. Everyone else had already been seated, and Olivia felt the weight of eyes as they entered the circular lecture chamber that had once been a throne room. Like an outdoor amphitheater, stone benches circled the center, rising higher and higher so that the king—or in this case, Dean Garmont and his spider-spangled robes—could be perfectly seen and heard. However, it also meant that she and Paisley could be perfectly seen and heard as they scooted past several boots and even more scowls to reach the Spinner section.

From Paisley, Olivia knew that the academy's enrollment was small compared to other learning centers, like Phlogiston Academy in Fyrton or Needle Pointe's Ties Institute. Still, with nearly a hundred apprentices packed into one room, it was the most people her age Olivia had ever seen. A third of the children wore Spinner yellow, another third Tiller green, and the last third, Forger black.

"Didn't the Gemmers send anyone?" Olivia whispered to Paisley as they squashed in next to the twins, Cami and Gabi.

"They did." Paisley pointed below. "She's there, between Scholar Hatchett, dean of Forgers, and Scholar Ravine, the Gemmer dean."

Olivia squinted down into the front row, where several adults in scholar's robes perched. It took her a moment to locate the lone speck of Gemmer blue scrunched between a bearlike man and a tiny woman in a bejeweled gown. Olivia sat back, slightly stunned. It was one thing to read that the Gemmers were the smallest guild, but it was another to see it in real life.

Excitement buzzed through the apprentices as Dean Garmont neared the end of attendance, and by the time he called out the last name (a Forger named Axel Zinc), the buzz had turned into a roar. Because whatever the first lesson of the first day of the first all-guild academy would be—flight? how to talk to wolves? invisibility?—it would be something grand and definitely more than just—

"A lecture!" Garmont clapped his hands together, ignoring the apprentices' obvious disappointment. "Deans Horatio Hatchett, Holly Barry, Rubi Ravine, and I have prepared a special seminar for you this morning entitled *Finding Ourselves in the Founding of the Guilds: The Founders: Part I*. Before we begin spinning storms or planting self-growing castles, we must learn our origins and how, from the darkness of the Lost Age, emerged a great civilization of craftsmen, artisans, and—"

FFFFFPPPPBBBBRRT!

Olivia's jaw dropped. Had that been— Did Dean Garmont just—?

Everyone looked as stunned as she felt. Everyone except for the blue-haired boy sitting behind Olivia and sniggering loudly. Then came another, slightly wetter *FFFFPPPTTTTTTTTTT.*

This time, the apprentices lost it. Laughter ricocheted against the stained glass windows, the sound so loud that *Finding Ourselves in the Founding of the Guilds: The Founders: Part I* was completely drowned out. Dean Garmont stood in the center of the arena, his lips moving, arms waving, but nothing could get their attention.

"Sam," Paisley giggled as she twisted around to admonish the boy. "How *could* you?"

Sam winked. "You haven't seen anything yet."

And they wouldn't, as an unexpected breeze whooshed by Olivia's ear, carrying a comb, a wooden cup, a palm-sized pouch, and a twisty bit of string out from Sam's seemingly infinite pockets.

The boy scrambled to catch them, but it was too late. The objects were already zipping through the air toward the center of the arena, where a woman suddenly stood, crossing two battle-axes over her head.

CLANG! CLANG! CLANGCLANGCLANG!

The apprentices' laughter stopped as each object hit the ax heads and stayed there, sticking to the blades like magnets. The woman whirled her axes down and examined her blades.

"A Tongue Twist," she said, beginning to walk up the steps toward Sam, "a Balding Comb, a Hic Cup, and a Gaseous Cushion." As the woman neared their section, Olivia realized that she was much older than she first appeared. Lines crowded her eyes, and what Olivia had mistaken for blonde hair was actually white. The same white, in fact, as the flour smudges on the frilly apron she wore over a chain mail shirt.

"What do you have to say for yourself, Samson Milliner?"

"I'm sorry, Provost," Sam squeaked. "I just—"

He stopped short as Provost Aquila Malchain shook her head. "I do not have time for this, Samson Milliner," she said. "And truth be told, neither do you." There was another swish, and suddenly one of the ax's dull ends was a hair's width from the emblem on Sam's chest. "What is on your tunic?"

"Uh," the boy mumbled, "a unicorn?"

Behind silver spectacles, the provost's eyes flashed. "And do you think there's a unicorn on your tunic because you are special?" She shook her head. "No. You have a unicorn as a reminder of what we have to lose."

With a suddenness that belied the woman's age, the provost jerked her axes upward and the chamber plunged into darkness. Muffled screams and squeals filled the air, but the apprentices quieted as the provost clanged her axes together and began to speak to the greater chamber.

"Four ages mark Arden. The Lost Age, that time before memory, when the world was still new, its seams not yet sewn, and monsters ravaged the land until . . ."

A curve of light suddenly shone in the rafters of the throne room, reflecting, or maybe even springing from Malchain's axes. It hung there like a crescent moon, and as Olivia stared at it, light dripped from its tips. As the moon's tears fell, they elongated, stretching into spiraling horns, flowing manes, and bright hooves. Unicorns etched from light galloped around the chamber, prancing among the seated apprentices and illuminating their expressions of awe. Olivia gasped as one unicorn galloped through her, momentarily warming her bones.

The provost shifted her axes again. Light smeared, forming into a silhouette of a girl crouched low over a unicorn's neck. The pair shook itself loose of the axes and raced toward the center of the arena, while the rest of the unicorns merged into a giant glowing serpent. The snake chased the Rider and her unicorn high into the rafters; then all three of them charged into a miniature sun. The convergence of light blinded Olivia, and by the time the black dots cleared from her eyes, the sun had gathered into a four-pointed crown.

"Thus, we entered the Royal Age," Provost Malchain continued, "an era that begins with the many nomadic clans of Arden uniting to crown Anders the First—and ends seven hundred years later with the overthrowing of the monarchy and the extinction of unicorns."

The crown of light split into four pieces that each shifted into one of the guilds' sigils. Olivia craned her head back to watch the love knot and oak leaf drift across the ceiling, floating over the apprentices like lost stars.

"The Guild Age," the provost said as she made her way back down the stairs, "three hundred years of stagnation, depleted magic, and distrust. A time that you were all born to but no longer live in, due to the bravery of one girl. A girl who sacrificed everything to piece together a fractured truth: unicorns could return, but only if the world changed. And so, we did. Spinners joined with Forgers, Tillers with Gemmers, and together, we all made it possible for the herds to gallop again. We abolished laws that separated us. We broke bread and shared stories."

Olivia frowned. She hadn't known the unicorns only returned because the guilds had worked together. Did Nan know? Olivia didn't think so. Nan was only a Traditionalist because she wanted to *protect* unicorns, but maybe if she knew that's what the Unicorn Academy wanted, too, she would forgive Olivia for enrolling.

"And yet," the provost continued, "it is easy to change for a single day. It is harder—much, much harder—to *keep* the change. Already, disagreement and distrust hound the Grand Council. But this newest age doesn't belong to them. It belongs to *you*. And you, my dear apprentices, will determine whether this is to be another broken age—or the Age of Unicorns."

The provost twirled her axes, and the sigils disintegrated into golden raindrops that showered down onto the apprentices' heads.

"In one year," the provost said over the awed gasps, "grandmasters will fill this chamber. On that day, all of your names will be placed into a helmet, and one will be drawn. That apprentice—that *one* apprentice—will be the academy's champion. They will have to pass whatever test the Grand Council sets before them and answer every question in order for the academy's charter to be renewed."

Shocked murmuring broke out. *One* champion? The provost couldn't mean—just *one*? But what if a Tiller was pulled and the test was a sword duel? Or a Gemmer was called to weave a flying carpet?

Malchain's axes raised. Everyone quieted.

"We do not know what will be asked or who will answer," she said. "That is why we must gain an appreciation for one another's talents. All of the guilds are responsible for the extinction of unicorns, and all of the guilds are responsible for keeping them now. Do not think of yourselves anymore as *just* a Forger apprentice or *just* a Gemmer apprentice. As of today, you are all *guardians*. Guardians of change. Guardians of the age. Guardians of unicorns."

The apprentices burst into applause, and Olivia clapped until her palms turned red. Every cell in her body tingled, as though the shower of light had seeped into her soul and lit up its corners to reveal a truth about herself Olivia hadn't known. A purpose she had never experienced. Looking around, she saw the others felt it, too.

With a final swing, Aquila Malchain, provost of the Unicorn Academy, returned her axes to their straps. The blades peeked from behind her shoulders like very sharp wings. She nodded to the apprentices and then strode out of the throne room, frilly apron strings swishing behind her.

"You heard the provost," Dean Garmont said as the other deans joined him at the center and the applause died down. "Apprentices, unicorn guardians—let's begin."

Once *Finding Ourselves in the Founding of the Guilds: The Founders: Part I* finished, the rest of the day was filled with small guild sessions. For Olivia, that meant String Theory, an hour of Defensive Knots, then a quick break for lunch before an afternoon filled with Stitch and Debate, and Animal Husbandry, where a sweet scholar named Miss Merino showed Spinners how to comb angora rabbits and told them to come prepared with shampoo next time, as they would be bathing the sheep.

When Olivia's teachers realized she had been raised away from Spinner life, they each assigned extra readings for her to complete before the next class. By the time the academy's bell tolled the evening hours, Olivia practically staggered under the weight of all the extra books and expectations. Still, she was pretty certain that if she ate dinner quickly enough, she would be able to carve out five minutes to post a letter to Laurel.

Laurel.

Olivia had thought her sister would be so furious she would come and make a scene at the academy, demanding Olivia to come back. She hadn't anticipated Laurel being so furious that she would totally and completely *ignore* Olivia.

Didn't she care that Olivia had abandoned her? Didn't she miss her? Olivia had spent the first week of Laurel's journeyman year utterly despondent, crying into daisy pots and writing sad poetry, while Laurel, on the other hand, seemed willing to just . . . let Olivia go. Maybe she wouldn't write, after all. Maybe she would give Laurel a taste of her own botanical.

Olivia was still debating it as she joined the press of

apprentices entering the Banquet Hall and slipped into line behind Cami and Gabi.

Since lunch earlier that day, new embroidery had appeared on the decorative tapestries, changing from "YOU CAN DO IT!" to "YOU SURVIVED!"

"Oh no," Cami said as they neared the front of the line and saw apprentices serving themselves from a single large pot. "They're using the Cauldron of Plenty again."

Gabi groaned. "I'd really hoped that was only for lunch."

At first, Olivia had been excited to see the large black pot at the back of the hall, another example of Tiller-Forger alchemy. Traditionally, Cauldrons of Plenty were meant to serve each individual the exact meal they most wanted. However, Provost Malchain had (rightfully) assumed that the kinds of meals most wanted revolved around sugar, and not wanting a schoolful of buzzing twelve-year-olds, she had requested that the Tiller and Forger apprentices spend the morning making some adjustments. Namely, fixing the cauldron so that it served each individual the meal they most *needed*. In the twins' case, the pot seemed to think they were in desperate need of iron. Everything that had been served to them had been spinach-based, including their pudding.

Olivia bit back a grin as across the room a string quartet of scholars struck up a lively tune. "I'll share," she promised. She'd been lucky to be fed a red-bean pie that tasted almost exactly like Nan's, except for a slight metallic aftertaste.

"Great," Gabi said, pushing Olivia ahead of her. "You first."

As Olivia picked up the ladle, a sudden commotion broke out from a table of Forgers. At first, Olivia couldn't see what was happening, but then a girl dressed in Forger black leaped onto the table and executed a grand split before spinning out into a graceful pirouette.

Then another.

And another.

"HELP!" the girl yelled as she sashayed her away across the banquet hall, knocking bowls and sending cups flying. "I CAN'T STOP!"

"She's wearing an Ever Dance Lace!" Cami said, clutching her twin's arm.

Gabi threw her hands over her eyes. "I can't watch!"

Olivia frowned. "What's so bad about dancing?"

"It's *eternal* dancing," Cami whispered. "If that shoe stays on she will never stop—not to eat, not to sleep, not even if her shoes fill with blood. She will dance and dance and dance until she's dead— Look out!"

Olivia lurched away as the girl, eyes wide in terror, thumped onto the serving table and leaped over the cauldron. And as she whirled past, Olivia realized the Forger wasn't just any Forger, but the girl she'd met at the Mender's shop. Suspicion crept along Olivia's belly as she strained to get a glimpse of the girl's boots. And the feeling only grew worse as she began to recognize the leaps and turns of the Green Thumb Reel.

A Tiller dance. A Buddle dance. A dance no Forger would know unless . . .

. . . unless a Tiller-born Spinner who had no idea what she was doing had accidentally cursed the lace. But, Olivia reasoned, it couldn't be *her* fault. If it had been, wouldn't the Forger have started dancing as soon as she put her boot back on? But when she asked, Cami shook her head.

"You can't dance without music. This is probably the first time the Forger's heard music since tying the lace!" She glowered. "I bet it was Sam."

Chaos reigned as some apprentices tried to help the scholars catch the whirling girl, while others only just managed to miss being kicked.

"APPRENTICES!" The large, bearlike Forger dean had suddenly appeared, the figures of Garmont, Ravine, and Barry right behind him. "MOVE TO THE WALL NOW!"

The tiny Dean Ravine notched an arrow to a bow and pointed it at the dancer.

"What's she going to do?" Cami gasped, clutching Gabi's arm as they fled to the perimeter. "I can't watch!"

Swish! Thud.

The apprentice collapsed onto the floor. Her shoulders rose up and down as she caught her breath—alive, unhurt, and, finally, still. A few feet away, a couple of inches of jute cord lay on the floor, expertly severed from the boot by Ravine's arrow.

The hall burst into applause.

"Wow," Cami said, still clapping. "I didn't even see Ravine *move*. She's fast!"

"Remind me *never* to get on her bad side," Gabi said, eyes wide, and Cami nodded in agreement.

Olivia didn't say anything. Couldn't say anything.

All her attention was fixed on Garmont, who had knelt down to pick up the bootlace and was now talking to the Forger girl. Suddenly, the girl looked up and pointed . . .

Right. At. Her.

Garmont rose to his feet. "Apprentice Hayes, come with me."

"We'll save you a seat," Gabi whispered, eyes wide. Olivia nodded, her mouth too dry to speak. She didn't know what she would have said to Gabi anyway. *Thanks, but I'm pretty sure I'm about to be kicked out and I'll never be allowed back in to sneeze, let alone eat dinner. Have a lovely life!*

Numb, Olivia followed Dean Garmont, her head spinning with possibilities. They were going to expel her, she was sure of it. After the provost's lecture on guild unity this morning, they wouldn't have any other choice.

"Sit," Dean Garmont said. They had entered what Olivia supposed must be the provost's study. An array of horseshoes, hand mirrors, and candelabras decorated the mantel above a smoldering fireplace. But as Olivia slid into a chair in front of the desk, it was the walls that held her attention. Or rather, the dozens of maps covering them.

There were the expected maps—the familiar outlines of Arden's veiny waterways, the crisscrossing of roads, the winding dots of star charts and trade winds, as well as more unexpected maps, such as the one noting every molehill in Greenwood Village and another showing continents Olivia had not even known existed. With a start, she realized that they were maps of a different world, or maybe even maps *from* different worlds.

Olivia had read of ancient travelers who had created passages out of Arden and into other worlds. And she knew Arden had had its own share of guests. Many even claimed it was because of two visitors, descendants of a long-lost prince, that unicorns had returned. But Olivia doubted that even otherworldly princesses could save her now.

"Am I being expelled?" she blurted out.

Garmont's eyebrows knitted together. "Do you want to be expelled?"

"What—no! Of course not! I—"

The office door opened and Provost Malchain strode in, her chain mail rattling ominously as she unloaded her axes into the umbrella stand and sat behind the desk. Her apron was gone, and her indigo housegown had been replaced by glittering armor. Steepling her fingers, she looked at Olivia, and the intensity of her gaze made Olivia feel like a nail about to be hammered.

"Olivia," Malchain said, "I am afraid we are here to discuss the rather serious matter of—"

"I didn't mean to!" Olivia burst out. "I don't know what I did to that bootlace, but I promise I didn't mean to hurt anyone!"

Malchain inclined her head. "I understand that you are new to Spinning and that it was unintentionally done. As Kessa Toll is no worse for wear, let us move on. We are not here to discuss shoelaces."

"We're not?"

"I'm afraid not," the provost said, her voice so solemn that Olivia wondered if someone had died. Her breath caught. Nan's cough. What if it wasn't the spilled goldenrod that caused it, but consumption? What if Laurel had told Nan Olivia had run away, and it had simply been too much for her heart? What if—

"Laurel Hayes is your sister, correct?"

The question dragged Olivia from her worry about Nan and plunged her into an ocean of anxiety for Laurel.

"What's wrong? Is Laurel all right?"

Garmont and Malchain exchanged a look, and then Malchain slid a news parchment across her desk, where a large headline marched across the top page:

UNICORN TRAPPER TRAPPED!

Olivia skimmed the article. Once. Twice. Thrice.

Only phrases stood out to her.

... youngest Tiller Master in three hundred years ... from the only family of Ambrosia brewers ... known for her steady hands during healing ... unicorn artifacts on her, including a sliver of rib and three unicorn hairs ...

The world fell away. Words lost their meaning.

"I don't understand," she whispered.

The fire popped, sending a momentary brightness across Malchain's face and revealing an expression both grim and pitying.

"There's been an arrest," the provost said. "The Prime Minister believes Laurel is the unicorn trapper."

CHAPTER THIRTEEN

The winter before Laurel left, a customer had paid Nan with a collection of short stories illuminated by an order of Forger monks. Most of the tales had been familiar to Olivia—children's rhymes about blind mice and monarchs wearing invisible clothes—but one had been new. A deeply tragic story about a lady whose true love was killed by wolves. The lady sobbed for fifty days and fifty nights until a unicorn took pity on her. Touching its horn to her cheek, the unicorn froze her tears in place. The frost spread, and as the rest of her turned to ice, the lady laughed because she no longer felt sorrow . . . or anything at all.

When Nan read it, she'd announced that it was too sad for little girls and put the book on the highest shelf, but Olivia had *loved* it. She'd spent the next several days standing in snowbanks imagining ice crystals creeping through her veins and frost gilding her bones. But now she didn't have to imagine. She knew.

The provost's pronouncement froze Olivia, chilling her to her core. Which was good.

Because girls with pink cheeks had to live in the moment and experience the world, while everything slipped off a girl of ice.

Olivia slid from one moment and into the next.

One moment, Malchain was informing Olivia that the Watch had questioned Laurel in Healer Hall and taken her into custody last night, but that this morning her cell had been found empty. The Watch believed Marguerite Hayes had broken her oldest granddaughter out of prison and they were now on the run.

In the next moment, a member of the Watch entered the office and demanded to know where her sister and grandmother were hiding. He threw questions at Olivia so quickly that her thoughts could barely keep up. But Olivia tried.

She explained that Laurel was so gentle she couldn't even kill the caterpillars in the vegetable patch! That it had been *Olivia* who had found the strands of unicorn mane they'd discovered in Laurel's pocket, and that her sister only had a sliver of unicorn rib on her because she'd taken it from Mayor Oakley—when *Olivia* had turned him into a mushroom. But the Watchman didn't seem to care or believe her.

Because the next moment, the Watchman removed a pair of handcuffs from his belt.

"Put those away," Provost Malchain said, her voice dangerously quiet. "Olivia is not yet sixteen. She is a *minor*."

"Yes, well." The Watchman shifted uncomfortably. "Unusual circumstances, you know."

"I do not know." Malchain's eyes flashed. "Louis, please escort Olivia back to her dorm. I require a private discussion with Watchman Spikes."

And so, Olivia found herself deposited back in her room by Garmont, the other girls suspiciously silent in their beds until she climbed into her own and drew the drapes shut. Then the whispers started.

Trying to ignore them, Olivia stared at the cave-like darkness above her. She'd imagined many things before. The stove's embers sprouting wings and transforming into a firefly. A spider's feelings as a broom dusted its home away. What it would be like to have magic. But she'd never, ever, in all her wildest daydreams, imagined Laurel to be a criminal. Even when they played Watch and Wraiths, Olivia had always been the wraith and Laurel the Watch. Her sister couldn't even *pretend* to break the rules.

"Do you think she helped her sister?" Olivia's stomach twisted as one of the twins whispered a little too loudly.

"Definitely." That was Paisley. She didn't even bother to lower her voice. "Remember last night? She *told* us they saw a unicorn."

It was quiet. Then—

"You think she was telling the truth?"

"At first I thought she was making it up," Paisley admitted. "You know, trying to seem all 'interesting,' since she just kept going on and on..."

Humiliation burned through Olivia. She'd thought her roommates actually liked her.

"But then I was wondering," Paisley continued, "how can someone from a no-place like Muddle produce the youngest guild Master in three hundred years unless..." She paused dramatically, clearly waiting for someone to ask. Cami obliged.

"Unless what?"

"She had help!" Paisley said. "Unicorn help."

"Are you saying—?"

"*Yes*," Paisley said emphatically. "Laurel Hayes cheated her way into becoming a Master by using talismans from the trapped unicorns— AAAHHHHEEEEEeemmmmmmpffff!"

There had only been the slightest swoosh of warning as Olivia's canopy drapes swished off their rail and launched at Paisley. The corners stretched out like the wings of a giant bat.

A giant bat that really, really wanted to hug Paisley.

Tight.

Olivia watched in horror as her once well-behaved drapes rolled Paisley up like a pastry sausage until all that was visible of Grandmaster Webster's niece were a nose, eyes, and a headful of hairbows that quivered with the girl's rage.

"What did you *do*?" Gabi shrieked as Cami ran to help Paisley.

Had Olivia done anything? She'd only meant to yank the drapes back to demand that Paisley stop talking about her sister—say whatever she wanted about Olivia but leave Laurel out of it—but she must have pulled a little too hard. Been a little too angry. Been a little too much.

"GGRAPPHPPPPPHHHHHRRR!" Paisley yelled through the fabric, which remained snug no matter how much Cami and Gabi pulled. "GLKMMMMFFFTT FFFFFFPYYYY!"

Olivia wasn't exactly sure what Paisley was trying to say, but she thought it was probably something along the lines of, "I'M GOING TO MAKE YOU PAY."

So, Olivia did the only thing she could think of. She turned—and ran.

Charging out of the dorm and through the darkened hallways, Olivia didn't stop as she skidded across the foyer, flung open the double doors, and threw herself into the night. She wasn't sure where she was going, she just knew that she had to get *away*. To get *out*. The gravel path shifted strangely beneath her toes, jabbing her bare feet, but Olivia didn't care. Her anger had melted away all the ice, and now her mind boiled with possibilities, schemes, and prison breaks.

Because one thing was certain: Laurel was *innocent*—and Olivia had to do something about it. She would commandeer the school's boat and row across the Rhona herself—aphids, she would *swim* across the river—she just had to talk to Laurel. *Find* Laurel. If she could do that, she knew they would figure out what to do next. Just like they always did, except—

Olivia skidded to a stop as she noticed three things in quick succession.

The first was that the gravel path no longer led to a leafy archway as it had this morning. Now it ended abruptly in front of a very thick, very thorny, very solid hedge.

The second was, despite the still night air, the hedge rustled.

And the third was that every nerve in her body was screaming at her to run away, *now*. Because the hedge wasn't a hedge at all.

A great roar of snapping branches and shredding leaves tore the air as a topiary lion—as tall as Nan's garden shed and just as wide—surged to its feet, each platter-sized paw boasting rose-thorn claws as long as butcher knives. The topiary shook its mane, sending twigs scattering into the air as it turned to face her. Where there should have been eyes were only shallow dents in the leaves, but Olivia could feel the lion contemplating her. *Hunting* her. She stumbled back.

The lion pounced.

Olivia screamed. The thorn claws stretched toward her—

"Down, Rosario!"

Olivia felt a leaf brush her cheek as the topiary twisted

and tucked into a somersault before sprawling awkwardly on the lawn. The lion sat up and quickly began to wash its viney tail as if to say, *I totally meant to do that.*

"My dear, are you all right?"

Olivia looked away from the topiary's rose-petal tongue and saw Holly Barry, dean of Tillers, rushing toward her.

"My goodness, there are reasons we have rules about staying in your dorm after candle snuffing! We let the topiaries out at night—"

"Topiaries?" Olivia said faintly. "Aren't they . . . murderous?" Topiary animals were just as hungry as *real* lions. And like real lions, enjoyed the taste of *real* blood. The thorn needles would kill her, her blood would soak into the ground, and the lion's tiny roots on the underside of its paws would suck her up along with any other nutrients in the ground.

"Yes, yes," Dean Barry said. Her long blonde hair fell loose down her back and swayed as she stood on her tiptoes to kiss the lion's leafy nose. "But that is one of the many advantages of having Forgers and Gemmers to work with. Deans Hatchett and Ravine are each able to provide special supplements so that the topiaries don't feel the need to, uh, *absorb* any other source of food. Isn't that right, you big smoosh bush?" She tickled the lion under its chin, right between two rose blossoms in its giant mane. "With the right tools, time, and care, topiaries are just as easy to train as ivy. Besides"—she looked at Olivia reproachfully—"Rosario would have let you through if you had a pass."

"Pass?"

"A note from the provost, myself, or another of the deans giving permission to leave the island. Anyone who doesn't have one will be stopped by a topiary." She patted the lion once more and sent him on his way. The moonlight played against his white-rose mane as he bounded toward a stag made of holly and a bear coaxed from pine.

"Aren't they marvelous?" Dean Barry murmured. She watched them with a dreamy smile for a moment before turning to Olivia. "Now, would you care to explain how Paisley became wrapped up in some rather restrictive drapes?"

Olivia burst into tears.

"Oh my . . ."

Olivia felt a hand wrap around her shoulders and guide her to a gazebo before gently pushing her onto a bench. "There, there, no harm has been done. Paisley is just a bit breathless, is all. Dean Garmont tickled the drapes and they released her right away. No need for tears, but if it feels better, let them come. Water is necessary for growth."

So Olivia did. Between hiccups and sniffles, she let her whole story pour out, and Dean Barry listened. When at last her eyes dried, Olivia said with a sigh, "I just don't know what to do."

"I think that is obvious," Dean Barry said, handing her a

handkerchief. "You will wash your face, put on some pajamas, and get a good night's sleep. Then, tomorrow, you'll go to class."

"Class? The Watch wants to put me in prison!"

"Provost Malchain has, shall we say, persuaded the Watch to her way of thinking." When Olivia frowned, Dean Barry explained, "Aquila has taken on all responsibility pertaining to you, your actions, and your whereabouts. So long as you remain in Unicorn Academy, you are under her protection. To put it bluntly, you may stay in school, you just may not *leave* school."

"So, I *am* a prisoner."

"School," Barry said, patting Olivia's knee, "is nothing like the penitentiary. Trust me." Something about the way Dean Barry said that made Olivia glance down at her hand. There, tattooed on the web between the scholar's left thumb and forefinger, was a green *A*.

Olivia's breath caught.

A for *alchemist*. The tattoo marked Dean Barry as a caught and convicted criminal.

Dean Barry delicately put her hand inside her scholar's robes and pulled out a scrap of paper. In the glow of the lantern flowers, Olivia saw that it was a topiary pass, useful from now until dawn. Barry stood up. "I believe I am supposed to instruct you to return to your room, but if I were you, I would wait until your roommate's soothing tea has taken effect."

"Thank you," Olivia whispered, accepting the pass.

The scholar gave one last dreamy smile, then left Olivia alone to her thoughts.

Leaning against the gazebo, Olivia let the night air dry her tears into a stiff mask across her face. The academy loomed in front of her, no longer a potential home but a prison meant to be survived. Olivia had been naïve to think she belonged here. The only place she'd ever truly belong was next to her sister, and she would do everything in her power to get back there.

She vowed it.

CHAPTER FOURTEEN

If Laurel and Nan had not been accused of trapping unicorns, Olivia's first full week at Unicorn Academy would have been a dream. To everyone's surprise—Olivia's most of all—she was good at Spinning.

Really good.

Her fingers, which had been so clumsy chopping turmeric, deftly threaded needles and twisted twine. And while she could never tell the difference between a butternut squash and a crookneck pumpkin, it took her less than a second to distinguish merino wool from angora. The other apprentices shifted in their seats, bored, as the scholars reviewed basic stitches and fabric names, but Olivia found everything *fascinating*.

She hadn't known so many kinds of fabrics and weaves existed in the world. She hadn't known the mathematical property of thread or Sean Specter's theory that the world was made of tiny, vibrating strings. Each little bit of knowledge was a door to a thousand more doors, and Olivia wanted to step through them all. She raised her hand during every lesson, asking questions and making more than one class run late. At the end of her first lacing class, Scholar Chantilly had held up her doily and called it an exquisite example of stitchery and had said she wouldn't be surprised if Olivia were able to lace herself a pair of flyable dragonfly wings by the end of the year.

Life should have been perfect.

But Laurel *had* been accused. And for every one of Olivia's accomplishments, there were a hundred whispers. Had Olivia sewn a unicorn tooth into her seams so that they hung so straight? Some mane into her lace? Because how else could a *Tiller*-born be the best in the class?

No one wanted to talk to her, let alone partner with her.

More than once, Olivia had to pair with the teacher, except for an unfortunate cat's cradle lesson where she'd been forced to work with Sam. It had ended with Sam calling Olivia a "carrot-brained snail" and Olivia slamming her portable loom over his head. She'd been assigned extra folding for a week, but it had been worth it.

It wasn't just the Spinners who avoided her. The Tillers seemed personally insulted that the Hayes sisters had been born into their guild. After a nasty bout with tongue-tie tea, she'd learned to stay clear of wooden cups. As for the Forgers, it was clear Kessa had told her classmates who was responsible for the dancing fiasco. Whenever they walked past Olivia, they would hiss at her, sounding like red-hot metal plunged into water.

It's not like she hadn't tried to apologize, Olivia thought irritably after a particularly large group of Forgers rattled their pots menacingly on their way to the kitchens.

On the second day of school, Olivia had gone to the one place she thought she might be able to feel better—and the one place that might hold a solution to her problem.

Entering the atrium of the Unicorn Academy library had felt like coming home. Bookshelves towered as tall as any tree in the Endless, and above, painted gray clouds drifted across the ceiling, creating that specific kind of coziness found on rainy days. Resisting the urge to fold herself into an overstuffed chair and escape into someone else's life, Olivia grabbed a book cart, but instead of wheeling her way to the second mezzanine, where the Spinner scrolls were kept, she kept walking. She walked past the Guild War Collection, the reading rooms, and the Royalty Wing. She paused a moment in the Tiller alcove, lingering next to a collection of tree stumps until a small group of Tillers exited the aisle. Then she moved on to the last and final room: the Unicorn Wing.

Olivia hesitated, her toes mere inches away from the door. If anyone saw her in this wing, it could very well be the biggest mistake of her life.

Well, the second-biggest mistake of her life.

The *actual* biggest mistake of her life was turning Mayor Oakley into a mushroom. If that hadn't happened, Laurel never would have had a unicorn sliver on her. She never would have been arrested. Which was exactly why Olivia had to look. *Had* to learn all she could about unicorns and their behaviors, their habitats and physiology, and yes, even how to capture a unicorn, so she could prove Laurel's innocence. Olivia stepped inside.

The Unicorn Wing was empty.

Olivia was too late. The provost, or maybe even the Grand Council itself, must have ordered the books removed in case . . .

Olivia's stomach tightened.

. . . in case the sister of an accused unicorn hunter got any ideas of helping said hunter.

CLANG!

Olivia jumped, almost knocking over her cart. Had she set off an alarm?

But when a second *clang* sounded, she realized it came from somewhere outside the room.

Backing out of the Unicorn Wing, she wheeled her cart out of the wing and into the hall, where the noise was even louder. Turning the corner, she saw Dean Hatchett directing a handful of Forgers who were latching metal cages around a shelf. The librarian hovered at the edges, watching the commotion and wincing as hammers got a little too close to the scrolls for comfort. When she noticed Olivia, she hurried over.

"So sorry," the librarian, a woman with exuberant curls, said breathlessly. "This will only take a minute, and then we shall return to our state of blessed silence and rain patter."

"What are they doing?" Olivia asked as she watched an apprentice secure a lock.

The librarian sighed. "It's the traveling collection. One has wandered away already. You haven't seen it, have you? *The Way Between* by Claudius Tripp? It's the only copy left in this world."

Olivia shook her head.

"Ah, well, it's bound to turn up eventually. We're on an island after all—no, not *those!*" the librarian yelped. "Those are the books on flight—they need to *breathe!*" She ran toward two hammer-happy Forgers and shooed them away.

Olivia was about to continue on when she spotted a familiar Forger sitting cross-legged on the library floor as she sorted a pile of nails. Before she could overthink it, Olivia pushed her book cart over to her.

"Hi, um, excuse me?" she said as she approached. "I'm Olivia."

"I know who you are." Kessa Toll didn't even bother to look up. "You're the girl who ruined my life."

That wasn't entirely fair, but Olivia had almost made Kessa dance to death, so Olivia decided to ignore it. "I just wanted to say sorry for—"

"Utter humiliation?" Now Kessa did look up at her, her eyes dark with fury. "Making me the laughingstock of the fencers? Trying to discredit my father?"

Olivia crossed her arms. "I am *trying* to apologize. I don't care about your father. I don't even know who he is."

"Please." Kessa rolled her eyes. "Everyone knows who my father is." Leaning forward, she swept the nails into a jar and stood up. "Just stay out of my way."

So, Olivia did.

She stayed out of everyone's way.

For the rest of that first week, Olivia went to bed early and got up even earlier, successfully avoiding ever having to see her roommates awake. Which was why, on the first rest day of week's end, Olivia found herself awake and dressed before dawn, her Spinner kit tied to her belt as she walked across the grounds and flopped herself under the branches of a friendly—and private—willow tree.

Making sure no one was around, she began to unwrap the parcel Dean Garmont had given her last night. Inside, he'd told her, were the objects the Watch had found among Laurel's possessions and deemed not dangerous.

There wasn't much. Aside from Nan's amber beads that she'd given to Laurel in honor of her mastership, there was only an Olivia-sized tunic that must have accidentally been packed along with Laurel's things and a glass jar of soil labeled Olivia—Day 29 of Eighthmonth.

Frowning, Olivia turned it over. It didn't look like anything special. Laurel collected hundreds of soil samples, after all. But why would this one have her name on it?

Tugging the drawstring of her Spinner Kit, she fumbled until she felt soft leather. Gently, she removed *The Account of Olivia the Observant: Apprentice to Tiller Master Laurel Haye*s. Flipping it open, she read through the first pages, sifting through her sparse notes to try to find some kind of answer.

There was none.

The only thing Olivia did find was a handful of *what-would-never-be*s. They buzzed at her as she flipped through the many more blank pages that would never be filled. She would never doodle daisies in the margins again while listening to Laurel interview a patient. She would never scrawl messy notes that Laurel would take one look at and have Olivia redo. She would never fill this book up to the very last page. Except . . .

Olivia paused.

There, on the very last page, written in emerald ink, was a single word in Laurel's round handwriting:

DONT

Triumph sparked through Olivia. So—Laurel *had* left her a clue! Her clever, brilliant sister must have suspected something when they returned to Healer Hall and had sneakily scrawled this secret message. A note that actually meant . . .

Olivia's triumph fizzled, then died. She stared at the letters, stumped.

Don't . . . go to the Academy?

Don't follow me.

Don't tell.

Don't—

"LOOK OUT!"

Olivia glanced up just in time to see a dagger slice through the willow leaves and land with a thud in the willow's trunk, a single hair's width from her ear.

What in Anders's name—?

The curtain of willow leaves whipped open, and a girl in a Forger's uniform yelped as she took in the scene. "Are you all right? Did I hit you? I'm so sorry! I thought it was too early for anyone to be out here! I thought it was safe to practice!"

"If you were aiming at me," Olivia said as she slowly edged away from the blade and stood up, "you missed."

"No!" The girl shook her head, and her chin-length hair whipped back and forth. "I mean, I *was* aiming, but not at you! I was aiming for the target." She pointed several yards away.

Olivia squinted. "You mean, that one in the completely opposite direction?"

The girl nodded unhappily.

"I thought Forgers knew how to throw daggers before they

could walk," Olivia said as the girl walked over to the willow and tugged on the dagger's hilt. It didn't budge.

"They do," the girl grunted, "but I'm not exactly a Forger. Not yet. I mean, I might be?"

Over her black uniform she wore a tool belt that looked a little too large, but maybe that was because she was so short. Her hair was so black it was almost blue, and cut short to her chin with bangs that framed a small nose and wide cheeks that now flushed a faint pink. Olivia understood.

"You're dormant!"

The girl shrugged. "So what if I am?"

"I've never met another dormant!"

The girl stared. "You're dormant, too? The provost said I was the only one in school."

"I mean, I *was*," Olivia corrected, and as the girl's face fell, Olivia hurried to add, "I only discovered I was a Spinner when I got here. I'm Tiller-born, from Buddle. Olivia Hayes."

The girl pushed bangs out of her eyes. "Violet Lee."

"You're Tiller-born, too? Why did the scholars put you in with the Forgers?" Olivia asked. "Were you always good at carving or, uh . . ." She racked her brain, trying to think what else a dormant Forger in a Tiller village might be good at. ". . . raking?"

Violet giggled. "Raking?"

Olivia shrugged. "Rakes have metal prongs! I don't know anything about Forging."

"Me either." Violet sighed. "To be honest, I think Provost Malchain is biased toward her own guild. But she said if my magic doesn't spark by the end of the quarter, she would have me try something else." With one last grunt and yank, the dagger came free.

Violet frowned as she inspected the nicked blade. "We're supposed to craft a dagger that will always find its mark," she said glumly. "Linna made one that can zigzag around trees, and Ignatius managed to make one that can hit a target underwater."

"Maybe you crafted it so it always flies in the opposite direction?" Olivia suggested. "King Charr IV gifted one to a courtier he suspected of rebellious intent."

"What happened?"

"The king was right. He woke up that night to see the courtier standing over his bed, the gifted dagger plunged backward into the noble's stomach instead of his royal one. So," Olivia said, "I'm just saying a Reggad—that's Dagger spelled backward, you know—can be incredibly useful. Can I try?"

Violet handed her the hilt. "Be my guest—"

THWACK.

Olivia grinned as Violet stared, open-mouthed, at the target, where they could just make out a new silver dot in its center.

"I thought you said you were a Spinner!"

"I am," Olivia said. "But I grew up next to the Endless, and when you can't Till, you have to find other ways to protect yourself from snakes and wolves and that sort of thing. I prefer a sling or slingshot, but I'm all right at knives, too. It's all about stance. Here, I can show you."

Violet didn't say anything. Instead, she was staring at the *Account*, Laurel's name shining clearly under Olivia's. If Violet hadn't realized who Olivia was, she certainly did now.

Olivia grabbed the journal and shoved it into her kit. "I know what you're thinking, but I am *not* a unicorn trapper—and neither is my sister. And if you don't believe me, then, then—" She couldn't think of anything inspired, so she said, "Just leave."

Violet was quiet, but then she smiled and said the most magical words of all. "Let's get breakfast."

CHAPTER FIFTEEN

With Violet at her side, life at Unicorn Academy improved. From the outside, they seemed like an odd friendship, their personalities as different as the sun and the moon—Olivia talkative and fanciful, Violet quiet and practical. But like the sun and the moon, they were a perfect pair, bonded together as the two outliers in the sky of sparkling, unproblematic, perfectly magical apprentices.

So, while Olivia still had to muddle through uncomfortable Spinner classes and deal with brassy Forgers and prickly Tillers, she now at least had a helpful finger when she needed to practice bow tying and someone to save her a seat in the throne room during the next all-guild assembly—which was good, because Olivia was late. Again.

"Sorry," Violet whispered as Olivia slid onto the bench next to her—in front of Paisley and the twins. "This was the only one with room for both of us. Just ignore them."

Easier said than done.

Olivia's suitemates, in an attempt to distance themselves from her notoriety, had gone to extreme lengths to make it very outwardly clear how they felt about rooming with the unicorn trapper's sister. Today, they each wore bright pink sashes with the words PROTECT OUR UNICORNS FRATERNITY embroidered across, and Paisley was *loudly* talking about when the next meeting of P.O.U.F. would be.

"Ignore them," Violet repeated and grabbed away the small button Olivia had just pulled out of her kit.

"It wouldn't do anything permanent," Olivia protested.

Violet blinked. 'That's not as comforting as you think. What exactly would that button do?"

But Olivia was spared having to answer as the chandelier dimmed and the curtains opened to reveal the most beautiful woman Olivia had ever seen. She perched on a stool, her long, canary-yellow gown draped around her with the careful precision of an artist. Next to her loomed a harp twice the woman's size, and as she lifted her hands to its strings, Olivia could clearly see the two armbands that marked her as journeywoman.

A quiet as complete and full as a robin's breast filled the hall, and then the harpist let the first note fly. It soared to the rafters, its wings growing and expanding until it filled the whole hall and then some. It needed more space and seeped into Olivia's eyes, ears, and then into that place where she felt her stories rather than just remembered them.

And as the theater, the academy, *the world* fell away, Olivia entered a new one created of chords that built themselves into slanting mountains, whistling wind, and the smell of dawn. If Olivia paid close attention, she could still hear the tinkling of the harp, but more real to her now was the morning call of the birds and button daisies beneath her slippers.

As Olivia stood, marveling at the composer's power to create, she realized she'd seen these particular mountains before. The music had carried her away to someplace and some*when* on Constellation Range.

And then—

A unicorn galloped into the meadow.

The stallion danced with the rising sun, its rays painting his flanks golden and turning his tail into a shining banner. Hooves hard as diamonds sent small tremors through the earth, and yet not a single blossom was crushed in his wake. Instead, the flowers grew bigger, creating a trail lush with color behind him and turning the mountain air so sweet that Olivia thought she might cry with wonder.

"*Oh*," Olivia said, and the unicorn's ear pricked. Midstride, he swiveled and, suddenly, he was facing the ridge. Facing Olivia.

Girl and unicorn looked at each other in joyful recognition.

The unicorn was a question she would always seek to answer, and the girl was a mystery the unicorn would always understand. They were true equals, halves of the same heart.

As they stared, the girl spotted herself reflected in the unicorn's eye, her own image dimmed by the bright gold of the bridle looped over her arm. Slowly, she reached out—but the unicorn reared. For a moment, it seemed as though the sun were whispering a secret to him. Then the unicorn let loose a call that rolled out across the mountaintop like a choir of bells, cacophonous yet joyful. His hooves hit the grass, and he was galloping again, thundering across the meadow and streaking into the peaks that were already fading away into balconies . . .

. . . and then Olivia was back in the music hall, now so quiet that she could hear how the entire audience held their breath and released it as one.

Apprentices and scholars alike surged to their feet, applauding so loudly that Olivia thought they must be shaking the very foundations of the chateau.

"That was incredible!" Olivia shouted to Violet, who still seemed dazed.

"What *was* that?" Violet asked.

"A Telling Harp," Olivia said, clapping her hands together even harder. "And she played *The Rider's Concerto*! It's an unfinished piece composed by Lady Elaina herself to capture the moment, the *very emotion* she experienced when she met her 'steed of stars.' It's the only bit of her work that survived the burning of the alchemists' libraries."

Olivia continued to clap as the next musician, a Tiller this time, took to the center. The following hour was one of chaos and laughter as the Tiller demonstrated the unique power of his pan flutes with the help of some volunteers. Mayhem reigned as each apprentice blew a note—and immediately grew ten feet tall or shrunk down to an inch, depending on which pipe they played.

Olivia enjoyed the fifteen minutes she spent on eye-level with the chandelier, even if she almost blew out a stained glass window of Princess Clarissa with a burst of laughter when she spotted Garmont taking a pan flute away from Sam, who'd clearly been trying to smuggle one out. Once all the pan flutes had been collected and accounted for (and everyone had returned to their appropriate sizes), Olivia eagerly took her seat, wondering what would be next. Maybe it would be the famed Cymbalists, a trio of earthshaking Forgers, or perhaps Dean Ravine would play a crystal flute.

Instead, Kessa Toll took to the stage.

"What's *she* doing?" Olivia whispered as the Forgers cheered. Since that awkward day in the library, Olivia had eventually learned who Kessa's father was: Donte Toll, Forger Grandmaster of Lumin City and commander of the city's Watch. He was also a staunch Traditionalist, which was why the Grand Council had voted him to be Secretary of

Education, so that he himself could set the academy's trial at the end of the year. The general thinking, Olivia had gleaned, was no one would *ever* accuse Donte Toll of making an easy test.

Violet shook her head as Kessa stood tall in the throne room. A single sconce glowed behind the apprentice, outlining her in gold and transforming her hair into a burnished halo. Tonight she wore flowing black trousers, and instead of a saber, a tarnished horn hung at her side. Quiet fell. Kessa brought the instrument to her lips and blew.

No sound came, but a great wind filled the hall. Candle flames flickered, and instead of blowing away from the wind, they leaned toward it, causing shadows to stretch long fingers. And beneath the wind came a whisper, like an echo's echo.

Olivia leaned on the edge of her seat.

The sound was haunting, but also . . . familiar.

It made her think of dark mountain passes and the setting sun and dark spaces between worlds. It made her think . . .

. . . of a unicorn trapped in a sinkhole.

She needed to get closer to the sound. She needed to understand it. She needed to follow it.

Olivia breathed in deeply, as though trying to suck the song in. The call replaced the sound of her heartbeat, then the rushing of blood coursing through her veins, and finally, the reverberation of her muscles as they tightened and pulled on her bones. Olivia *was* the call, and she *must* return to it—

TTTTTTTTEEEEEEEEEEEEEEEEEWWWWWWWWWTTTTTTT!

Olivia threw her hands over her ears as the stained glass windows of the throne room shattered. Shards of broken glass rained down on the benches and would have injured them all . . . if anyone had still been in their seats.

Instead everyone, from the shortest apprentice to the tallest scholar, was on the stage, crowded around Kessa. Olivia was standing right next to Kessa, though she had no memory of rising from her chair and walking, or even deciding to go there at all.

"Well done, Kessa; excellent breath control." Dean Hatchett strode toward the front while slipping a pair of whispering willow buds from his hairy ears. Behind him followed Ravine in her typical glittering garb, with a plain clay whistle still on her lips. When Hatchett nodded at her, Ravine blew again.

TTTTTTTTEEEEEEEEEEEEEEEEEWWWWWWWWWTTTTTTT!

This time, the glass swirled up into the air and clinked back into the windowpanes, recreating Princess Clarissa, who looked none the worse for breaking.

"Thank you, Rubi," Hatchett said, coming to a stop. His voice was soft for such a large man. While shorter than Garmont, Hatchett was easily an entire barrel's width wider than the skinny Spinner. Muscles corded his arms and scars crisscrossed his hands. The dean of Forgers should have been terrifying, but he moved with a gentle carefulness that reminded Olivia of the large mastiff who would let Buddle's toddlers ride on his back.

"You have just experienced the pull of a Luring Horn. Now, do not be alarmed," he said, looking at the Spinners and Tillers around him. "Most horns are unable to lure anything larger than, say, a rat."

"We're bigger than rats," an anxious-looking Tiller said.

"This Luring Horn is different from any other," Hatchett reassured the apprentices. Reaching for the horn, he flipped it to reveal a circle with a five-pointed star pressed into the silver.

"See this?" Hatchett tapped the star. "Usually, one would expect a guild's sigil to be here, but this mark indicates the horn was crafted *before* the founding, when every individual had their own special sign. It is likely that this is the *first* Luring Horn ever crafted, and therefore the most powerful. Copies are never as inspired." He turned it right side up again and returned it to Kessa. "Remind me, how long has this instrument been in your family?"

"Ages," Kessa said, caressing the horn. "But it's spent the last thirty years in a cupboard. Daddy thought it was broken and almost melted it down before I played it."

Scholar Hatchett nodded. "In the case of musical instruments, magic is released twice. First, when the instrument is crafted. When a Forger sees a bar of silver and knows how to hammer it just right so that its sweetest, most alluring song can spring forth. The second is when the musician plays it."

"But humans aren't magic," Paisley said, crossing her arms. "Magic is in the material. We just release it."

Hatchett smiled. "Who is to say we *aren't* material? Not all would agree with me, of course. But when a musician plays, they use their own breath and their own hands to make an instrument sound. It's *Apprentice Toll*—her skill, her passion—that makes the horn sing."

"Go Kessa!" someone (a Forger) shouted from the edges, and the cheer set the rest of the guild whooping and hollering, while Kessa stared down at her feet, a small smile playing across her lips.

After taking a few more questions and with a final round of applause to the performers, the scholars dismissed the apprentices. Excited chatter surrounded Olivia as they flooded into the hallways and up the staircases. Some spoke loudly about their experience meeting the unicorn while others, Tillers, wondered if they could figure out how to carve their own pan flutes. The only two who didn't seem enthralled were Violet, who hadn't spoken a word since the Luring Horn, and Olivia, who kept turning over what Hatchett had said:

Apprentice Toll makes the Luring Horn sing.

A horn so powerful it could call an entire academy to it. And if it could do that, who else could it call?

What else?

Before the Blastachio exploded, Olivia heard a strange call in the mountains. A sound she'd thought was just the wind between peaks, but now . . .

. . . what if it had been the Luring Horn's call?

. . . what if Olivia had been lured into a unicorn trap set by Forgers?

. . . what if *that* was the secret Kessa's shoelace had tried so hard to hide?

What if, what if, what if.

Reaching the Spinners' Wing, she waved good night to Violet and practically floated into her suite. Ignoring the usual nightly chaos of the others tying up their hair, Olivia fell into bed, not bothering to change into her pajamas. Her brain was thinking too much, too fast. She rolled over to look out at the night sky and studied the dark patches on the moon.

No matter which way Olivia spun the story, Kessa was definitely hiding something.

CHAPTER SIXTEEN

"No." Violet shook her head. "Absolutely not."

It had been two days since the musical demonstration, and two days since Olivia could think of anything other than the Luring Horn. Its echo dragged at her like an anchor, tethering her to that moment and calling her to reexamine the sound again, and again, and again.

"It's not *that* bad of an idea," Olivia protested as she leaned against the willow's trunk and peered through its leaves. She caught a glimpse of the academy's hives, where Forgers were swinging tin smokers.

"Close it!" Violet urged. "I told Scholar Hatchett I was having cramps; he'll make me try to lull the bees if he sees me out here."

Olivia let the leaves fall back into place. "You should try. Maybe your Forger magic will spark today."

Violet shuddered. "And if it doesn't, I'll get stung. So no, thank you. The only idea worse than that is *your* plan. I'm *not* going to spill putrid perfume on Kessa's boots."

"But it's so simple!" Olivia protested as she fiddled with her thimble. It was a new habit she'd developed after learning about all the mishaps that could happen if a Spinner twirled her hair. "You can 'accidentally' do it during class. They'll smell so bad she'll have to wash them and leave them outside overnight. And then we can *borrow* the bootlace—"

"Shh!" Violet said as a sudden gust of wind blew and the willow leaves lifted to reveal a girl crouching a few feet away, scooping up some pebbles into a tin pail. Her honey-brown hair was pulled into a high ponytail that puffed like a squirrel's tail and revealed a necklace of white stone around her brown neck.

Olivia exchanged an uneasy glance with Violet. Had the girl overheard them?

The girl let dirt fall from her hands, then stood and moved a few more feet away. She seemed to be mumbling to herself, and the wind caught her words, blowing them back to Olivia.

Olivia frowned. "Is she saying 'bones'?"

Violet listened, then shook her head. "She's saying 'stones.' That's Tourmaline."

Olivia looked again. So *that* was Tourmaline l'Ore, the only Gemmer at Unicorn Academy. She should have guessed. Only a Gemmer would wear glasses with rose-quartz frames and have so many rings on her fingers. Olivia watched as

Tourmaline ambled away, and only when she was sure the Gemmer was out of earshot did she turn back to Violet.

"So," she said with her most winning grin, "are you in?"

"*No!*" Violet threw her hands up. "Even if we *did* steal Kessa's bootlaces, why do you think they would prove the Tolls are behind the unicorn traps?"

"Because they're bootlaces," Olivia said matter-of-factly. "Sarah Loomway wrote that if you want to know a person, you have to walk in their shoes. Laces are good at holding on to both feet *and* memories. Plus"—she shrugged—"we're not stealing it. Just, you know, borrowing it."

Violet opened her mouth, but Olivia spoke faster. "Your alarm bell isn't going off," she said, pointing to the tiny copper bell Violet was busy polishing, "It can't be such a terrible idea."

"The alarm bell is quiet because I'm not a Forger." Violet sighed. She prodded the bell. It rolled—silently. Violet buried her face in her hands and groaned. "This is such a waste of time."

Olivia's heart squeezed. "Did you ask Malchain if you can transfer? It would be fun to have you in Spinning classes."

"Yeah." Violet's palms muffled her voice. "But she says I need to give Forging at least one more week."

"One week?" Olivia began to pace. "That doesn't leave us time to implement the plan—"

Violet's head snapped up. "Olivia, why would the Tolls want a unicorn, anyway? They're powerful already."

"Because people who have power always want more power." Olivia waved a hand impatiently. "That's how all the stories go! I've thought a lot about this. Maybe Donte Toll wants the unicorn to increase his chances of becoming Prime Minister. Being able to draw from a never-ending supply of unicorn mane would make all your craftings exceptional. Or"—she shrugged—"maybe he's just trying to make Prime Minister Martinson look bad so she can't win again."

Violet finally set her essay down. "Say all of that is true and Grandmaster Toll *did* make Kessa lure a unicorn into a trap, there is still one major flaw in your plan."

Olivia crossed her arms. "What?"

"Kessa doesn't have that lace anymore. Garmont does, remember? He confiscated it."

Olivia stared, and Violet groaned. "You forgot."

Olivia had. It was one thing to *borrow* the lace from Kessa. It was another to *borrow* from a teacher. Especially when everyone already thought she was related to a thief.

Olivia was still mulling over this latest snarl when she arrived at History of Spinning later that afternoon. History was the perfect time for mulling, as, so far, they hadn't even gotten to when humans inhabited Arden. Scholar Yarnly was *still* in the glacial ages and moving forward as fast as, well, a glacier.

Today, however, was different. The neat rows of tables had been rearranged into a circle, and at the center stood a single spinning wheel. It looked like any other wheel Olivia had seen, except maybe a little ricketier.

"Nooo," Paisley moaned as she entered the classroom. "If we have to review the basics of wheels again, *I* will unravel. We've all been spinning since we were three. Well," she said, with a sideways glance toward Olivia, "*most* of us have."

"I can assure you, Paisley, that if you attempted to spin on this wheel without first knowing its name, you wouldn't live to see sunset," Dean Garmont said as he swept into the room. "There's been a change in today's schedule, as this wheel will have to return to Prophecy's Keep tonight."

Prophecy's Keep. Olivia's breath caught. Did that mean . . . was this—?

Dean Garmont nodded his head significantly as the class stared at the wheel. "Yes, you are indeed looking at the Wheel of Destiny. I see many of you are familiar with the legend. Samson—"

Sam, who'd been whispering to Bard, froze.

"—would you like to refresh the class?"

"Uh, all right," Sam said, scratching the back of his head. "The original owners were Loquacious and his twin Garrulous. They spent their lives in competition, obsessed with being first—first to be born, first to marry, first to slay a bloodsucking beast. Obsessed with knowing who would ultimately win at life, they commissioned a spinning wheel upon which they could spin out their futures. The twins raced, each trying to look out farther and farther, each trying to have the longest fate. They spun and spun, pouring more of themselves into their growing yarn with each turn, until they had spun not just their future into the thread, but their fingers, their bones—"

"Yes, thank you—"

"—their muscles, their eyeballs, *everything*, until there was nothing but a flesh-colored pile of wet thread," Sam finished.

Silence filled the classroom, and Olivia looked at the wheel with a new wariness.

"Indeed," Garmont said. "However, no need for any of you to worry about becoming a skein of skin today. Most of you won't be able to spin your fate to next Tuesday, and perhaps one of you, if you are extraordinarily talented, might even catch a glimpse of Wednesday."

After a quick review of spinning basics, Garmont directed them to take out their prepared lamb's wool. ("Lamb's wool is the easiest to spin futures into," he reminded the class. "Wool, like the creature it comes from, is happy to follow your lead.")

One by one, each apprentice approached the Wheel of Destiny and sat upon the three-legged stool. No one managed to spin for more than a second or two except for Paisley, who held on to her future for seven seconds and Spun into Tuesday morning. After each turn, the apprentice would hand their inch of yarn to Garmont, who then would consult the *Telling Tome* and decipher for the class what the lumps and bumps foretold. They learned Cami was destined to eat soup tonight, while Garmont cheerfully informed Sam that he should be sure to carry an umbrella to his next class. Finally, it was Olivia's turn.

She sat down and raised her hand to the bobbin, then froze.

"Olivia," Dean Garmont said. "Is something wrong?"

"What if . . ." she whispered, but her mouth was too dry to continue. She licked her lips, and this time she managed to get out, ". . . my *sister*."

A sympathetic expression appeared on Garmont's face, as though he could see into the clouds of thought darkening her mind. What if she spun the answer to Laurel's fate? What if her string said she was destined to see her sister behind bars for the rest of her life . . . or worse?

"Knowing your future can affect the present," Garmont said, voice gentle. "Once armed with knowledge, you can prepare for anything, yes?" He waited for her to nod and move her hands into position. When she was ready, he said, "Start with your first memory, and go from there."

Dry-mouthed, Olivia nudged the wheel.

Click-clack-click-clack

She let the wool slip from her fingers and wind around the bobbin. The fleece was as soft as her babyhood blanket, and a memory of warm hands and a heart beating beneath her cheek wrapped her tight.

Click-clack-click-clack

A black shawl, draped over her shoulders. The feel of Laurel holding her chubby hand tight.

Click-clack-click-clack

Olivia, the wool, and the whirring wheel spun into one. Memories—more like impressions, really—slipped by, a fast-flowing stream that picked up speed as they moved closer and closer to the Now.

Click-clack-click-clack

Wool thread stitching Laurel's apprentice badge around the sleeve of her blouse.

Click-clack-click-clack

Wool thread stitching a second badge.

Laurel hugging her tight, before leaving Buddle with the other journeymen.

Click-clack-click-clack

Laurel coming home.

Click-clack-click-clack

Green grass and sunlight flowed between her fingers. A girl running across a mountain range toward three shining unicorn hairs.

The wool suddenly felt sticky. It clung, hobbling her hands, dragging her down into a chasm, a void, a strange place between—

CLACK!

Olivia was thrown loose as the wheel stopped, halted by Garmont's hand.

Silence filled the room as the apprentices stared at Olivia and the strange, *long* tangled mess on the bobbin that was her fate.

"Perhaps a bit too enthusiastic," Garmont said as whispers and one or two giggles punctuated the classroom, "but an excellent start. Let's take a look." After a few pokes and twists, he consulted the book. His thick brows lowered . . .

and lowered . . .

and lowered.

He flipped through several pages, then flipped back. The class grew restless. Olivia saw Paisley whisper something to the twins, who looked at Olivia and sniggered. Bard scooted his chair a few more inches away from her, as though her messiness was contagious. The only apprentice who didn't stare at Olivia was Sam, and that was only because he was too busy rummaging through his Spinner kit, muttering about a lost umbrella.

Worry turned Olivia's stomach. Garmont must have seen something utterly horrendous to push his brows down that far. She wasn't sure she *wanted* to know, but she *had* to know.

"Dean, what's my—" But she was cut off as the academy bells clanged and Garmont snapped the book shut, Olivia's yarn still in its pages.

"Scholar Yarnly asked me to remind you your project on the First Filament is due at the end of the week. Your class tomorrow will resume as usual." With that, he strode out of the classroom, taking Olivia's fate with him.

There was a scrape of chairs as the rest of the apprentices gathered their belongings, chatting about their futures and wondering when their fates would come true.

"Why do you think I need my umbrella for Animal Husbandry?" a concerned Sam asked. "There's not a cloud in the sky. But maybe I should stay inside and skip class? Or I could . . ."

Olivia didn't hear the rest of Sam's plan. She was out the door, sprinting after Garmont.

The halls between bells were haphazard at best and jammed at worst as apprentices from all guilds hurried to their next lesson. Olivia ducked to avoid being accidentally jabbed by a rack of wire clothes hangers and dodged a Tiller carrying a potted palm to reach the end of the hallway, only to discover that the next corridor over was entirely empty.

Olivia sighed with relief.

It was the scholars' corridor. Now she knew exactly where Garmont would be. She made her way to the seventh door on the right, where the dean's door stood slightly ajar. As Olivia reached to knock, she heard a voice in the room.

"I don't care what that council says, Louis. The signs are there."

Olivia paused. That sounded like the provost. Stepping to the side, she peered through the crack and saw Provost Malchain sitting at Garmont's desk while he poured water from an ever-warming kettle into a mug.

"And Nadia's not listening?"

"Of course not," Malchain sniffed. "The Prime Minister rarely listens to me these days. She is too busy—" She cut off. "Are you paying attention?"

Olivia shifted slightly to see Garmont across the room, carefully shutting an armoire before locking it shut, but not before Olivia could see what was inside: a collection of cords, ribbons, and trim of all lengths hanging in neat rows, including one very familiar, very sliced bootlace.

"Of course I am," Garmont said. "Let me just close the door, and you can tell me more."

Olivia slunk back and stayed flush against the wall until she heard the *click* of the lock. Holding her breath, she counted to three, then scurried back the way she came, positively giddy. How *lucky* she was to have seen what she saw. How positively *fortuitous*.

It was almost—Olivia thought to herself as she exited the academy and made her way to the stables, where a sopping wet Sam stood covered in soup and Paisley and the twins giggled—*like fate.*

CHAPTER SEVENTEEN

In the end, Violet agreed to help, but only because, as she was quick to point out, Olivia was going to break into Garmont's office no matter what.

"Where were you?" Violet asked as Olivia ran down the scholars' corridor toward her a full hour later than they had agreed.

"Sam." Olivia rolled her eyes as she bent over, hands on knees, to catch her breath. "He 'accidentally' loosed moths into the yarn room." Taking one more big breath, she pulled herself upright. "Do you have it?"

Violet nodded and flashed a small gold key.

Shivers prickled across the back of Olivia's neck, the good kind, the kind she got when Nan would tell tales of the Huntress and her Hounds. While the key's top had been hammered into three crossing loops, the end of it was as toothless as a baby's smile, the hallmark of a Skeleton Key. Olivia had practically fallen off the willow root when Violet said she might be able to get her hands on one. The tricky keys could open almost any lock, and while not exactly contraband, they weren't considered polite.

Violet bounced on the balls of her feet and peered down the hall over Olivia's shoulder. "Garmont might be back any moment. Maybe we should wait until tomorrow?"

"And give the *real* unicorn trapper another night?" Olivia shook her head. "We are unicorn guardians, remember. Besides, I know exactly where the lace is now. What if he moves it later?"

Violet still looked doubtful, but she handed the key to Olivia, who inserted it into the lock. The gold warmed in her hand, feeling sticky and soft, like candlewax.

Click!

Olivia grinned. She pulled the Skeleton Key out and saw that its three new teeth were already melting back into its stem, ready to slip into more locks. She handed it back to Violet and turned the knob. The door opened.

"See?" Olivia whispered. "Quick as a rip. Let's go."

A single silk lantern glowed on the dean's desk, providing just enough light to navigate the crowded study without stubbing their toes on an extraneous coatrack or wayward mannequin. Some might have called Garmont messy, but Olivia could tell by the way piles of fabric were lumped on shelves and patterns cluttered the windowsill that Garmont was simply *enthusiastic*.

"Which cabinet?" Violet whispered, and Olivia pointed across the room. While Violet got to work, Olivia browsed the objects on a nearby shelf of things that had clearly been confiscated. Olivia recognized most of them as belonging to Sam, including the Gaseous Cushion from the very first class and the almost-pilfered pan flute from the music demonstration.

"Olivia!" Violet's panicked whisper cut across the dark. "The key! It's stuck!"

"What do you mean?" Olivia asked as she hurried across the room to join her.

"I mean," Violet said, her voice tight, "it's *stuck*. I can't get the key out of the lock, and I can't let go of the key!"

Olivia reached out to try herself, but drew back at Violet's hiss. "No! What if you get stuck to the key—or me?" Violet blinked rapidly. "Garmont's going to see me! I'll be kicked out! Then I'll never get—"

"Your magic," Olivia finished, her stomach twisting. She *never* should have asked Violet to help. Olivia felt as withered as a worm, as tiny as a beetle, as useless as—

Wait.

As tiny as a beetle.

Olivia sprinted for Sam's dedicated shelf and grabbed the pan flute.

"Blow," she instructed Violet as she thrust it under her nose.

"But what if—" Violet stopped short as they heard someone in the hallway cough and then heard the knob turn.

Garmont had returned.

Violet looked like she might faint.

"Do it," Olivia hissed, eyes glued to the door.

Violet pursed her lips, then blew. Olivia couldn't hear the note—it was far too high for any human to hear—but she knew instantly her plan had worked. One second Violet was standing there, and in the next, she and her key had disappeared. Unless, as Olivia did now, you looked closely at the lock, where she could just make out a tiny figure with a flash of gold in her hand disappear into the black of the armoire's keyhole.

And not a moment too soon, as Dean Garmont entered the room.

"Olivia?" Garmont pulled on a silk cord, and the hundreds of silk lanterns dotting the ceiling glowed to life. He stared at Olivia, and Olivia stared right back.

For the first time in her life, she had absolutely nothing to say.

Luckily, Garmont spoke first. "I should have known." Sighing, he crossed the room to sit on the upholstered chair behind his desk, then studied Olivia. Which was good. Because if he turned his head ever so slightly to the right, he might spot a certain armoire that now had the end of a bootlace dangling from its keyhole.

Olivia sucked in. Violet had done it!

Now they just had to get out of here before the pan flute's

charm wore off. Which would be soon. Olivia didn't want to think of how soon.

"Sit down," Garmont said, waving toward a chartreuse pouf in front of his desk.

That was the last thing Olivia wanted to do, but she didn't have much of a choice. She sat.

Garmont steepled his fingers, looking her squarely in the eyes. "I suppose," he said after a moment, "you are here to steal back your fate."

Olivia tried not to show her relief. She hadn't been sure what she was going to say, and Garmont just provided her with the perfect excuse. Before she could say anything, however, something tapped.

Garmont looked around the room. "Do you hear that?"

Tap-tap!

Out of her periphery, Olivia could plainly see a three-inch Forger apprentice using a bootlace to rappel down the armoire in full view. Every few inches, her feet tapped the wood. Quiet—but not quiet enough. So Olivia did the only thing she could think of.

"I don't think *stealing* is the right word," she blurted out. "It's *my* fate. Can I have it back?"

Nan would have admonished her for her tone, but Garmont didn't look mad. In fact, he looked sheepish.

"My apologies," he said. "You are correct; however, I am sorry to say that I no longer have it. It's at Prophecy's Keep."

"What?" For the first time, Olivia stopped paying attention to the armoire. "Why?"

"All tangled fates must be taken there for examination," he explained. "The Keepers are tasked with detangling them and comparing them to the prophecies that have compiled over the years. Once they are finished, I assure you that it will be returned to you, fully intact.

"Now, seeing as this has been, shall we say, a fateful day, perhaps we should call it a night." He stood up and gestured toward the door, as though he meant to usher her out.

But she couldn't leave, not without Violet, who was . . .

Olivia's pulse quickened as she glanced at the armoire. Where was Violet?! Neither bootlace nor apprentice was anywhere in sight.

"Dean," Olivia said quickly, "can't you tell me *anything* about my fate?"

Garmont shifted, and somehow, Olivia knew that whatever he said next would be a lie. Or at least, not the whole truth.

"I'm afraid not. I'm not trained in futures. Besides, fate is a funny thing. Sometimes knowing our fate is what brings it into existence. Take Sam, for instance. Had he not known he would need an umbrella, he would have taken the usual route and avoided the kitchen and their soup cauldrons altogether."

Something pushed on the toe of Olivia's slipper. She looked down to see Violet clambering up, using her laces as handholds. Keeping her foot very still, Olivia twitched her skirt forward and the fabric fell to the floor, covering her toes and her tiny friend.

"All right, then," Olivia said, standing up as carefully as she could. "Have a good night!"

Garmont frowned. "You don't have any other questions?"

"Nope," Olivia squeaked, unable to keep the panic from her voice as she shuffled toward the door. "Good night!"

"Is something wrong with your foot?" the dean asked.

"I—I stepped on a pin earlier," Olivia fibbed, and minced into the hallway.

She shuffled a few meters down the teacher's corridor, then bent over and gently picked up Violet before running toward a secluded alcove furnished with several potted ferns. She set Violet down five seconds before the girl shot up like a magicked weed.

"Are you all right?" Olivia asked as Violet immediately plopped onto the tiled floor.

"I think so," Violet gasped. "Though I think I might—" Her lips clamped shut, and then she leaned over a potted fern and vomited into the clay pot. Olivia reached into her kit and pulled out a small bottle of water and handed it to her friend.

"Thanks," Violet said after she'd taken a few sips. She leaned against the pot, her eyes closed. "I never want to be, or feel, that small again." She popped an eye open. "There was a *spider* in there, Olivia! With huge, liquid eyes! I thought it was going to eat me, but I threw the key at it and it ran away. Olivia!" Violet's expression was stricken. "*I left the key!*"

"We'll figure something out," Olivia said firmly. "But look on the bright side. You got Kessa's bootlace, right?"

"Yeah," Violet said, her voice still shaky. She unwrapped the lace from around her wrist and handed it to Olivia.

Olivia looked at the silk cord braided in shimmering whites, icy blues, and palest lavenders that all looped together to create an intricate knot in its middle.

It was obviously beautiful.

It was clearly magical.

But it wasn't Kessa's bootlace.

CHAPTER EIGHTEEN

"Maybe this is a sign," Violet said, still hovering behind Olivia's shoulder as Olivia stared down at the knotted, useless string in her hand. "Maybe the stars are telling us to leave Kessa alone."

"You don't believe in signs." Olivia felt hard and tight, like a kernel held over the fire. She squeezed the string, and its knot pressed into her palm.

"Yeah, but . . ." Violet fidgeted, then looked at her toes, then up at the rafters. "I'm not so sure what makes *you* so sure Kessa is the unicorn trapper, you know?"

"I never said Kessa *is* the trapper, just that she has something to *do* with the traps." Irritation seeped through Olivia. How did Violet not understand? How did she not *get* it? Laurel would have understood. She didn't mean to say this last part out loud, but she must have, as Violet's frown deepened.

"I get that you want to help Laurel," Violet said slowly, cautiously, the same way Olivia talked to the nanny goat on bath day. "You're a good sister. But have you considered that maybe you want to help her so badly that you're seeing a story that just . . . isn't there?"

Olivia squeezed the cord so hard, the knot cut into her hand. *"What do you know?"*

Olivia had never heard her own voice sound like that. So cold that the words burned her tongue and numbed her brain. That was the only thing that could explain the horrible, terrible sentence that lashed out next. *"You're just a lackie."*

Violet's expression went blank, and before Olivia could say anything—before she could take it back—Violet reached out. "Then I'll just take that bootlace back."

"No," Olivia yelled, stepping back, but it was too late. Violet's fingers had wrapped around the cord.

She pulled.

The knot slipped—and the world turned white as a blizzard gusted into Unicorn Academy.

Olivia stood frozen to the spot as snow and ice blasted the walls, the tapestries, the portraits, the chandeliers, *everything.* Cold wet pummeled Olivia's face, and the wind howled as the blizzard expanded, reaching down corridors and up staircases with long, icy fingers.

A Wind Knot.

They had stolen a Wind Knot from Dean Garmont's office.

Olivia had read that Wind Knots were relatively common in Needle Pointe, the bustling Spinner city tucked at the end of a river and the start of a sea—the perfect place for an experienced sailor to trap a breeze or a storm with a few twists of twine. They were useful on the open sea. They were deadly inside a castle. And Olivia had absolutely no idea how to put the blizzard back. But she'd have to try.

"Run!" she croaked to Violet, but Violet hesitated. *"Go!"* Olivia insisted. "You're not a Spinner. You can't help!"

Violet's eyes flashed. "Because I'm *a lackie*, right?"

Before Olivia could apologize, could say she didn't mean it at all, Violet turned heel and vanished into the swirling whiteness that had consumed the fifth floor. Olivia wished it could swallow her and her terrible words up, too. Because the worst part was that her words hadn't done anything to banish the truth Violet had spoken.

Because Violet was right. Olivia did see things that weren't actually there—unicorns in sinkholes, friendship in classmates, a place in the world.

Olivia *needed* Kessa to be the trapper because if she wasn't, then Olivia had no other idea for how she could help her family.

In the distance, Olivia heard shouts and the slamming of doors as apprentices woke to a blizzard in their room. She tried to loop the cord, to put the snow and cold and howling wind back into a knot, but her fingers were red and the cord stiff with ice.

"ATTENTION, APPRENTICES!"

Olivia jumped, almost skidding across the icy tiles as Provost Malchain's voice reverberated from within the suits of armor lining the hall.

"EXIT AND FIND YOUR DEAN OUTSIDE. THIS IS AN ORDER."

Olivia tried one more time to bend the cord, but it would not twist. She was out of time.

Shoving the cord into the snowy dirt of the potted fern, she raced to join the rest of the apprentices skidding and slipping toward the grand foyer. They looked more excited than scared, wrapping their bathrobes tightly around themselves as they hurled snowballs at each other and used shields and wooden trays to slide down the snow-covered steps and onto the front lawn.

Dean Garmont appeared on the marble steps, a giant silk fan in each hand. With graceful arcs, he herded the snow and wind in front of him, directing the flakes into a stream above their heads before settling them into the river beyond.

Next to him, Hatchett moved large piles of snow with his bellows, while Ravine laid her hands against the cream-colored stone of the academy. The air was filled with a gentle hiss as the stone warmed, melting away any ice or snow that touched it. The only dean not assisting with the dissipation of the blizzard was Barry, who had her hands full with the topiaries, which had never before seen so many rule-breaking children at one time.

"DROP THE APPRENTICE. DROP HIM! GOOD, ROSARIO! NO—NO, FOCUS!"

Olivia saw the lion topiary put down a giggling Tiller apprentice and take after a group of Forgers, who shrieked with glee as they ran from his rose-thorn paws.

At last, the blizzard thinned and only a few snowflakes drifted in the air, glittering in the torchlight. The topiaries sat still, encircling the apprentices as they were counted by the scholars. When everyone was accounted for, Provost Malchain took to the marble steps.

"It's late and I need everyone to return to their dorms—quietly and quickly. Now." She fixed the crowd with a steely look. "Please be assured that we will be looking into who released the Blizzard of 556, and that there will be consequences."

Though there was no way for Malchain to spot her in the crowd, Olivia held her face carefully blank while her insides squirmed. How had everything gone so catastrophically wrong?

As the apprentices jostled back up the steps and into the academy, she spotted Violet trailing behind a group of Forgers.

Olivia began to jog. She might not have gotten the proof Laurel needed, but she could make one thing right. Weaving between the other apprentices, she tapped Violet on the shoulder.

"I didn't mean it!" she said as Violet turned around. "I'm so sorry. You're the most resourceful person I know. You're *not* useless."

Violet waved a hand impatiently. "Listen, I think you are right."

Olivia frowned. "What? How can you say that about yourself?!"

Violet rolled her eyes. "No, I mean, I think you're right about Kessa. I think she is up to . . ." she stopped, glanced around, then mouthed, *trapping*.

Olivia's eyebrows shot up. "Really?"

Violet kept her voice low as they jostled past the statue of King Anders in the foyer. "When you first met Kessa at the Mender's, she was already enrolled in the academy, but she didn't take the ferry with you, right?"

"Right."

"So," Violet said, nodding toward an open window, where they could make out the silhouettes of the topiaries. "How did she get off the island—and back in time for class—*without* sharing the ferry with you *and* without setting off the topiaries?"

Olivia stopped in her tracks. Violet was right. The topiaries would see anyone who tried to cross by boat or by air, which left only one other direction. Olivia stared down at her feet, or rather at the rocks *under* her feet, and felt a smile spread across her face.

She looked back up at Violet. "I think we're going to need some help. Gemmer help."

CHAPTER NINETEEN

Help, however, was hard to find.

Specifically, Tourmaline l'Ore, the one and only Gemmer apprentice in the entire Unicorn Academy, was hard to find. She wasn't at the Banquet Hall for breakfast, lunch, or dinner, and when Olivia and Violet visited the library and explored the grounds during meals, they never came across her. Nor did they see her in the hallways between classes or at any of the all-guild assemblies. It was as though she had vanished—which made Olivia all the more certain that Tourmaline was exactly who she needed to speak with.

"I bet Tourmaline's using secret passageways to move around the academy," Olivia said to Violet as they made their way outside. Only half an hour ago, they had all woken up to paper birds showing them a revised schedule and advising them to wear fireproof clothing.

"Olivia." Violet sighed, tugging her cloak around her.

"First you think Kessa is using a secret tunnel to sneak off the island to trap unicorns, and now you want me to believe Tourmaline is using tunnels to skip class?" She shook her head. "You're tunnel-obsessed."

"We live in a castle," Olivia pointed out. "Castles *always* have secret passages."

"Maybe Tourmaline just has a cold," Violet suggested as they hurried toward the wild meadow just beyond the manicured lawns of the estate. "Or she's on an excursion with Ravine. The dean hasn't been around, either."

Violet was right, Olivia realized. She fiddled with the thimble in her pocket, trying to remember when she'd last seen the dean of Gemmers. Most likely, the blizzard, five days ago. She wondered what kind of Gemmer lessons might require a learning excursion off the island. Lava brewing? Earth quaking? Or . . .

Olivia's breath caught.

. . . sinkhole digging.

Olivia didn't know much about Gemmers—no one did, really. They didn't often visit the lowerlands. Many said it was because they were too arrogant to rub shoulders with the other guilds, but others claimed that the Gemmers' great citadel was falling apart and they couldn't spare anyone as they worked to keep their home intact.

Could *that* be reason enough to trap unicorns?

But when Olivia floated her latest thought to Violet,

Violet just laughed. "If that's the case, you can ask Ravine now—look!"

They had rounded the gazebo that marked the end of the formal gardens. Most of the school was there, chatting with friends and sneaking glances at the mound of something white and sparkly on the grass. At first, Olivia thought the mound was snowballs left over from the blizzard snow, but on second look, she realized that it was a tower of carefully stacked glass orbs. Anytime a curious apprentice drew too near, Dean Ravine arched a single black brow, and the offending apprentice ran away.

"Yes, yes, we are outside, very exciting," Dean Garmont said, walking through the apprentices and toward Ravine. "Gather round—no, come on, boys! It's just a bee! You've all seen one before!"

Too late. At the mention of *bee*, all the nearby Forgers and Spinners ran away screaming, while a couple of Tillers raced forward, hoping to herd the pollinator to their garden patches. Having grown up with Nan's hives, bees didn't faze Olivia, and so she stayed put, watching as Ravine selected a glass orb. The scholar held it to her lips, whispering something. Then she lifted the orb high above her head and smashed it into the ground.

Light flashed, and then Ravine's voice filled the sky:

"YOU HAVE UNTIL THREE TO BE SILENT—OR I WILL TURN YOU TO STONE AND YOU WILL BE SILENT FOREVER."

The apprentices didn't need the count of three. Silence fell, and the words rolled away like thunder because, Olivia realized, that's exactly what they had been. The lightning had carried Ravine's whisper the same as it carried thunder in its wake.

Garmont sighed. "Was that entirely necessary?"

Ravine lifted an elegant shoulder and smiled sweetly. "They're paying attention now."

Garmont looked like he might say something else, but instead he turned to the apprentices and clapped his hands. "Listen up! After last week's unseasonable blizzard, Provost Malchain has asked us to prioritize elemental magic—specifically, storms."

"That sounds dangerous," a Forger said, and Olivia couldn't help but nod in agreement.

"It is," Ravine said. "But I'm willing to risk you."

Even though the comment was not directed at Olivia, Olivia couldn't help taking a step back from the formidable dean.

"We aren't going to brew a *whole* storm," Garmont said, ignoring his colleague, "just a single part: lightning. Rubi just demonstrated the usefulness of Lightning Messages. It is the fastest way to send information, though not the most secretive. Can anyone else tell me another reason why it might be useful to have lightning on hand? Yes, you, then, go on."

"It rejuvenates fields," a Tiller said. "Lightning breaks

apart the air, mixes ether into the soil, and fertilizes the crops. Powdered lightning is often used in quick-grow formulas."

Dean Garmont nodded. "Very good. Anyone else?"

Cami raised her hand and noted that lightning woven into bandages could help a patient's heart, and then a Forger mentioned how a sword hammered with lightning would be impervious to rain and never rust.

"Excellent examples," Garmont said. "Let's now— Yes, Olivia, you have another example?"

"No," Olivia said, pasting a bright smile on her face. "I have a question, though it's probably for Tourmaline." She paused and made a great show of looking around for the Gemmer. "Where is she?"

"Tourmaline," Ravine said, stepping in front of Garmont, "is where she is meant to be. I am sure I can answer whatever question you have." The tiger-eye gems that had been stitched onto the Gemmer's robes suddenly seemed to gleam with predatory intent.

Olivia gulped, but it was too late to back out now. Quickly, she thought of a second question. "Er, what do Gemmers use lightning for?"

Ravine didn't bother to reply. Instead, she stooped down and began to dig where the lightning had struck the ground. Soon she began to pull, and a moment later something slid free. At first, Olivia thought the dean had pulled up some roots, but then she saw that the "roots" were rigid, and where the dirt had been knocked off, Olivia could see straight through them, as though they were made of . . .

"Is that glass?" Olivia asked.

The scholar grunted. "When lightning strikes, it transforms sediment into glass." Gently, she blew on the glass, warming it with her breath. Then she began to reshape it.

"Lightning-made glass can hold many things," Ravine said, "including lightning itself. The same way only a diamond is hard enough to carve another diamond, only lightning can trap lightning." She held out her hand, and Olivia saw she had coaxed the roots into an empty glass orb.

"Usually," Ravine continued, "Gemmers have to wait for a storm to fill a bottle, but by jumbling our talents today, we can skip that step."

The air again began to hum, not with lightning this time, but excitement. The apprentices had never before been allowed to jumble magic, and as Olivia looked at her fellow academymates—the Forgers, Tillers, and Spinners—she again felt the sparkle of the provost's welcoming words: *Guardians of unicorns.*

Ravine looked over at the other deans—Garmont, Barry, and Hatchett. "Ready?"

Garmont spread out a small rug on the grass, then took off his boots to reveal the fuzziest pair of wool socks Olivia had ever seen. Closing his eyes, Garmont stepped onto the rug and began a strange, shuffling dance. His hair swayed, then rose, spreading in all directions and making him look like an absent-minded alchemist. Next to Olivia, Violet mumbled something.

"What?" Olivia whispered back.

"Static electricity," Violet said, pointing to Garmont's feet, where blue sparks crackled between his socks and the rug.

Olivia frowned. She hadn't heard that expression before. "Static wha—" She broke off as the blue sparks suddenly converged and raced up Garmont like a vine on a trellis. He brimmed with newly formed lightning.

"Now!" Garmont shouted, and Hatchett leaped forward, a conductor's metal baton at the ready. Light zipped from Garmont to the outstretched baton, and then Hatchett was swirling it, wrapping the lightning tightly around, the same way Olivia wound thread around a spool. The bolt fought him, but soon it had twisted into a glowing coil. Hatchett flicked it off the baton, sending light zagging into the orb that Ravine promptly corked shut.

"And that," Ravine said, holding up the humming, glowing ball, "is how you trap lightning in a bottle. Who would like to try?"

They all did, except Violet.

"I'm going to be electrocuted," Violet said, eyes wide under her black fringe, as the others sorted themselves into guilds.

"I'll make sure I'm your partner," Olivia reassured her, but Violet looked like a ghost as she drifted toward the Forgers.

Soon, the deans asked the Forgers and Spinners to form two lines, with the Tillers circling them, ready to call moisture out of the surrounding leaves if anything should accidentally catch fire.

Clutching the pair of fuzzy socks Garmont handed to her, Olivia stood on tiptoe to find Violet standing third in the Forger line. Trying to maneuver to the same spot, Olivia slid in right behind Sam. But as she made to move, someone skirted the gazebo, then darted down the path that led into the Unkempt Woods. A someone with fluffy hair and pink-quartz glasses. *Tourmaline.*

"Olivia," Garmont called. "You're first!"

Olivia jumped. Distracted by Tourmaline's appearance, she hadn't noticed the line shift. Instead of standing third, she now stood at the very front. And instead of looking at Violet in a Forger tunic that was just a little too big, Olivia found herself staring at Kessa Toll.

A smile spread across Kessa's face. It had the opposite effect of most smiles and made Olivia want to curl up into an acorn cap and bury herself in the ground till next spring. But that, unfortunately, didn't seem to be an option.

"Dean," Olivia said, turning to Garmont, who had just finished laying out the tapestry between them, "I wanted to partner with Violet, since—"

"Dean Hatchett thought it best Violet sit this one out," Garmont said, nodding over to where Violet now stood with the Tillers, looking utterly horrified. Olivia raised her eyebrows and jerked her head in the direction of the path, trying to tell Violet to follow it, follow Tourmaline, but Violet shrugged and mouthed the word *sorry*.

She had no idea what Olivia was trying to say. Olivia forced herself to pay attention to Garmont, who was finishing up some advice Olivia had completely missed.

"Ready?" Garmont asked.

Kessa slipped a silver headband into her voluminous curls. "Ready," she said, eyes flashing as she accepted the baton from Hatchett and stepped toward Olivia.

"On the count of three, then," Garmont said, moving out of the way and leaving the girls to face each other. "One!"

"If you say *anything*," Kessa hissed in a voice too soft for anyone else to hear, "my father will send another storm your way."

"Two!" Garmont called.

Olivia's mind scrambled, trying to make sense of Kessa's threat. Another storm. *Another.* Which meant there had been a *first* storm. Which meant—

"Three!"

Olivia stepped onto the tapestry and dragged a foot across, feeling for the movement of the tapestry's wool as it marched its way back and forth across the vertical weft threads, forming line by line a complete picture. A complete story. Her imagination raced.

Forgers, in the mountains, metal shovels gleaming as they dig.

Kessa standing with them, about to blow the Luring Horn, just as the Dandiloon's great puff floats over the peaks.

Donte Toll, sinister in matte-black armor, raising his broadsword to the sky.

Facts, not stories, Nan always warned. But as Olivia crouched, jumped, and swirled, the facts stacked themselves into a story Olivia wished she'd never read: Grandmaster Donte Toll had sent the storm after the Dandiloon.

Olivia almost stumbled as she realized the true reason why Grandmaster Toll would want the Unicorn Academy to fail. He needed his daughter, the only player of the Luring Horn, to be free from promises to the Prime Minister so she could travel . . . so she could collect.

Olivia swayed, dizzy with the revelation. She suddenly felt too big for her skin. She crackled with anger. She zipped with knowledge. She sparked with lightning.

Too much lightning.

"Olivia! *Let go!*"

Olivia's eyes opened, and she spun to a halt directly in front of Kessa. The harvested lightning crackled around her arms and nipped at her braids, desperate to be loosed. All Olivia needed to do was reach a hand out to Kessa's baton. But Olivia did not want to give this girl anything.

"*NOW!*" someone yelled above the sizzling sparks.

Unless Olivia wanted to fry herself, she had no choice. She reached for Kessa's flourished baton. Heat flowed away from her, straining toward the metal, but then—

CRACK!

Blue heat engulfed Olivia. Suddenly, she was on the ground, back flat against the earth while Ravine knelt next to her, holding Olivia's fingers in the dirt.

"What's happening?" Olivia mumbled. She felt shriveled, like the skin of a baked pumpkin.

"I'm grounding you," Ravine said. Her long black braid fell over her shoulder, and its paintbrush end tickled Olivia's arm as the scholar measured her pulse. "The lightning did a doubleback and struck you. The earth should draw out any extraneous sparks. Can you sit up?"

"I think so," Olivia said. Her head throbbed, and a dull pain radiated from her left hip. She set her hand there and felt the steel thimble in her pocket. The lightning must have aimed for it.

The air smelled like it had been toasted. Rolling onto her side, she saw a smoking pile of fringe—all that remained of the tapestry. Just beyond it, Dean Barry directed the remaining apprentices to smother several small fires that had broken out.

"I did this?" Olivia asked, horrified.

"No," Ravine said grimly. "Only metal directs lightning, and only a Forger can direct metal." Seemingly satisfied, she pulled Olivia's hands out of the dirt and wiped them on a towel. "Dean Hatchett has escorted Kessa to the provost's office and then she will be sent to the Forger barracks to pack up her things."

Panic looped around Olivia's ribs and drew tight. "Pack up her things? You mean—Kessa is being expelled?"

"We can't have apprentices attacking other apprentices, especially not in class. Her father will collect her tomorrow." Ravine stood up and offered Olivia a hand. "You should probably go to the infirmary."

Tomorrow. Kessa was leaving tomorrow. Which meant that tomorrow, she would be free to roam Arden with Grandmaster Toll. And Olivia was sure that in a matter of days, there would be fewer unicorns. She was *sure*, but she didn't have any proof. And she was running out of time to collect it.

She. Needed. Tourmaline.

"I'm all right," Olivia said, waving off Ravine's hand as she scrambled to her feet. After assuring the dean she did not need any assistance, Olivia took the dirt path back up the hill to the academy and its infirmary. As soon as she passed the gazebo, Olivia checked to make sure no one was watching her, then hiked up her skirt and ran into the Unkempt Woods.

CHAPTER TWENTY

The Unkempt Woods had been properly named. Unlike the Endless, with its ancient oaks and clearings, the Unkempt Woods was a knot of brush and thorns. But Olivia knew how to read a forest floor, and Tourmaline's path was as clear to her as any sentence. She followed the Gemmer's trail of snapped twigs and crushed sorrel, bleeding hearts, and alumroot until she arrived at the foot of an old stone wall. Though it was three times Olivia's height, she didn't spot it until she stood only a few feet away. Ivy hung heavy on its stones, and the wood of a single arched door had silvered with age.

It was the perfect place to hide, and without another thought, Olivia pushed her way into the walled garden. Except it wasn't a garden at all.

It was a graveyard.

Goose bumps prickled down her arms as Olivia took in the moss-covered tombstones and cracked mausoleums. The air here felt ancient, like time had gone soft around the edges. Like maybe things buried in the ground might not always *stay* in the ground.

Olivia pulled her sling from her Spinner's kit. Just in case. She began to explore, pausing occasionally to read the names. The farther in she went, the older the dates, until she reached a section where the grave markers were so old, wind and time had wiped them clean. Still, there was no sign of Tourmaline.

The closest thing she saw to another living human was a statue of a lady and a bridled unicorn. The lady's braids and curls tumbled down her back. Her garb was that of long ago, the founding days, when draped togas were in style, and the sculptor had carved a thousand pleats into the stone. The unicorn's neck arched over the lady's shoulder, protecting his rider from the skeleton creature at its hooves. Intrigued, Olivia crouched to take a closer look, wondering what it was supposed to be. It was about the height of a tall goose, with arms absurdly long for its body. The sculptor had given it a thin, serpentine neck. A neck that now twisted toward Olivia.

It wasn't a statue, after all.

Olivia screamed as bone scraped against rock and the monster leaped onto the marble unicorn. Balancing on the unicorn's head, it spread its arms wide, each one six feet in length and ending in sharp points. Its skull, though small, protruded forward into a hooked beak. Its neck swiveled again, and without soft tissue, vertebrae clattered against each other as the creature fixed empty eye sockets on Olivia.

Olivia trembled at the macabre sight, but she managed to fit her thimble into her sling and whirl it around her head.

Any second, the skeleton would leap.

Any second, those claws would tear into her, shredding flesh into ribbons.

Any second . . .

But now several seconds had passed, and the skeleton stayed where it was. Staring at her. Olivia knew she should let the thimble fly and run, but she couldn't. So far, the skeleton had done nothing but look at her.

The sling slowed, then stopped.

Silence filled the cemetery as Olivia and the skeleton stared at each other.

"What are you?" Olivia finally croaked out.

"That's Ghost."

Now Olivia *did* scream as Tourmaline l'Ore suddenly stood next to her.

As far as Olivia could tell, Tourmaline hadn't walked up or popped out from behind a gravestone. She simply, inexplicably, was suddenly just *there,* pink quartz glasses on her nose, necklaces draped around her neck, and a tight smile stretched between two round cheeks.

"How—how did you do that?" Olivia sputtered.

"Family gift," Tourmaline said as she pulled out one of her longer necklaces, with a single black opal pendant at its center. Want to see?" she asked, and before Olivia could reply, she held it up and began to swing it back and forth, intoning in a deep voice, "You are getting verrrrrry sleeeeeepy. You will forget that you ever saw me or Ghooooost—"

"Are you trying to mesmerize me?!" Olivia asked.

"Grit." The smile fell from Tourmaline's face. "It's not working?"

Olivia frowned. "What's supposed to be happening?"

"You're supposed to be forgetting all this"—Tourmaline waved her hand—"and deciding you really want to go to the Banquet Hall and eat some chocolate."

"I hate chocolate."

"Really?" Tourmaline said as she shoved the pendant back under her neckline. "Weird, but that doesn't matter. If I'd cut the opal right, you would have craved it."

"You also would be a criminal." Olivia crossed her arms. "Mesmerizing opals are illegal."

"It's nothing personal." Tourmaline twisted a ring on her finger. "But I have to protect Ghost—hey!" Tourmaline's excuse was cut short as the straps of Olivia's thrown sling wrapped quickly around the Gemmer's fingers, binding them tight. Tourmaline tried to shake the ties off, but they only clung more tightly.

She scowled at Olivia. "That's not nice."

"It's nothing personal." Olivia kept one eye on Tourmaline while trying to find the skeleton. The thing had disappeared. "But you're the one who keeps trying to curse me—I'm assuming that ring does something?"

Tourmaline tugged once more at the binds, then seemed to give up. "Yeah," she admitted. "It turns back time."

Olivia blinked. "That's fantastic!"

"That's what I thought, too." Tourmaline sighed as she leaned against a tombstone. "But when you turn back time, you don't *remember* that you turned back time—and you do the exact same thing you did in the first place. It's totally useless." She sighed. "If you're going to keep me tied up, can you at least give Ghost his lunch? He gets grumpy if he's malnourished." She nodded toward Olivia's feet.

When Olivia looked down, she almost jumped. The skeleton had sidled up next to them and was now staring up at the girls. Though the skull was expressionless, the angle of it clearly said, FEED ME! "What exactly does Ghost eat?" Olivia asked, trying to keep her voice steady. "Human flesh?"

"Ha! You're funny." With her unbound hand, Tourmaline fished out a clay bottle from her cloak. "Ghost doesn't even have a stomach."

Handing the bottle to Olivia, she told her to uncork it. As soon as Olivia did, the cork shifted, growing and stretching into a large, shallow bowl. Following Tourmaline's instructions, Olivia tilted the bottle and milk flowed out. As soon as it was full, Ghost splashed in, flicking milk over himself like a bird bathing in a puddle. But Ghost wasn't a bird.

"What is he?" Olivia asked.

"Isn't it obvious?" Tourmaline asked as she picked up a sharp rock and began to saw at the sling's straps. "He's a fossil."

"But fossils . . ." Olivia licked her lips, her mouth suddenly dry. "They're *dead*."

"I know." Tourmaline looked up from her sawing. "I brought him back to life."

Olivia had learned at too young an age that there were some things even magic could not undo. Telling an orphan otherwise was just cruel.

"Good luck with that sling." Olivia stood up and shoved the bottle back at Tourmaline. "Only a Spinner can get it off." She stomped toward the stone wall. "You are going to have to find someone else to do that, and listen to your jokes."

"But," Tourmaline said, "I'm not joking."

The vulnerability running through the Gemmer's voice tripped Olivia up, forcing her to stop. Standing still, surrounded by graves, Olivia weighed her options. She didn't have many.

Tourmaline was the only Gemmer apprentice at the school, and Olivia doubted Ravine would be willing to discuss secret tunnels with her. Then there was the *Kessa* of it all. With Kessa expelled, her Luring Horn would be let loose upon Arden and its unicorns without any restrictions.

Facts, not stories, Nan always said. Maybe Olivia had spun an unfair story about Tourmaline. Maybe the Gemmer really did believe that she'd raised Ghost from the dead, even though resurrection was impossible.

Impossible . . . like an invisible sinkhole.

Olivia almost flinched. If only Laurel had believed Olivia the night of the sinkhole. If only Laurel had *listened* to Olivia, then maybe the Toll family would already be under arrest. Maybe the unicorns of Arden would already be safe.

Taking a deep breath, Olivia faced Tourmaline. "How did it happen?"

Tourmaline stopped sawing at the leather binds, her expression wary. "It's a long story," she warned.

Olivia plucked the sharp stone from Tourmaline's hand and let it drop to the ground. Then she sat at the base of the unicorn statue and pulled the Gemmer down next to her.

"Good," she said, taking Tourmaline's hands and beginning to pull at the sling. "Because this is going to take some time."

It was, according to Tourmaline, all her little brother's fault. If he hadn't told her about the abandoned eaglets on the south side of the Queen's Nose, Tourmaline never would have found herself sneaking out of Starscrape Citadel at midnight, rope in hand, ready to scale the cliff.

"Hang on," Olivia interrupted. "Why didn't a grown-up do that?"

"They said the eaglets weren't worth the risk," Tourmaline said, and her many necklaces and bangles practically jangled in fury. "Can you believe it? Not worth it—*eagles!* They do so much for us—pick carcasses clean! Eat mice! Give us feathers! Without them, our arrows would never fly straight. Anyway, Basalt wouldn't leave me alone, so I said I would help. But six-year-olds aren't the best scouts, because he was wrong. Mama and Papa Eagle were there, and they were *not* happy to see me. They attacked, and I slipped—well, more like plummeted—off the cliff."

Olivia gasped. "Your ropes didn't hold you?"

Tourmaline shook her head, sending the jewels in her chandelier earrings dancing. "It's more like I didn't tie my knots right." With her free hand, she gestured at the sling Olivia was unbinding. "Something like this would have been useful, but"—she shrugged—"I fell."

Tourmaline described how her body had slammed against the rock face again and again, her life—Mama's hugs, Papa's scratchy kisses, her brother's laughter, winter days swimming in hot springs, enchanted nights singing in the marble halls—flashing before her eyes. With one last desperate effort, Tourmaline grabbed for anything—grabbed for *everything*—and her palm slammed into a shallow outcropping.

"I knew I wouldn't be able to hang on forever," Tourmaline

said. "And there were still hours until morning, and anyone could spot me from a window in the Citadel. I started to cry, and that's when the stone beneath my fingers rippled. The tiny ridges I managed to grab? They were the ridges of *bones*. They started to bob, like they were twigs in water and not in solid stone. Then the rest of Ghost surfaced."

"I would have screamed," Olivia said. She gently tugged the final knot, and the sling slipped from Tourmaline's hand into Olivia's waiting palm.

Tourmaline shook out her fingers. "I did. But with Ghost's help, I was able to pull myself onto the outcrop and wait for morning. That's how Papa found me, squatting on the cliff's face like some sort of curly-haired spider, a pile of bones at my side." The humor faded from the Gemmer's voice as she neared the end of her tale. "I got my wish, though. Now my little brother leaves me alone. *Everyone* leaves me alone. No one wants to be around a girl who can bring bones back to life. I'm creepy." She said the last two words lightly, but Olivia knew that sometimes, the lightest words hit the hardest of all. "When Aunt Rubi suggested I go to the academy instead of my cousin," Tourmaline continued, "no one complained."

"Aunt Rubi—Scholar Ravine is your aunt?!"

"My mother's youngest sister." Tourmaline nodded, scratching Ghost under his chin bone. "She's the only one not scared of me. Maybe because she's so scary herself." She glanced at Olivia. "But it's all an act, you know. Aunt Rubi only pretends she doesn't care about the Unicorn Academy, because she cares so much it *hurts*. Before the unicorns returned, Aunt Rubi used to sneak off the mountain and disguise herself as a Forger just so she could buy a new scroll for the Citadel's library. Until her, we had nothing new to read for three hundred years. Not a *single* new idea." Tourmaline made a face. "Aside from me, she's the only one who sees Ghost as a wonder, not a problem. And you're not a problem at all, are you Ghostie-Toastie?" Tourmaline scratched Ghost's skull and the bones leaned into her hand.

"What was Ghost?" Olivia asked, watching the strange tableau. "Before . . ." She drifted off, not wanting to say *before he died*. It sounded rude. So she settled on, "Before he came back?"

"Not sure," Tourmaline admitted. "Aunt Rubi and I are trying to figure it out. Right now, I'm leaning toward a drakon."

"A what?"

"They're a kind of animal that died out long before humans existed in Arden," Tourmaline clarified. "We still find their bones in mountaintops sometimes. We think they looked like a salamander with wings, but they were probably more closely related to unicorns."

Olivia frowned. "How? Last I checked, unicorns don't look like flying lizards."

Tourmaline giggled. "Obviously! I only mean that drakons,

like unicorns, were *born* from magic. They're *pure* magic. The guilds didn't make them."

Olivia stared at the skeleton, mulling Tourmaline's words. *Creatures born, not made.* There were plenty of fantastical creatures in Arden, but aside from the unicorn, guildsmen were responsible for their creation, like the academy's topiaries, or chimeras, the copper creatures that Forgers and Tillers rode into battle.

"Arden is full of strange bones left behind by the creatures that used to roam long before the guilds ever existed," Tourmaline continued as Olivia tied the sling onto her belt. "At the Citadel, we call them Originals."

"And you think Ghost might be some kind of Original?" Olivia asked.

"He might be," Tourmaline said. "But he's not sure himself. Fossils are just impressions of bones; they don't preserve memory." Her thumb ran up and down Ghost's bumpy vertebrae. "We spend a lot of time here, though," she said, looking around at the graveyard. "I keep hoping he'll see something—a name, a rune, anything—that will help him remember who he was. What he was."

Olivia smiled at Ghost. He was cute, in a creepy, bony kind of way. "I didn't know what I was for the longest time," she told him. An idea began to form, and she reached for the indigo pouch hanging next to her sling. "You said that he used to have wings?"

When Tourmaline nodded, Olivia got to work.

She'd snagged a bit of the Dandiloon's fluff before they'd left the mountains, and now she twirled it between her fingers, coaxing the fibers to spin together and lengthen, growing longer and longer until she had yards of thin white thread. She held it up to Ghost's eye socket. "May I?"

The fossil stayed still, skull devoid of any expression. Just as Olivia wondered whether Ghost could hear without ears, he stretched out his humerus, radius, and ulna—or, as people who hadn't grown up in Nan's apothecary called them, arm bones. Using the bones as both weft and loom, Olivia wove the dandelion thread into a tight fabric. She only paused once to put on her thimble—still warm from the lightning strike—so she could better push the shuttle through the tight spots between the phalanges. When she was done, she sat back to admire her work.

The fabric wings were so delicate she could see through them to the unicorn statue beyond. But the dandelion fibers were strong, like the bones they were woven on, and she could feel them vibrating in excitement, ready to ride the thermals again. She made one last tuck, then nodded. "There. Try that."

Ghost hunched, shoulder blades jutting forward, and then a great gust slammed into Olivia as the fossil beat his wings and launched into the sky.

"You're doing it!" Tourmaline whooped.

Triumph radiated through Olivia as she watched Ghost's tailbone disappear into the cloud cover. She'd done it. She'd *healed*. When all of this was over, when the Toll family was apprehended, the unicorns safe, and Nan and Laurel cozy at home, Olivia could join them behind the apothecary counter. They could be *Hayes and Hayes and Hayes*—after Nan had gotten over the shock of having a Spinner granddaughter. Which she would, because Olivia was going to make everything right.

"Tourmaline," Olivia said as she tried to get her thimble off. It wouldn't budge. "I have a favor to ask you."

"Anything," Tourmaline said, her smile rivaling the radiance of her jewels as Ghost dove out from the clouds only to shoot back up again.

"Are there tunnels around here that might lead off the island?"

Tourmaline looked at Olivia, and her eyes sparkled. "Meet me at midnight, and I'll take you into the catacombs."

CHAPTER TWENTY-ONE

The rest of the afternoon held some of the longest hours of Olivia's life—right up there with the time she'd had a stomach bug during Starfell festivities and had spent all day as a miserable snail on her bed. Not only because Olivia was acutely aware that Kessa's hours at the academy could be ticking to a close, but also because for the first time since she'd started Spinning, all of her work had gone very, very wrong.

In Pattern class, her scissors wouldn't cut correctly, no matter how many times she sharpened them. Instead of piecing out beautiful crystals for snowflake lace, her designs showed faces with fangs and three eyes. And when she'd tried to pull a bit of embroidery floss through brocade, the needle had grown hot, burning her fingers and singeing her hoop. She'd managed to stop the fabric from bursting into flames, but not before all of the gold chain stitch she'd meticulously wrought the day before melted, turning her flowers into smeared suns.

And most wrong of all: she could not get her thimble off.

No matter how hard Olivia tugged, twisted, or prodded, the steel thimble would not budge from her middle finger.

That night, as she coaxed her pillows into an Olivia-shaped lump under her covers and tiptoed out of her dorm and into the darkened corridors to meet Tourmaline, Olivia finally thought she knew why.

Somehow, Kessa had used the lightning to curse Olivia's thimble.

But Olivia couldn't tell any of the teachers—not without getting Kessa into even *more* trouble. Until Olivia had firm proof Kessa was sneaking out of school to capture unicorns, she did not want to give the scholars yet another reason to expel the Forger, making it even easier for her to lure unicorns to their doom.

Olivia made it through the hallways without any trouble; her Be Nimble Candle, at least, had worked perfectly. Each time a scholar on night patrol neared her candle, their eyes had grown heavy with sleep as they breathed in the scent of chamomile and sweetest dreams that Olivia had woven into the wick—giving Olivia and her kerchief-covered nose just enough time to slip by unnoticed.

She arrived at the statue of King Anders first, and Violet

arrived a few minutes later, her own Be Nimble Candle burned to a nub.

"I had to hide on the second floor," Violet whispered through her kerchief as her flame flickered and died. "It didn't work on Scholar Rivet. She has a stuffy nose."

Tonight, Violet wore pajamas of ash gray, and the color highlighted the circles of worry beneath her eyes. "Are you sure we can trust Tourmaline?" Violet had not been happy when Olivia had filled her in on what happened after Olivia had left the magic jumbling class. And she'd been unhappier still when Olivia told her that she'd revealed everything she suspected to Tourmaline.

"Yes," Olivia said. "Trust me, you'll like her."

"I'd like her better if she'd show up," Violet muttered just as a third voice whispered, "Here!"

Olivia almost dropped her candle—and Violet *did* drop her candle—as Tourmaline appeared out of thin air. Again.

"How do you *do* that?" Olivia hissed.

"Told you," Tourmaline whispered. "Family gift." She extended her hand and pointed to the third ring on her right pinkie finger, a thin band of gold cupping a chip of dull gray stone. "Misdirection ring, made of magnetite, a mineral that can be found in volcanos, the ocean, and the human brain. When polished properly, it can repel others from looking at you. See?"

She twisted the ring, and even though Olivia *knew* Tourmaline was right there, every time she tried to look at the Gemmer, her eyes slid over the space.

"And if I turn it upside down . . ." Tourmaline must have done so, because Olivia could suddenly see her again.

"That's why we could never find you in the halls," Violet said, speaking for the first time. "You've been using your ring to hide you and your, um . . ." She eyed Ghost, who stared back the only way he could: unblinkingly. ". . . dragon, Olivia said?"

"It's dra-*k*on," Tourmaline corrected, "but I'm starting to think he wasn't a drakon. Ghost is scared of fire, and drakons breathed fire, so that doesn't really make sense. Are you ready?"

Without waiting for an answer, Tourmaline mumbled something to Ghost. The fossil launched himself from her shoulder toward the statue. One bony talon struck the gemstone tine of Anders's crown, and as he circled back to Tourmaline, the tiles under the statue's feet clinked, twisted, then sank down into the earth, constructing a narrow, spiraling staircase.

A narrow, spiraling, *dusty* staircase, in which a single Forger apprentice–sized boot print was clearly visible on the top step. *Kessa.*

Tourmaline coughed and waved a hand in front of her nose. The dank smell of wet stone and earth wafted into the hall. "I'm glad that worked."

Violet's eyebrows disappeared under her bangs. "You mean, you weren't sure it would?"

"I had a hunch," Tourmaline said, watching Ghost soar up into the rafters of the foyer. After a thousand years encased in rock, he did not seem keen to return. "There's an ancient Gemmer saying: *'If Anders stands there; gates beware.'*" At the girls' confused expressions, Tourmaline explained, "Arden is full of tunnels, and most of their entrances have a statue of King Anders guarding the entrance."

"Guarding from what?" Olivia asked.

"Let's find out." Tourmaline flashed a devilish smile, then disappeared down the first spiral.

Violet looked at Olivia. "I'm not sure about this."

"We'll be fine," Olivia whispered back with more confidence than she felt. "I have my sling."

"It's not that," Violet said, eyes troubled. "But if we actually *do* find a tunnel that leads off the island, you're not allowed to leave Unicorn Academy, remember? If we're caught—if *you're* caught . . ." She didn't have to finish the sentence. Olivia knew what she meant. *Prison*.

But if Olivia *didn't* follow Tourmaline into the academy's belly, it would be Nan and Laurel who would one day languish in a cell. And then there were the unicorns. It *always* came back to the unicorns.

"We won't be caught," Olivia said, and began her descent.

By the time Olivia and Violet reached the bottom, Tourmaline had lit a Gemglow. The sapphire's light washed everything it touched in ghostly blue, illuminating an arch here, a roughly hewn pillar there, and the corners of several stone boxes.

No. Not boxes. Sarcophagi, coffins carved from rock. Leaning forward to examine one more closely, Olivia made out the etching of a man with curls cresting over a simple circlet. His hands were folded peacefully at his chest, and a ring with a five-pointed star had been carved on his left index finger.

"Who were they?" Olivia whispered, despite the fact that there was no one around to overhear.

Tourmaline leaned forward, examining the edge of a stone coffin. "They are carved from the same stone as the academy's foundations," she said, voice awed. "If I had to guess, I bet they are Anders's Thousand."

"Thousand what?" Violet asked. She'd stayed by the stairs, her arms crossed in front of her, as though she were trying to keep her heart from leaping out.

"Anders's army of a thousand warriors," Olivia said, surprised that Violet didn't know that. These brave men and women had gone after the Devourer, but none had lived to see the next day. Reverently, she touched the corner of the box in silent thanks, then looked at Tourmaline. "Where now?"

Tourmaline held up her sapphire Gemglow. "This way."

They followed the Gemmer. Until now, Olivia had never known so much darkness could exist. It didn't help that darkness magnified sound, making the shifting of pebbles sound like the patter of feet, or that creatures had been carved onto the pillars. There were unicorns, of course, along with fish-tailed melusines, tiny figures with butterfly wings, and something that matched Tourmaline's description of a drakon, along with other, more monstrous creatures.

"Gross," Tourmaline said, coming to a stop. Olivia peered around her shoulder to see that three archways loomed in front of them, but only one was blocked by a door—a large, round one of dark-blue rock. No handle had been carved on it, but something else had: a large snake that circled its tail down and around and back up to its—

"Is it *eating* itself?" Olivia asked.

"Seems like it," Tourmaline said, her voice tight with distaste. She prodded the door, first with her hand, and then she unhooked her earring—a small, dangling prism—and held it up to her eye as she peered at the door.

"It's magically sealed," she said finally, and lowered the prism. "There's no way Kessa could have gotten through. So"—she pointed at the archways on either side—"it's one of these."

Olivia was about to ask which one they should try, when Violet suddenly gripped her arm and whispered, *"Did you hear that?"*

Holding her breath, Olivia listened for whatever had made Violet's voice sound so strained. She'd expected to hear the light pitter-patter that had seemed to be following them, but instead she heard something completely different.

"*Grrrrrrrrrrrrrrrrrrr-ooooooooooooooooowll.*"

The sound thrust Olivia back to a winter twilight on the edge of the Endless. She and Laurel had been gathering kindling when they'd heard the hunting cry of wolves. But then there had been a whole forest of trees, a talented sister, and a powerful grandmother between Olivia and the pack.

In the tunnel, something glinted in the dark: wolf eyes.

Before Olivia could think, her sling was in her hand, whirling above her head—

"Don't!" Tourmaline yelled, but it was too late. The pebble soared into the darkness and hit with a resounding *CRACK!*

Olivia tensed. That wasn't the sound of a pebble hitting flesh. She'd missed, and now the wolf knew it was in danger. Its growl intensified, and the entire tunnel seemed to rattle with the creature's rage.

"GET BACK!" Tourmaline shouted, and pulled Olivia and Violet from the opening just as the tunnel collapsed.

Grit pelted Olivia's skin. She threw her hands over her head, trying to protect herself from falling debris as the ground vibrated with impact. The tunnel's demise might have lasted one minute or a hundred, but by the time stones stopped falling, the second archway was entirely blocked. No one would be able to get in—or get out.

"Everyone all right?" Tourmaline asked. Her voice was

calm, but the light of the Gemglow wavered as her hand shook. Carefully, Tourmaline placed it on the ground.

"I'm fine," Olivia said, though she wasn't sure if she was. In her panic, she'd collapsed an ancient tunnel and almost killed them all. "I'm so sorry, I—"

"No." Tourmaline shook her head and pulled off her dust-speckled glasses. "I should have warned you. The stones in there felt tired, like they only needed the gentlest of invitations to collapse."

"We need to go back," Violet said. She still stood where Tourmaline had pulled her and seemed unable to stop staring at the fallen rocks. "There's no way Ravine didn't sense that! If anyone realizes Olivia snuck out—"

"Aunt Rubi isn't at the academy." Tourmaline rubbed her spectacles with the hem of her tunic, then squashed them back onto her nose. "She spends each new moon in Lumin City, fulfilling the grandmaster duties for Jewel Way. That's why I said to meet me *tonight*; I'd never be able to leave if Auntie wasn't gone. We share a suite."

"Then we have to keep going," Olivia said. She clicked her thumbnail against the steel of her thimble-covered finger. "Laurel, Nan, the unicorns—they can't wait another month! Especially since Kessa leaves tomorrow." She looked at Tourmaline. "Where does the other tunnel go?"

"East," Tourmaline said. "Under the river. It's the only one that does. If Kessa has been using a tunnel to sneak into Lumin City, this is the one she would take."

"And is *this* tunnel tired?" Violet asked.

Tourmaline shrugged. "It's younger than the other tunnel. I think we should be fine." She scooped up her Gemglow, and this time the light was steady. "Shall we?"

"What about the wolf?" Violet asked. "What if it gets out?"

"That rockfall is thick," Tourmaline assured Violet as she beckoned them to follow. "It will take days for anything to dig out."

Olivia wished she felt comforted. But as they entered the tunnel, she thought she heard a *skritch-scratch* behind them. A sound like claws scraping against rock.

"Let's pick up the pace," Tourmaline said.

For the next half hour, they trooped through the dark. It was hard not to jump at every kicked pebble, every drop of water. After all, anything could be at the end of the passage: a horde of angry Forgers; a trove of unicorn snares; maybe even the missing unicorns themselves.

The dark thoughts tangled and swayed around Olivia like seaweed, cold and slimy, distracting her so that she didn't realize that the passage had started to slant upward until they turned a corner and saw stone stairs leading up to a square of light outlining a trapdoor.

"Where are we?" Olivia asked.

"Not sure," Tourmaline said, "but we were walking long enough to have made it under the river." She stepped to the side and waved Olivia toward the stairs. "After you."

"I'm first?"

Tourmaline and Violet looked at each other, and for the first time, they seemed to be on the same page. Violet smiled. "Definitely."

Olivia tiptoed up the planks. When she reached the top, she tried to peer through the trapdoor's cracks, but she couldn't make out anything except candlelight. She pressed her ear to the wood. Silence. She lifted the door up a few inches.

She was not in a secret Forger artillery. She was not in a unicorn's cage. Instead, she was in a small cellar, with shelves running along every wall and up to the ceiling, where a single paper lantern shone from the beams.

And she was alone.

"All clear," she whispered to the girls below, then lifted the door free and let it clatter to the ground before heaving herself out. Tourmaline popped up a second later, while Violet emerged slowly, as cautious as a moth leaving its cocoon.

"Where are we?" Violet asked. "It doesn't look very Forger-y. Or smell Forger-y. There's no smoke."

"But there are treasures," Tourmaline said. She pointed to a porcelain vase that had broken and been repaired with melted gold. Above it, on a hook that would typically hold links of sausages, hung a wind chime made from pieces of a crystal flute. "Check this out!" Tourmaline blew on it, and the shards clinked together, making beautiful music even in this shattered state.

As Olivia moved around the shelves, she realized that the cellar wasn't really a cellar at all, but a gallery of broken things. But that wasn't quite right. These things weren't broken. They had all been—

"Olivia?" Violet's voice wavered as she pointed to a repaired china cabinet stuffed with books. Olivia squinted, trying to make out the titles in the dim light. When she finally worked out the words, she wished she hadn't.

The Unicorn's Lament: Songs of Entrapment

The Art of Unicorn Bones

One Hundred and One Uses of Unicorn Horn

On and on the titles marched, each one more horrifying, more specific, and more gruesome than the last. Bile burned Olivia's throat. They had found the unicorn trapper, and she knew exactly who it was.

From somewhere up above, hinges creaked. Olivia, Violet, and Tourmaline froze as a narrow shaft of light shouldered into the cellar, followed by voices.

"This way," the Mender called.

CHAPTER TWENTY-TWO

Tourmaline acted first. "Grab my shoulder!"

Olivia and Violet stumbled over, weaving between displays to get to her. As soon as they both gripped her, Tourmaline twisted her ring.

"Are we invisible?" Olivia croaked.

"Unnoticeable, I think," the Gemmer whispered. "But I've never tried hiding more than just me and Ghost."

"No chances," Violet said grimly, and tugged the three of them to the ground and under a desk. Sandwiched between her friends, Olivia tucked herself into her knees and tried not to gasp for air as the staircase groaned under footsteps. *Many* footsteps.

The Mender—friend to the Unicorn Academy, Olivia's very first Spinner teacher—*was the unicorn trapper.*

Or, at the very least, the Mender was working with the unicorn trapper. Olivia's thoughts galloped wildly, seeking to fill in the missing pieces. The night of the musical demonstration, Kessa had said her father thought the Luring Horn was broken. Maybe the Tolls had come by the Mender's shop to see if she could fix the horn, and then the Mender had begun her diabolical unicorn trapping plans in order to . . .

But there, her ideas stopped.

. . . to Mend something unmendable? But what could possibly be important enough to fix that she'd risk poaching unicorns? Before Olivia's imagination could dream up an answer, several shoes appeared in her line of sight, and the murmuring of conversations grew crisp and clear.

". . . The flute doesn't belong to you. It belongs back at the Citadel."

Next to Olivia, Tourmaline flinched. Olivia knew why; she had recognized the speaker, too. Dean Ravine. Her stomach turned. The Tolls *and* the Mender *and* Rubi Ravine *and* all those other voices . . . The unicorns stood no chance.

Her family stood no chance.

"Move along," a deep voice said, and Olivia watched as a pair of riding boots with spurs approached the desk. "The Prime Minister expects our report to arrive in an hour. Mender, the map, please."

As the Mender's magenta slippers padded away, Olivia felt a finger poke her ribs. She scrunched her neck around to see Tourmaline mouth, *The Prime Minister.* Olivia nodded back. She'd caught that, too. Unless the Prime Minister, who had fought so hard to return unicorns to Arden, had suddenly turned on the herds, this was *not* a secret meeting of unicorn trappers. But then . . . who were they?

Judging by the several more pairs of shoes—Tiller galoshes, Spinner slippers, and practical Forger boots—that gathered around the desk, Olivia guessed they were alchemists, people willing to mix materials together to create something new. The Prime Minister had been the head of a secret alchemist camp before she'd become Arden's leader, and so Olivia assumed these grown-ups squashed in the Mender's cellar in the earliest hours of the morning must be the woman's personal friends.

The Mender's slippers returned, and then Olivia heard the whisper of linen unrolled above them. Violet pressed against Olivia, while Olivia pushed back into Tourmaline, who herself was trying to keep her own toes tucked under the table. Unnoticeable didn't mean unsteppable.

The riding boots shuffled even closer, and then their owner's voice became louder as he leaned over the desk.

"Thorn Barley says that more disappearances have occurred in Springmill, Bloomsbury, Overgilt, Nicklton, and Burnmore," Riding Boots said. There was a strange familiarity to the list of names, though Olivia could not place why that would be. Springmill and Bloomsbury were Tiller communities, of course, but the others were Forger settlements she knew nothing about.

"And in Constellation Range," Riding Boots continued, "by these falls and then again here, here, and here." Riding Boots stepped back, and more feet shuffled forward so their owners could get a better look.

"So many," someone murmured. "And there are no updates on the girl?"

Olivia's fingers curled into her palm. They were talking about Laurel.

Riding Boots grunted. "None."

"How is that possible?" another demanded. "How can a girl and an old woman be slipping past the finest seekers of Arden? Past even *you*, Anvil?"

"The answer," the Mender interrupted in such a supercilious voice that Olivia knew she *must* be looking down her nose, "is obvious, even if you do not want to face it."

The Mender's hem swished gracefully as she made her way to the head of the desk. "At the Prime Minister's request, we have all emptied libraries, scoured histories, studied fragments, and conversed with every manner of thief to try to understand what could possibly contain *unicorns*, the very creatures that call the moon their mother and stars their siblings. What guild could possibly forge or grow or spin or carve anything that could contain such magnificence?"

The Mender let the question linger, allowing it to grow larger and heavier, until Olivia thought the cellar's floorboards would sag with its weight. "I didn't have an answer until this afternoon," she finally said, "when all of Lumin City heard Rubi's . . . *thundering.*"

Ravine's emerald-studded boots shifted. "The apprentices weren't listening."

The Mender continued, "The same way only lightning can hold lightning or a diamond can carve a diamond, only pure magic can trap pure magic. And if only pure magic can trap pure magic . . ." She took a deep breath. ". . . then only a unicorn can trap another unicorn."

Silence fell. Then—

"Impossible," someone rasped.

"Nett's right," a woman agreed. "Unicorns are *incapable* of doing wrong! If they could, then they wouldn't *be* unicorns. They are all that is good, that is pure, that is *life.* You're saying a unicorn *betrayed* its herd? An *evil* unicorn? *Impossible.*"

"Yes," the Mender agreed, her voice rising above the growing dissent. "It *is* impossible. Which is why the girl is the key. With the help of her grandmother, Laurel Hayes has discovered how to *control* a unicorn. And now she is using its magic to trap and contain the others. *That* is how the Hayeses keep slipping away. And our job, as Nadia's trusted friends, is to figure out *how*, before Arden's unicorns are lost forever."

Conversation began in earnest. The advisors tossed around theories, solutions, rumors, and possibilities, but Olivia couldn't follow any of them. The most she could do was sit still, clenching her fingers into a fist and focusing on the cold thimble digging into her palm. Because if she thought about anything else, she would explode out from under the desk, giving Tourmaline and Violet away as she yelled at these so-called councilors all to leave her family *alone*.

That Laurel was *innocent*.

That if they wanted to find a trapper they should look at—

"What about a Luring Horn?" a woman in slippers asked, almost as though she had heard Olivia's screaming thoughts. "Donte's been bragging about his daughter's ability. Could the two families be working together?"

Olivia stiffened. Next to her she felt Violet do the same. But the Mender responded quickly.

"Not possible. Donte brought the horn to me shortly before the school year began, thinking it was broken. Unicorns have been disappearing since long before Kessa could make it play."

The air rushed out of Olivia's lungs. She'd been wrong. But maybe the Tolls had been lying about the timeline—

"Besides," Ravine added, "Provost Malchain had all the deans examine the Luring Horn before allowing Kessa to bring it within the academy's walls. It's a powerful instrument, but it is silver, through and through. We could not detect any . . ." She paused, searching for a word. ". . . *unicorn magic* within it."

Olivia shivered, understanding Ravine's pause. *Unicorn magic*. She meant unicorn body parts. Ground bone, a drop of blood, a piece of heart—all would enhance the potency of a crafter's work.

"The Watch found a fragment of unicorn rib and strands of mane on Laurel Hayes," Scythe said, setting off another round of muttering.

"But it was *just* a sliver," Ravine said. "I doubt that and some strands of hair could control an entire unicorn, no matter how well Laurel utilized them."

A long sigh emanated from Anvil. "I wish it were only that which points in Laurel's direction, but there's more. Nettle, can you show them?"

Olivia heard a soft *clink* above her head.

Someone sniffed, and then the Mender said, "That's Ambrosia, isn't it? Or, to be more accurate, vials that once contained Ambrosia. There's only some residue left."

"We found them on Constellation Range," a young man wearing moss-woven slippers—Nettle, Olivia assumed—said. "Not too far off from the herd leader's last known whereabouts."

"And what," Ravine said, sounding grumpy, "is Ambrosia?"

"That's the question, isn't it?" Nettle replied. "It's the most powerful Tiller botanical ever brewed, but only the Hayes family knows the recipe. For now. Sena and I are taking one of the vials to Woven Root, so that the alchemists there can try to distill the ingredients. This one, we'd like you to give to Dean Barry so she can investigate further."

There was another clink as Olivia assumed the vial transferred hands.

"We're hopeful that between Woven Root and the academy, we can figure out what's in it," Nettle's companion, Sena, added. "When we asked Healer Hall, they said Laurel claimed the Ambrosia fell out when her Dandiloon hit a storm, but that didn't explain the rest of it."

"The rest of what?" Dean Ravine asked.

"Wherever a unicorn has disappeared, my patrol has found traces of Ambrosia in the soil," Anvil said. "And the disappearances, well, you've seen. They're everywhere."

Silence again filled the cellar. Olivia could barely breathe. Keeping her head down, she stared at the dusty floorboards.

Ambrosia. Controlled unicorns. And, somehow, Laurel at the center of it all.

Finally, Anvil cleared his throat. "Thank you, all, for coming at such late notice. If that is it, I'd best go write my report. She's expecting it tonight."

Slowly, people drifted toward the stairs, the creaking planks drowning out their words, until at last the door clicked shut.

Tourmaline scrambled out from under the table. "We have to get back to the school! Aunt Rubi can't know I snuck out!" Sweat beaded Tourmaline's upper lip. She looked sick. Violet, too, seemed feverish. Red splotched her cheek, as though the information shared had slapped her. Olivia wasn't surprised. What they had overheard . . .

Which was why she had to see.

Instead of heading to the trapdoor, where Tourmaline waved at her frantically, she looked at the map of unicorn disappearances spread across the table. The familiar outline of Arden stretched in front of her, sketches of all the major cities, towns, villages, and even, in the most northwestern corner, Buddle. But she wasn't looking for home.

She was looking for a pattern.

And to her dismay, she found it.

The black marks that swirled across Arden, marking the places where unicorns had vanished, formed a familiar shape. Familiar because it matched the dried flowers Olivia had so carefully pricked into a whale-ish shape on the map above her bunk.

Now Olivia understood why Springmill, Bloomsbury, Overgilt, Nicklton, and Burnmore had sounded so familiar.

Laurel had visited them all.

Melancholy stalked the girls as they wove their way back through the tunnel, pressing a cold nose against their ankles as they passed the engraving of the snake, squeezed by the stone coffins, and moved up the stairs and into the academy proper.

Tourmaline shot across the foyer and toward the steps that would take her to the Gemmer suite in the astronomy tower, but Violet lingered, her expression all too knowing. All too kind. Olivia couldn't bear it.

"See you tomorrow," Olivia said, tying her scarf over her nose and lighting the Be Nimble Candle before Violet could say anything.

Olivia drifted down the hall, as aimless as the candle's smoke. She was barely there. Most of her was still in the cellar, staring at that map. When she reached her dorm, she slid into bed and closed the drapes but didn't blow out her candle. Instead, she reached for her beloved *Actes des Ardenians*, which she kept beneath her pillow.

She turned to the front page and touched her mother's name in her father's handwriting. If they had lived, would she feel less alone now? Or would they, like Nan and Laurel, have excluded her from the family's secret?

Secret*s*.

After all, there was more than one secret they had been hiding from her.

The Ambrosia recipe.

The locked drawer in Nan's desk of various guild craft and jumbled magic.

And now, Nan and Laurel were somewhere out in the wide world doing . . .

Well, whatever it was they were doing, Olivia knew it couldn't be what the Prime Minister's inner circle believed it was. Olivia turned the page and took in the inked illustration of the Rider and her unicorn. She wondered if Lady Elaina had ever felt lonely as the one and only unicorn rider.

Olivia traced the outline of the stallion's ears. Somehow, she didn't think so. The Rider, after all, always had her unicorn, even at the end, when they drowned in sun's fire. Her finger continued to follow the forelock, from which sprung its spindly horn, then down to the unicorn's nose, where the Golden Bridle wrapped around its muzzle.

Olivia froze.

The council—they were wrong. Time before memory, something *had* been crafted that could tame a unicorn. *Control* a unicorn.

Lady Elaina's Golden Bridle.

CHAPTER TWENTY-THREE

"... So you see, it *can't* be Laurel or Nan," Olivia whispered to Tourmaline the next morning at breakfast.

The Banquet Hall was empty except for a few Tillers who were up to check on the garden frost. The next Spinner class wasn't until later, when they were supposed to meet the Forgers at the cobbler's bench. The Spinners were to explain to the Forgers the theory behind Seven League Boots, while the Forgers would be attempting to craft a set of iron studs that could be used both to decorate the boots and to ensure that the boots could always find north. Olivia had come across many tales about Spinners so dizzy from crossing seven leagues—or twenty-one miles—in a single step that they had lost their sense of direction and accidentally stepped the wrong way into a bog of quicksand.

But Olivia couldn't wait until midmorning to share her latest theory with Violet. She couldn't bear her friend thinking her sister was a unicorn trapper for one more hour than necessary.

As soon as she'd heard the first bird chirp, Olivia had flung herself out of bed and rushed through the corridors toward Violet's dormant room near the kitchens, only to discover that the Forgers had been woken an hour before to practice sword glowing and were now running laps around the academy to build endurance. Violet would be busy for at least another thirty minutes.

Olivia decided to eat breakfast while she waited, and to her surprise had found a sleepy-looking Tourmaline in the middle of the Banquet Hall, staring miserably at her bowl of porridge. When Olivia asked why she was up, Tourmaline said Aunt Rubi's seismograph had detected a funny tremor last night and now she wanted to investigate as soon as possible.

"She's finishing some clay tablets for the Prime Minister," Tourmaline had yawned. "And then I get to pretend I've never seen the catacombs before."

This was all the prompting Olivia had needed. She launched into her early-morning revelation, practically vibrating like a violin string.

"Only a Forger or a Spinner or some combination of the two could craft a golden bridle," Olivia continued. "And Nan and Laurel—*they're both Tillers!* It *can't* be them."

She took a bite of her oatmeal and looked at Tourmaline

expectantly, but the Gemmer only blinked blearily back at her. With the bags under her eyes and pinched expression around her mouth, she looked closer to death than even Ghost.

Tourmaline mumbled something.

Olivia leaned forward. "What?"

"I said," Tourmaline repeated as she brushed a honey-brown curl behind her ear, "or they could have found the Golden Bridle."

Olivia was already shaking her head. "Not possible. *The Golden Bridle burned up in the sun.* If we can figure which Forger or Spinner is capable of crafting something like that, then I think we've found the unicorn trapper."

"Olivia." Tourmaline suddenly looked more awake. "Do you have someone in mind?"

"Noo-ooo," Olivia said slowly, but it wasn't quite the truth. She had an idea. Or two. They weren't particularly nice ideas, but they were better than believing the Hayes family business was *unicorn trapping*. She took a deep breath. "Do you remember what the invitation to the academy said?" When Tourmaline shook her head, Olivia recited, "*The Unicorn Academy of Artistical and Magical Learning shall provide the highest quality of instruction led by the most talented and innovative artisans from across the land.*"

"Olivia," Tourmaline said, taking off her pink glasses and rubbing her eyes. "Are you saying—"

"Yes," Olivia said. "I think whoever made the Golden

Bridle, whoever is trapping unicorns, must be one of the scholars here, in this school."

Before Tourmaline could respond with a *You're absolutely right, Olivia! You solved it!* Olivia heard someone shout her name across the hall. Turning, she saw Violet sprinting toward her, her short black hair mussed like the edge of a raven's wing.

"Good, you're done," Olivia said, scooting her mug of pomegranate juice toward Violet. "Tourmaline and I have something to tell you—"

"Grandmaster Toll just arrived!" Violet gasped out.

"So?" Olivia nudged the juice closer. Violet looked like she was on the verge of passing out. "We knew he was coming. That's why we wanted to prove Kessa was the trapper before he came to collect her and let her loose on Arden's unicorns. But"—Olivia forced a laugh—"that was ridiculous of me. Because all this time—"

"No, you don't understand," Violet said, shaking her head. "Grandmaster Toll is here, *but Kessa isn't!* She wasn't at sword practice. The others told Dean Hatchett that she wasn't feeling well, but they were just covering for her. When we woke up, Kessa wasn't here!"

Olivia's heart began to pound. "Did anyone say where she was?" she asked, remembering the sound of footsteps in the catacombs. The footprint in the dust. The scratch behind the tunnel . . . where they had trapped the wolf.

Violet shook her head. "No one knows. Olivia, I think—"

"—I do, too," Olivia said, just as Tourmaline said, "Kessa is in the catacombs."

Olivia's chair toppled toward the ground. "We have to go—now!"

The Forger may have cursed the thimble on Olivia's finger, but that didn't mean Kessa deserved to be wolfmeat. And, less honorable, but no less true, if they *didn't* get Kessa out of the catacombs before Grandmaster Toll discovered the scholars had not only lost his daughter but that she had been in mortal danger, there was an excellent chance he, as Secretary of Education, would shut down the school before there could even *be* a trial.

Violet ran to the Forger barracks to distract the adults, while Tourmaline and Olivia sprinted to the foyer. They were lucky it was still early and the hallways relatively empty. Racing toward the abandoned statue, Olivia pulled out her sling and fitted a button into its pouch.

Plunk!

The button hit the point of King Anders's crown, and just like last night, the spiraling staircase revealed itself. Unlike last night, however, the smell emanating from the mouth of the catacombs had taken on a metallic scent . . . one not dissimilar to blood.

Olivia took a step back. "Tourmaline, what is that? Tourmaline?" She turned to see the Gemmer a few steps away, her usual rosy undertones suddenly gray. Minutes ago, she'd looked merely tired, but now she looked positively ill. "What's wrong?!"

Tourmaline closed her eyes. "The rocks down there. They feel . . . wobbly. They're making me dizzy." She sat down with a *thump* and pulled her knees to her forehead. "I don't think I can walk."

"Wobbly as in they might collapse?"

"Yes—no, I mean, maybe?" Tourmaline seemed dazed. "Something's shifted since last night."

Olivia thought through her options. It didn't take long, as there were only two. One, stay here with Tourmaline, or two, go on without her. And Kessa, for all her snobbiness, didn't deserve option one.

"Put your ring on," Olivia whispered. "I'll be back soon. If I don't come back in half an hour, tell Ghost to get Ravine."

Curled at Anders's feet, Tourmaline nodded miserably and handed her the Gemglow.

Olivia tucked the gem at her waist, where it swung shadows into the catacombs as she climbed down and began to weave through the stone coffins. Perhaps it was because Olivia wasn't a Gemmer, but the gem's light wasn't as strong as last night. Or maybe that was due to the smoke that hung in the air. It mingled with the dust, stinging her eyes and coating her nostrils. Now the metallic smell was so strong she could taste it on her tongue.

Olivia ran faster.

Two minutes later, she had passed through the sarcophagus chamber. Ten minutes later, the three doorways loomed before her. They were not as they had been left.

The stone snake carved onto the middle door still chewed its tail, and the way to the Mender's workroom remained clear. But the blocked tunnel was no longer blocked.

Boulders lay scattered around the tunnel's mouth like crumbs in a giant's beard. But what had wiped them away so easily? Her heart hammered against her chest, and after securing a second button into her sling, Olivia crept forward.

"Watch it!"

"AHHHHHHHHHHH!" Olivia swerved to the side, narrowly avoiding stepping on a glowering Kessa Toll.

The Forger sat on the ground, her back against the tunnel wall and her black hair brown with dust. Her face, too, was dirty, except for a few places that Olivia guessed had been cleaned by tears. It wasn't hard to see why Kessa had been crying—her ankle had swollen to the size of a melon.

"Where are the scholars?" Kessa asked, looking past Olivia into the dark. "Are they coming?"

"It's just me," Olivia whispered. "Come on, we have to get you out of here. Can you stand?"

"If I could stand," Kessa snapped, "I would have already left."

Silently, Olivia counted to five, then asked, "Can I see?"

Kessa's mouth thinned, but she nodded. Olivia untied the Gemglow and set it on the ground, then crouched beside the Forger. She had seen many ailments in Nan's apothecary, and this was either the worst sprain she'd ever seen or a complete break. Ever so gently, she touched Kessa's toe. The Forger screamed.

"Shh!" Olivia ordered, covering Kessa's mouth with her hand. "There's a wolf down here!"

Kessa pushed her hand away. "No, there's not."

"Yes there is—" Olivia broke off as Kessa, rolling her eyes, pulled a tiny flute out of her front pocket and began to play. But what poured forth wasn't the cheery notes of a songbird but a long, low *Gggggggrrrrroowlllllllllllllllllll.*

The *wolf's* growl.

Olivia stared. "It was you! You—you tricked us!"

"So what if I did?" Kessa said, removing what Olivia now realized was a Mimiccolo from her lips. "You were spying on me, and I didn't collapse a tunnel on *your* head—oof." She broke off as a wave of pain cascaded over her face.

"This is ridiculous," Olivia snapped, plunking onto the ground next to her. "Yell at me later, but we need to get you upstairs. Your father is here!"

"Already?" Kessa bit her lip.

"Yes," Olivia snapped. "And if we don't get you upstairs, he'll discover the scholars lost you and he'll convince the Grand Council to shut down the academy, and that might not matter to you, but to me—and Violet and Tourmaline!—it means *everything*. Now, will you let me help you?"

Without waiting for an answer, Olivia pulled out a cotton bandage with strength and cleanliness woven into it. She didn't trust herself to heal Kessa's bones magically, but Nan had taught her how to tie an ankle tight enough that if Kessa looped an arm around Olivia's shoulder, they might be able to get out of here before Grandmaster Toll realized the scholars had lost his only daughter.

"This might hurt," Olivia warned. Kessa didn't say anything, but she nodded. Olivia got to work. She wrapped the bandage, tugging the cloth snug as best she could. She was clumsier than usual, her thimbled finger getting in the way. Though Olivia couldn't tell in the dim light, she thought that the thimble looked bigger. Had it always reached past her first knuckle? Or was the smoke making her see things?

Kessa said something, but Olivia couldn't make it out. Shaking her head, she looked away from her thimble and back at the Forger. "Sorry, what was that?"

"I said, the academy matters to me, too. You know it does."

Olivia frowned. "How would I know that?"

"Because," Kessa winced as Olivia moved the bandage higher, "you know my secret."

Olivia froze, wondering if she had been right all along. "What secret?"

"That I don't want to be a fencer. I want to be a musician."

Kessa's face suddenly crumbled. "Then you mocked me by turning my Win Every Bout Lace into an Ever Dance Lace!"

Olivia stared, horrified. "*That's* what you think I did? I promise, I didn't mean to braid the Green Thumb Reel into your lace, and I *definitely* didn't mean to make fun of you."

Kessa had turned to the wall, so all Olivia could see was one ear and the glint of a gold earring, but she had the uncomfortable sense that Kessa was crying.

"I'm sorry," Olivia said. "Mending your bootlace was the first bit of magic—well, the second, really—I ever did. But it was the first time I intentionally Spun. I didn't know what I was doing, I was just following the music in your lace."

"Music in my lace?" Kessa repeated.

Olivia nodded. "Shoelaces catch moments, the same way a net catches butterflies. There were so many songs tangled in there, your lace practically sung an aria to me! I don't think it enjoyed forcing your feet to fence."

"The bootlace never forced me to fence." Kessa sniffed. She still didn't look at Olivia, but at least she was talking. "It just helped me. A *lot*. I'm pretty hopeless without them. Daddy was planning on tutoring me himself this year, but then the whole Unicorn Academy ruined his plans. So he bought the laces for me, and I promised I would keep them on at all times, but one snapped the very first day of school, and I didn't know what to do. Dean Hatchett found me crying, wrote me a pass, and I skated over with my Frosting Blades before the sun even rose."

"Dean Hatchett knows you wear cheating laces?!"

"I like to think of them as survival laces," Kessa said, some of her old loftiness coming back into her voice. "And yes. As the former head of the Investigators, he's really good at spotting . . . *unusual* magic."

Olivia hadn't realized that Hatchett had been an Investigator, a member of the guards who once patrolled the roads and waterways between villages, making sure that each guild stuck to its own and confiscating any jumbled or, as Kessa would say, *unusual* magic. She wondered how he'd come to be a teacher at an academy that promoted the very thing he'd spent his life guarding against, but as her thimble finger slipped again, she had a more pressing question.

"Wanting to be a musician is not a big secret," Olivia pointed out. "Seems a bit extreme to curse me just for thinking that I might know about it."

"Curse—?" Kessa blinked. "I didn't curse you!"

"Yes, you did," Olivia said, pausing in her bandaging to shove her thimbled finger under Kessa's nose. "You struck me with lightning and now my thimble is stuck."

"No." Kessa nudged the finger away and leaned her head against the rock wall. "Or if I *did* curse the thimble, I didn't mean to. But wanting to be a musician and not a fencer *is* a big deal when you're the only child of Grandmaster Donte

Toll, the best at everything deadly and dangerous. It's why I've been practicing in the catacombs."

Pride seeped into Kessa's voice. "I discovered the entrance to them myself, using an explorer's Bat Pipes. When played correctly, I can *see* how the sound waves bounce off solid objects and can chart unseeable places. Anyway, I come down here almost every night. The catacombs are deep enough that no one can hear me play and also big enough that I can practice attack music. If I can prove to Daddy that songs can pierce a heart just as deeply as a sword, then maybe he'll let me keep playing."

"Attack music," Olivia repeated. "Would that have anything to do with all the smoke?"

"Yeah," Kessa admitted. "It took me all night, but I finally found a rock with enough tin inside it that I could Forge an explosion." She grimaced. "I didn't control it very well, though. The tunnel cleared, but sediment hit me. I heard my ankle pop."

And destabilized the tunnel enough to make Tourmaline dizzy, Olivia thought, but didn't say. She focused instead on the final twists of the bandage, mulling over Kessa's story. It was different from her own. Olivia wished for nothing more than to be exactly like her family, to be a great physician like Laurel, her parents, Nan, and all her ancestors, while Kessa wanted to be free of her family's trodden paths. Funny how the grass was always greener on the other side of the fence, and the tree, as Nan would say, was always taller than its branches.

"Twenty-nine minutes!" Tourmaline's voice whispered as Olivia, Kessa's arm looped around her neck, reached the top of the stairs. "The provost just walked by with Grandmaster Toll!" Tourmaline must have twisted the ring, because Olivia could suddenly see the Gemmer standing right in front of them, her eyes frantic.

Kessa jumped. "How in forge fire did you—"

"I have a plan!" Olivia interrupted. "Tourmaline, how do you feel?"

"Dizzy."

"Great." Olivia nodded. "Take my place and help Kessa to the infirmary. Tell the scholar on duty that you fainted while Gemming and that Kessa bravely caught you before you hit the ground—but not before one of your rocks accidentally fell on her ankle."

Tourmaline crossed her arms. "If I must," she sniffed. Then, turning to Kessa, she added, "Just so you know, I expect *several* customizations to my chain necklaces in exchange for making myself look so clumsy."

"If I'm not expelled, sure," Kessa said, still staring at Tourmaline, clearly trying to puzzle out how she hadn't noticed her before.

"But how can Malchain expel you for an honest mistake?" Olivia said. "You said the lightning strike was an accident, and she didn't expel me for accidentally Spinning your laces."

"I don't think Malchain wants to expel me," Kessa said as she put an arm under Tourmaline's shoulder. "It's Daddy who is insisting she follow the handbook. This way, he doesn't break the clause that says every grandmaster must have at least one relative enrolled, *and* he gets me back home where there's no chance I can embarrass him."

"Then it's all right, then," Olivia exclaimed. "Tell your father that if you are expelled now, people will wonder why *I* wasn't. That they might start to wonder more about your laces, and I doubt he would want anyone to look too closely at them."

"You know," Kessa said, a slow smile spreading over her face. It was the first time Olivia had ever seen her smile. "I always heard Spinners were twisty, but I didn't know they could be steel-sharp, too. That just might work."

The next evening found Olivia, Tourmaline, and Violet tucked into their corner of the library, the pine cones in the fireplace burning merrily as they worked on the next day's assignments.

"May I?"

Olivia looked up from her text to see Kessa, looking

surprisingly nervous. Without a word, Olivia scooted over, and Kessa sat down. Violet handed her a mug of cocoa while Tourmaline—fully recovered and enthusiastically eating through a tin of lavender cookies—offered a corner of her blanket. Whether it was the fire, the hot chocolate, or something else, Olivia warmed as she looked at her circle of friends. Because that's what they were now. And she knew that together, they could face anything.

Which was good, because by the end of the week, Olivia's thimble still hadn't come off. Instead, it had lengthened, dripping down her finger and casting her entire hand in steel.

PART III

Are you sleeping, are you sleeping,
Forger child, Forger child?
Warning bells are ringing, warning bells
* are ringing,*
Get ye gone, get ye gone.

—The Brothers Tin Household Songs and Tales

CHAPTER TWENTY-FOUR

Winter appeared overnight when a snowstorm dusted in and the Rhona froze over. For one glorious morning, apprentices snuck out to skate up and down the river while the topiaries skidded after them. Classes only returned to normal once Ravine heated the rocks to melt the ice and Malchain threatened an academy-wide detention if they didn't return to their classrooms *immediately*. But after the initial excitement of snow wore off, the reality of dirty slush and drafty corridors sunk in.

    A weariness seemed to infect both apprentices and scholars—even Sam seemed too tired to stir up trouble. The Tillers struggled the most as their classes moved indoors and their attention turned from harvesting to canning. The sounds of swords clanging in the academy became common as Forgers moved their fencing practice into the ballroom. Meanwhile, Spinners were asked to knot warmth into carpet tassels on top of their usual assignments, and Olivia found herself falling behind.

With a steel-clad hand, her work grew sloppy. The metal was flexible enough for her fingers to bend but did not allow the same dexterity as warm skin. Everything took ten times longer, and anything with metal went wild when Olivia touched it. Pins wove around her fingers like hungry cats, and the eyes of needles kept winking shut, making them impossible to thread.

And then there were the elbow-length gloves Olivia wore to hide her condition. Dean Garmont's eyebrows had risen when Olivia refused to remove them in class due to her need to "sharpen her other sensory perceptions," but he had allowed the gloves to remain. They made it hard to hold a shuttle and easy for Paisley to mock her, but the gloves kept her secret. Olivia only took them off when she was sure no one aside from Violet, Tourmaline, or Kessa was around.

Over the last week, each of her friends had tried to remove the thimble. Kessa had wielded a crowbar, attempted to charm it with her flute, and had even smuggled a potato peeler from the kitchen to try to shave it off. Tourmaline tried to scrape it with a diamond, but aside from a few scratch marks, there was no change. Violet suggested water and soap until Kessa pointed out that might make it rust, and the only thing worse than a steel hand was a *rusted* steel hand. And so the iron crept higher up Olivia's wrist.

"I really think you should tell Malchain," Violet said, not for the first time.

They were huddled next to their usual library fireplace. Kessa had her case of flutes out and was meticulously polishing them, while Tourmaline frantically tried to finish an essay with the words PEARLS: THE WORST GEM EVER written at the top.

"Why are they so bad?" Olivia asked, trying to change the topic but also genuinely curious.

Tourmaline, her legs swung over the chair's arm and her essay propped against her knees, peered over the parchment. "At the end of the day, a pearl is just a piece of grit that wanted to make itself feel special—and at what cost? The poor oyster!" Tourmaline shook her head. "Pearls are mean, through and through."

"Interesting," Violet said, not sounding the slightest bit interested. "Olivia. Tell Malchain."

Olivia sighed. "I don't want to give the Grand Council any reason to shut down the academy," she said, looping yarn over a knitting needle as she worked on a scarf for Ghost. She hadn't seen the fossil since the first snowflakes gusted in. Without skin or fur or scales or feathers, he shivered constantly, creating an unnerving rattle wherever he went. According to Tourmaline, he'd darted straight back into the Gemmer tower and was now nesting among her fuzziest sweaters. He refused to cozy up by the fireplace with them due to his fear of fire.

Tourmaline shrugged. "I wouldn't worry—"

"You never do," Violet sighed.

"—because I bet I can find a chisel in Stonehaven that can shatter it off," Tourmaline said, scowling back down at her essay. "How do you spell *presumptuous*?"

Olivia smiled as Violet spelled the word out for Tourmaline, but inside, she felt like a scrap of fabric, a bit of material that didn't fit into the design. Tomorrow, everyone would be going home for Starfell, the holiday when Arden passed directly under the hooves of the unicorn constellation and stars streaked across the sky. Tourmaline and Dean Ravine would trek back to Stonehaven for the weekend, and they would be taking Violet with them. Provost Malchain had, at long last, accepted that Violet was most likely not a Forger and yesterday had assigned her to the Gemmer guild.

So far, Violet had just as much Gemming talent as a slug, but Tourmaline said her aunt was hopeful that Violet visiting Stonehaven, surrounded by Gemmers and rocky wonders, might awaken something within her. Olivia hoped so. She hated that Violet's magic still hadn't revealed itself. She knew exactly how isolating it could be. But the few times Olivia had tried to discuss Violet's guild status with her, Violet always found an excuse to leave.

"And I'll check my father's shelves," Kessa promised. She would only be a mile away at her family's forge in Alloy Alley.

Olivia, of course, would be staying on the island, as per Provost Malchain's agreement with the Watch. She wouldn't be alone, though. Dean Barry had invited her to spend the break in her cottage on the grounds. The Tiller scholar's brother and his husband were coming to celebrate with their four small children, and Dean Barry had promised there would be plenty of nutcrackers, fizzy tea, and even, she'd said with a wink, a Green Thumb Reel.

"Could you please stop, Kessa?" Tourmaline said, not looking up from her essay. "It's really hard to concentrate when you're whistling like that."

Kessa paused in her polishing. "I'm not whistling. What are you talking about?"

Tourmaline shook her head. "That sound!"

The other three paused, and without the click-clack of her knitting needles, Olivia heard it, too. A strange metallic clanging and it seemed to be coming from—

"The window!" Olivia gasped. "Look!" Above the rooftops of Lumin City, a flock of chimera soared into view. All pretense of working disappeared as they all raced to the windows.

Here were the chimera of Olivia's storybooks—the great battle beasts of old. She caught glimpses of elephant tails, bear ears, antlers, hooves, paws, and all manner of wing: insect, fowl, and mammal. The copper animals crescendoed through the clouds and over the Rhona. As they drew closer to the academy, Olivia could see saddlebags and packs strapped to their haunches and a human rider upon each one.

"Alchemists!" Tourmaline whooped. "It's Woven Root!"

"No," Kessa corrected. "Parliamentarians wear indigo. They're wearing scarlet and green. That's Ember Seed—Olivia, I bet someone there can get your thimble off!"

It couldn't be more perfect—a camp full of alchemist Forgers used to seeing strange things and who had absolutely no idea who Olivia was. But before she could sweep Ghost's scarf into her kit and pull on her gloves, the suit of armor in the library's back corner cleared its throat, and the provost's voice echoed out through the visor.

"Good afternoon, academy guardians! As you may have noticed, we have some guests! Ember Seed Troupe was originally set to visit us after Starfell, but due to a conflict, they have decided to grace us with their presence today. While lessons will be postponed, I ask that you use this extraordinary opportunity to explore what a career in alchemy could mean for you. Behave yourselves . . . or else." The visor fell silent, and Olivia squeaked with excitement.

"Let's go!"

"I can't," Tourmaline said, looking miserably down at her essay. "I have to finish this or Aunt Rubi will make me shovel coal all holiday. But I should be done soon—I'll meet you there?"

After promising to buy Tourmaline a chocolate swan, the

other girls rushed outside to join the throng of apprentices making their way toward an arch of pine boughs wrapped with red ribbon. Alchemists in crushed-velvet gowns and furs stood near the entrance, handing out small favors and party hats. Olivia eagerly accepted a paper unicorn horn and plopped it onto her head before grabbing two aluminum crowns and shoving them toward her friends.

Kessa leaped back. "No way are you putting that on me."

"They're not that ugly," Olivia protested.

"Never put strange metal on your head," Kessa snapped. "You don't know who'll be able to read your mind or walk into your dreams."

"Excuse me." Violet crossed her arms. "Read our minds?!"

"Not easily," Kessa amended. "But it *is* possible. Most Forgers can only manage Metal Telepathy with someone of close kin, someone with the same iron in their blood, but you never know. That's why we all wear protective charms." She tugged her right earlobe, and Olivia noticed again the tiny gold shield sparkling against her black skin.

"All right, then, unicorn horns for all," Olivia said, exchanging the circlets for paper cones. "Glorious spring, am I smelling parsnip pastries?" She was, along with roasted hazelnuts, hot berry cider, and balls of fried dough dusted in flavors such as "joy," "exaltation," and "supreme bliss." Once the girls had properly loaded up, they began to explore. Every few feet there was something new to see or buy or taste or smell:

carved rubies filled with perfumes, levitating cakes, lanterns that illuminated secrets, and best of all, a tent full of books.

"There's no time to browse," Kessa said as Olivia dragged them toward the tent. "We have to get that thimble off!"

"Just five minutes," Olivia promised. "I want to see if they have anything about, you know"—she lowered her voice—"the bridle."

Olivia had not forgotten the Golden Bridle. Just as the thimble clung to her finger, she clung to her theory that the *real* unicorn trapper must have found a way to reforge Lady Elaina's Golden Bridle. Her friends, however, thought otherwise.

Kessa groaned. "I've already told you—no one can replicate the Golden Bridle as it was. All the artifacts that date back to the Lost Age were made when the world was young, its potential untapped, and everything was still new. There's power, you know, to being the *first* of something."

As a youngest sister, Olivia did know that. And as a sister, she had to clear Laurel's name.

"Five minutes," Olivia repeated, and slipped inside. The scent of dusty scrolls, paper, leather, binding sap, and thread wrapped around Olivia like the fluffiest bathrobe. Haphazard towers of books and scrolls lay about, many made of the usual parchment and leather, but there were others made of silver and glass, gold and bark, and even a few with shalestone covers and clay pages. Unlike the other tents crowded with apprentices, this one was empty aside from a Tiller scholar who was browsing a selection of illustrated books and a Forger scholar asking the seller if he knew the name of a scroll with red handles.

Olivia waited as patiently as she could, using the time to look at a display of Hollow Books. She'd never heard of this alchemy before, but the display card in front explained that each book contained a single mistake that, when fixed, would fuse the pages together to reveal a secret compartment. *Perfect,* the card proclaimed, *for storing a lover's lock of hair, a family heirloom, or a bad report card.*

"Olivia!" Kessa was in front of her again. "I found someone who can help!"

Olivia glanced at the seller. He was still speaking to the scholar.

"We have to go." Kessa tugged on her arm. "He only has a few minutes!"

"Go on," Violet said. "I can ask."

Olivia's arm practically flew from its socket as Kessa yanked her out the exit, between tents, and through crowds. Olivia only narrowly avoided colliding with a sword swallower, but at the cost of bumping a snake plant charmer, whose plants began to rustle violently. Kessa ignored it all and only stopped when they reached a chimera corral. An elk chimera with owl's wings frolicked in the snow while several others drank from olive oil–filled troughs. Next to the fence stood a wooden hut, and without bothering to knock, Kessa pulled Olivia through its door.

"Ring-a-ling!" Kessa called, but if someone replied, Olivia couldn't hear them over the loud hammering. She couldn't see anything, either, except for thick smoke and a hazy red glow. Kessa pulled out her tiny flute and blew a few quick notes. The smoke swirled away, clearing a path to a teenage boy hunched over a bit of copper at a forging oven.

His hair was soot black and his arms were sinewy with muscle. He wore a pair of wire-rimmed glasses and a red handkerchief over his mouth.

"Joust!" Kessa called, pulling the flute away from her lips as a true smile broke over her face.

The boy stopped midswing. Above his kerchief, his eyes widened, then crinkled into a warmth that rivaled the forge.

"Pipsqueak! Move your bolt, you're in the way." The girls stepped aside as he reached for a long, skinny spike hanging on the wall behind them.

"Who is he?" Olivia whispered as Joust began to scratch a whirling design into the copper.

"My cousin," Kessa whispered back.

"Her favorite cousin," Joust called without looking up from his work.

Kessa rolled her eyes, but her smile gave her away. She was more than happy. She was relaxed. "Joust upset the whole family when he dropped out of Phlogiston Academy to study etching," Kessa explained. "Now he's a chimera keeper. His specialty is reptile scales. The serpent chimera shed constantly and always need larger skins forged for them." Joust held out the copper scale, then added a few more lines before dunking it into a fizzing solution.

"Done," Joust said at last, pulling off his gloves before removing his kerchief to reveal a chiseled jaw, Kessa's nose, and a dazzling smile. He was tall, dark, and utterly handsome. "How can I help you?"

"Olivia had an accident," Kessa said, pulling Olivia forward. "Go on, show him."

Olivia peeled off her glove. She heard Joust's sharp intake of breath as he took in the gleaming steel skin. *Never* had her mistake felt so heavy.

"Lightning-struck, I see," Joust said after a moment. "May I?" When Olivia nodded, he took her hand in his and led her to a bench near his forge. (That was the reason—and the *only* reason—Olivia suddenly felt flushed.) From his Forger belt, Joust unhooked a gauge, a pair of tweezers, and what looked like a large nail file, and began to examine her arm. Olivia wasn't sure what he was doing, but he must be doing *something*, because her skin felt all tingly where he touched it.

"I was thinking you could put some of your etching acid on it," Kessa suggested helpfully from where she hovered next to him.

"I could," Joust agreed, "but then Olivia would have no arm at all."

"But you can get the thimble off, right?" Olivia asked.

"No," he said, letting go and sitting back. "But I think *you* can. I've only seen such powerful craftsmanship from a grandmaster. And you're just a first-year apprentice?" Joust whistled. "You, Olivia, are a talented Forger."

CHAPTER TWENTY-FIVE

"But I'm not a—"

Pain shot across Olivia's foot as Kessa stepped on her. *Hard*.

"I'm as surprised as you are, Olivia," Kessa cut in, before turning to Joust and loudly whispering, "She *never* completes her assignments."

"I don't blame you." Joust smiled at Olivia. "I found the months of forging nails and practicing wire cutting incredibly dull. But it's important to set the foundation so things like this"—he gestured to her arm—"don't happen."

"The foundation," Olivia repeated. "The *Forger* foundation."

Joust nodded and turned her hand over. "It's funny, but I've never seen a thimble so dedicated to someone. It is extremely loyal to you. That's why it keeps creeping up your arm. It wants to protect you."

"From what?"

"The lightning, and after that, who knows?" He shrugged and let go of her hand. "Metal isn't like humans. It doesn't have emotion, but it is very impressionable. You just need to convince the thimble that you're safe. Once it warms up to the idea, you should be able to talk it down."

"You—you want me to calm the thimble?"

Joust smiled. "Sing it a song, give it a hug. Whatever you do to make yourself feel better."

As the Toll cousins withdrew to the far side of the hut to give her some privacy, Olivia looked at her hand. It gleamed red in the forgelight, reminding her of the campfires she'd sat around with Nan and Laurel.

Whatever you do to make yourself feel better.

Usually when she felt bad, she went to Laurel. But at the mere thought of her sister, the steel's grip tightened.

"All right, all right," she whispered to the thimble. "No thinking about Laurel. How about . . ." Olivia closed her eyes, thinking. Books always made her feel better. They reflected the world, just like metal did. "Time before memory," she began, "in the ages long since lost, the wind blew across a barren land. It had been exiled from its world, but it still carried with it the sound of laughter, the scent of water, and five seeds."

As Olivia told the tale of the First Tree, she felt the thimble heat, warming ever so slightly. Her palm tickled as the steel slowly receded down her wrist. By the time she reached the end of the story, the thimble had reshaped itself around her finger's first knuckle. Olivia tried to pull it off. It held fast.

"A little more," Olivia prompted. "Come on—oh, all right! You can stay, but you have to be as tiny as possible—and no spreading unless I ask, got it?" There was a final tickle, and then Olivia held out her hand, admiring her new steel fingernail. It felt nice, like a perpetual hug. A reminder that she was never alone, so long as she had stories.

"Pretty," Joust said, coming over to look at her hand. "Are you sure you don't want it completely off? You don't want people thinking you're a Spinner."

"Ha," Olivia said weakly. "I'm fine. Thank you, Journeyman Toll."

"Call me Joust." He winked, and Olivia blushed.

"Joust really thought I was a Forger?" Olivia asked Kessa a few minutes later as they wound their way through the fair, looking for their friends.

"He just assumed so because that thimble really, really likes you." Kessa grimaced. "Thanks for not telling on me. I trust Joust, but if Daddy hears a rumor that I can use lightning to Forge protective metal . . ." She shook her head. "I'll be forced to become an armorer."

Olivia understood what Kessa was saying, but she needed one last reassurance. "So, just to be *cuttingly* clear, you don't think there's a chance that I actually *did* Forge the thimble?"

Kessa didn't stop walking, but she did glance down. "How

could you? You're a Spinner! It is impossible to belong to more than one guild. It's Anders's First Principle of Magic."

She gestured to a nearby stand with a small sign that said Guardian Gardens. A Tiller woman was busy watering a rosebush while a man wearing a Forger's leather apron stuck a few gold nuggets into its pot. A moment later, the thorns on the bush began to look more gold than green.

"Alchemists need each other to practice their craft," Kessa said. "They can't work alone."

"I know." Olivia bit her lip. "But with all the issues I've been having with my scissors and pins—"

"The thimble's fault," Kessa cut in. "You heard Joust. A thimble is forged to protect, and it didn't want you to accidentally cut yourself." She began to wave. "Look, there's Violet!"

Olivia turned, hopeful she'd find a book tucked under Violet's arm, but no luck. The only thing the bookseller had given Violet was a suggestion to utilize the academy's library . . . which, of course, they already had.

"Sorry," Violet said again, brushing a snowflake out of her bangs.

Olivia tried to smile. "Maybe I'll find something about the Golden Bridle in Dean Barry's cottage."

"Why would Dean Barry have something?" Kessa asked, stopping to pull a few coins from her tool belt and handing them to the merchant selling hot berry cider.

Olivia shrugged. "She was convicted for jumbled magic back in the day. Maybe she has a book about the alchemy of Lost Age objects."

But even as she said it, Olivia didn't believe it. Dean Hatchett, a Forger and a former Investigator of said jumbled magic, seemed *much* more likely to be a unicorn trapper than cheery Dean Barry, but Olivia wasn't about to suggest *that* in front of Kessa again.

The girls explored the fair until dark, and when the sun set, the alchemists ushered the apprentices back through the archway for one last spectacle—a wild show of flying chimera riders darting through fireworks.

The display dazzled, burning onto Olivia's retina, and when her vison cleared, she saw that Ember Seed and its fair had disappeared, leaving the apprentices staring at the edge of the Unkempt Woods. The only sign that the alchemists had been there at all was a newly planted holly sapling with bright red berries. Except the berries weren't berries at all, but embers that burned without burning.

The next morning, trunks were shut, farewells were said, and all the apprentices stood in line waiting for the sleighs that would take them across the frozen river. Snowflakes dotted the air as Olivia hugged Violet tight and waved goodbye to Kessa. She was just wondering if Tourmaline had slipped past her when she heard someone call her name. Turning, she saw the Gemmer bounding down the steps. "Where did you go?" Olivia asked. "You never joined us yesterday."

"I forgot to give you your present!" Tourmaline huffed.

"What?" Olivia frowned. "I don't have—"

"Happy birthday!" Tourmaline said loudly, then threw her arms around Olivia and drew her in for a hug. "There's lots of light we cannot see," she whispered as she slipped something into Olivia's pocket. "The holly—"

"Tourmaline!" Dean Ravine appeared behind her niece. Her black braid had been wrapped around her head, giving the tiny woman a few more inches. Still, she was now exactly Olivia's height.

"Tell *Holly* hi for me," Tourmaline said, stepping away from Olivia.

"That's Dean Barry to you," her aunt admonished, and shooed the Gemmer toward the horse-drawn carriage where Violet was already sitting.

Putting her hand in her pocket, Olivia pulled out Tourmaline's prism earring. She held the crystal up and the morning sun hit it, splitting the light and scattering rainbows onto the snowy steps.

CHAPTER TWENTY-SIX

Starfell in Barry's cottage was lovely—which only made it a hundred times worse.

Every tradition, from stargazing to singing to eating comet pies, only emphasized what Olivia had lost. So when the last day of break arrived, she felt only relief. Her friends would be back tomorrow, and she hoped they had managed to ask their families about golden bridles. Violet and Tourmaline probably wouldn't have had much luck at Stonehaven, but there was a good chance Kessa might have uncovered something in her father's private collection.

Olivia's perusal of Dean Barry's shelves had been unfruitful, but there was still one last place to look. Excusing herself for the privy, Olivia left the Barry family's tableau of happiness—Dean Barry cooing to her succulents, Baker Barry whipping cloudberry mousse with his husband, the Barry children playing Watch and Wraiths on the kitchen floor—and slipped into the dean's workroom.

The smell of soil and green made Olivia want to cry. It smelled like Nan. It smelled like home. Like Bumblebee Apothecary, the walls were lined with shelves, and every shelf was full. But not with books. Jars and vases nestled together next to gardening supplies and bits of twine. The only book was a cookbook entitled *The Magic of Cooking*, and the only other paper in the workroom was a few loose sheets filled with equations and dirt smudges on the potting table.

Olivia turned to leave, but as she did saw she had missed a small desk hidden behind the open door. An intricate contraption of thin metal pipes and glass decanters preened on top. It looked more like it should belong in Dean Hatchett's or even Ravine's office, and Olivia hurried over to look. She was only a pace away when she spotted the cracked vial on the desk.

Without thinking, Olivia picked up what had once been a full bottle of her Nan's Ambrosia, and as she did, saw a piece of paper beneath it. A letter, or rather, a draft of one, with many scratch-outs, but Olivia could see enough:

REPORT FOR THE PRIME MINISTER
VIAL II.

<u>Mission</u>: Extract the ingredients from the residue of Ambrosia in Vial II (of two), located in Constellation

Range on the 30th day of Eighthmonth of the fourth year of the unicorns' return.

Result: Inconclusive.

Interpretation: Impossible though it may appear, the botanical has been so thoroughly blended that it appears to be one single substance. However, all testing reveals a high concentration of unicorn magic. It is as though this vial were once filled with unicorn blood or unicorn tears or unicorn bile or liquefied unicorn or

Olivia dropped the report, unable to read on. Unable to breathe. If she understood correctly, Dean Barry believed that Olivia's family was not only trapping unicorns but . . . *harvesting* them.

She had to get out. Scrabbling for the doorknob, Olivia practically tripped into the hall. From there, she could hear the Barry nieces and nephews laughing raucously as they played and the sound of Baker Barry's husband strumming the guitar. No one would miss her.

Grabbing her cloak, Olivia slipped out the back door. She welcomed the blast of cold, relishing the numbness that made it impossible to think.

As she trudged across the grounds, snow began to fall, gently at first, then it picked up, erasing the land but not, unfortunately, the report Barry had sent to the Prime Minister. With reluctance, Olivia angled herself in the direction of the Barrys' cheery, candlelit windows. It was only when she arrived at the foot of the holly bush that she realized she'd mistaken the glowing red berries for the windows.

When Ember Seed had planted the bush a week ago, Olivia had been able to see across its top, but now it loomed high above, almost as tall as a rooftop. Snow covered the berries, diffusing their pink light across the ground, where Olivia noticed a set of footprints.

Her brows furrowed.

As far as she knew, only she and the Barry family were on the island for Starfell. And whoever was out there must have come by recently, as the fast-falling snow had already partially covered Olivia's tracks. Funny, too, how the footprints led *into* the bush, but there were no footprints leading *out*.

"Hello?" Olivia called into the snow. "Is anyone there?"

No one responded, but Olivia felt a memory stirring, and then she remembered Tourmaline's strange goodbye. She'd told her to say goodbye to *Holly*, but before that, she had said something about the holly bush. And before that she'd said . . .

"'There's lots of light we cannot see,'" Olivia murmured, and reaching into her cloak, she pulled out the prism earring Tourmaline had slipped to her. She hadn't worn it yet—what was the point of a single earring?—but now she wondered if Tourmaline had meant it for her *ears* at all.

Holding up the prism, Olivia peered through—and almost dropped it.

When she looked through the crystal, the berries' light extinguished, and without their light shining in her eyes, Olivia could see an arch in the hedge. Putting out a hand, Olivia tried to feel for the entry, but razor-sharp leaves cut into her skin, and she yanked her hand out.

Taking care to hold the prism tight this time, Olivia held it up again.

The archway reappeared. But where there should have been the Unkempt Woods, she saw instead a meadow. One that looked like the one she stood in now, except for the fact that the snow only powdered the grass and the stars above twinkled, not a snow cloud to be seen. And beneath the stars, suspended above the field, a firework burst. It sparkled silently, never falling, never extinguishing, as though it had been frozen in time.

Because it had been.

Olivia had only come across one mention of frozen time before, in a tale about a Tiller boy who accidentally drank a potion that would make him sleep for a hundred years. His parents' grief had been so sharp that they had managed to fold time in on itself, creating a small wrinkle in the world where everything stayed put. The Tiller's parents secured the fold with a briar hedge, then drank the potion so they could wake with their son, unchanged, in a hundred years' time.

The alchemists of Ember Seed Troupe were more than just entertainers, it seemed.

Still looking through the prism, Olivia reached a hand out again. Now she knew exactly where to put it so the leaves did not scratch. Turning slightly sideways, Olivia walked through.

Immediately, she realized she'd missed the biggest difference of all.

What she'd assumed was snow was actually thousands of tiny white flowers with bell-shaped heads. They crisscrossed the meadow, swirling toward the center, where a creature a shade brighter than the petals lay asleep at its center.

It looked like a horse, though it was both stronger and more delicate than any horse ever could be. Tulip-shaped ears. Seafoam mane. Diamond hooves.

The creature looked like a unicorn.

Except.

Olivia choked on her breath.

Except where the spiraling horn should have ended in a perfect point, there was an angry jag, like lightning. Like the tops of mountains. Like a bite.

CHAPTER TWENTY-SEVEN

A hand grabbed Olivia's shoulder.

Olivia screamed.

The hand moved from her shoulder to her mouth while Olivia tried to pull away.

The footprints.

She'd forgotten about the other set of footprints. The footprints of the person who'd done this to the unicorn. The unicorn trapper.

"Calm yourself, Olivia," ordered Provost Malchain.

The Forger's white hair rippled down her back, free of its usual braids. Instead of her typical dress, she wore a suit of white-gold armor, and for once, her axes weren't peeking out behind her shoulders. But that was only because one was already in her hand—the hand that was not currently covering Olivia's mouth.

"If you promise not to scream, I will remove my hand,"

Malchain whispered. "It's important not to disturb the unicorn."

Olivia nodded, but as soon as she felt the provost's hand lift away, she took a deep breath and—

—the provost's hand went back over her mouth again.

"Olivia," Provost Malchain chided. "I do not condone lying in my students. I do acknowledge how this situation may appear to you, of course."

Reaching under her breastplate, Malchain pulled out a tin of hard candy. Olivia recognized the citrus-y smell: Loose-Lip Lozenges, usually given to people to ensure they would be perfectly honest.

Provost Malchain popped one in her mouth. Clearing her throat, she said, "I am not the unicorn trapper, nor do I hold any ill intent toward the creature or toward you. Now, if I release my hand, will you stay quiet?"

Olivia nodded, and the provost withdrew her hand. "Excellent."

Olivia licked her lips. "But how—?"

"—did the unicorn come to be here, in our meadow?" Provost Malchain gazed out, face solemn. "Last week, two alchemists found this poor creature galloping the edges of Arden, utterly wild, her horn already as you've seen. When they told the Prime Minister, she ordered the unicorn be brought here, under the protective care of myself and the deans. Between the five of us, we will be able to keep the unicorn safe and asleep."

"But why is it so important to keep her asleep?" Olivia asked, looking at the unicorn. Her ears twitched as she dreamed. "Is she sick?"

"In a way," Malchain said. "This particular unicorn may have been found, but she is still lost. With her fractured horn, she's . . . well, she's not a horse, obviously, but she's no longer quite a unicorn. She is, shall we say, betwixt. It is best for all that she remain asleep until her horn can be restored."

"But the unicorn—she can be healed?" Olivia asked. "The horn *can* be mended?"

Several seconds passed before Malchain spoke. And when she did, her voice was quiet. "We do not know. As far as the histories tell us, a living unicorn's horn has never been broken before. In the past, the only way to separate a unicorn horn from a unicorn was in death."

"You mean—"

"Slain, yes." Malchain nodded. "Unicorns are immortal unless killed, and while a unicorn slayer might reap the benefits of unicorn flesh, the slayer is also cursed for eternity. However, if someone were to learn how to sever a *living* unicorn from its horn, then they hold the core of the unicorn's power and face none of the consequences."

Malchain's words were familiar, and memories from the Mender's cellar swelled within Olivia. "You think the hunter is using the missing horn to control and trap more unicorns?"

The provost looked at Olivia sharply. "The Prime Minister's *trusted council* believes that, yes," Malchain said, and the slight emphasis told Olivia that Malchain knew exactly *where* Olivia had come by that information and was choosing to ignore the *how*.

"But it is my belief as well," Malchain continued. "Whomever holds the unicorn's horn is most certainly the hunter." The provost slid her ax back into its holster and adjusted her breastplate. "Come, let's leave the unicorn to her dreaming and return you to the cottage."

Olivia, however, had one more question. One that she didn't think she could bear to ask, but in this tiny frozen pocket of time, she found her courage. "Provost?"

Pausing at the arch, Aquila Malchain turned. "Yes?"

"My family has brewed Ambrosia for three hundred years," Olivia said. "And for the majority of that time, there were no unicorns to be found in Arden. Whatever Ambrosia is, it's not *possible* for it to contain . . . unicorn remains."

The provost inclined her head. "Recipes change, just as people do."

Malchain's words were like mold, soft, spreading, dangerous. They clung to Olivia as they waded back through the snow, knocked on the cottage door, and Dean Barry shooed her off to bed. They settled into the damp, dark places of her brain, eating away at what she knew to be true: Laurel was innocent.

People change, the mold crooned. *You have.*

Olivia tapped her thumb against the steel of her fingernail and felt the heaviness of the quilt across her feet.

Laurel had changed, too.

She'd seen it at the cottage. Noted it. Marveled at it that night in Bumblebee Apothecary, when she'd said with an unfamiliar smugness, *Physician Heliotrope thinks I'm on to something* big—*a complete rethinking of how we look at potential in soil."*

And the sister she knew, the Laurel she'd grown up with, never, ever, ever would have left Olivia alone in such a mess. She'd have left *more* than a book with a single, grammatically incorrect word—

Olivia sat up so quickly, her bed creaked and the Barry niece closest to her shifted. Reaching for the nightstand, she grabbed her pouch and plunged her hand inside until she felt the hard corners of *The Account of Olivia the Observant*. She pulled it out and flipped to the page: DONT.

Heart pounding, she reached for her pen to fix the mistake that Laurel would never, ever have made. Not without a reason.

Between the N and the T, Olivia inked in an apostrophe—the symbol used for missing letters. A symbol for something hidden in between.

As soon as the pen's nub lifted from the page, the book became heavy.

Olivia's heart pounded as she turned the cover.

The blank pages had fused together, creating a single thick page into which a hollow had been carved. But instead of a note explaining all that Laurel had done and where she was now and how Olivia could join her, something else nested in the newly formed nook.

A small spiral, no wider than her palm and just as long as her hand. It looked like a seashell, except it gleamed like no shell ever could. Its point was perfect, but its base was jagged, like a puzzle piece. Like mountaintops. Like lightning.

The unicorn's missing horn.

CHAPTER TWENTY-EIGHT

Olivia did not tell a soul.

Not Provost Malchain. Not Dean Barry. Not Kessa or Tourmaline or Violet when they returned the next day with descriptions of Stonehaven's diamond decorations and Alloy Alley's street dancing festival.

Olivia couldn't—*wouldn't*—say anything.

Not until she talked to Laurel.

"You owe me, Olive Pit," Laurel had said so very, very long ago when Olivia had turned the mayor into a mushroom. But it was more complicated than sisterly love or familial loyalty.

Whomever holds the unicorn's horn is most certainly the hunter, the provost had said.

And yet . . . Olivia had the horn, and she was definitely *not* the hunter.

But who would believe her? Parliament would throw her into prison (or worse), and the unicorn hunter—the *real* one, whoever it was—would still be free. Still be stalking unicorns.

Olivia's imagination spun several explanations for Laurel, more than a dozen excuses, and even one possibility where she had just dreamed the whole thing up. But none of her stories lasted any longer than a chopped knot. Certain truths kept slicing through.

The Mender's map.

Ambrosia.

The unicorn's horn.

It *always* came back to the unicorn's horn.

Sometimes Olivia believed the horn was proof Laurel couldn't be the hunter, couldn't be responsible for the missing unicorns, since she hadn't possessed the horn in weeks. But then an oily thought would rise up and slickly say, *Unless she has* more *unicorns*.

"Are you mad at us?"

Olivia, slung over a library armchair, looked up and blinked. Either she'd been reading too much and completely destroyed her eyes, or else Tourmaline really *was* standing in front of her, wearing the most ostentatious gown Olivia could possibly imagine.

Jewels clung to her friend like raindrops—blue diamonds, pink rubies, smoky sapphires, violet amethysts, ember topaz, and apple-green emeralds. The only bit of noncolor was the bonelike cape that draped around her neck and around her shoulders. The skull-clasp at the base of her throat lifted, and if it were possible, Olivia would have sworn Ghost winked.

"What are you wearing?" Olivia asked.

"No." Tourmaline crossed her arms. "The question is what are *you* wearing? Even *Kessa* dressed up for the party tonight!"

Olivia looked past Tourmaline's blinding apparel to see Kessa and Violet standing behind the Gemmer. Violet was dressed in a lavender tutu with amethyst clips in her black bangs, while Kessa looked more or less like her usual self, except her black leather tunic might have been ever so slightly shinier.

"The party?" Olivia repeated, and as she did, a fuzzy memory of Tourmaline informing them earlier that week that she expected them to attend some sort of midsemester celebration in the Gemmer tower. Olivia hadn't paid attention because she already knew she wouldn't go. Ever since she'd seen the sleeping unicorn and its fragmented horn, Olivia had spent every minute awake scouring the library for a cure.

While the academy's library had been emptied of books exclusively about unicorns, she was still able to glean information about them in obscure footnotes and appendices. And even if they didn't explicitly mention unicorns, she thought that maybe she might find some clue, some hint of how to mend a unicorn's horn within the many tomes of Spinner sewing. Quilting seemed like a good start—patching together pieces to make something complete. But then again, so had veil-knitting, button-making, and a bit of Forger work known as zipper-making—but none of them had led anywhere.

If she could just figure out *how* to reattach the shard to the sleeping unicorn's horn, she could fix all her problems. The unicorn would know herself again and be able to share with the grandmasters *who* had done this to her and *how* and maybe even *why*. Olivia could clear Laurel's name, save the unicorn, and be a hero.

Be accepted.

Belong.

She had no time for parties.

"I'm sorry," Olivia said, looking back to Anne Patchitt's *The Qualm of Quilts*. "But I really need to—"

"No." Tourmaline glared through her glasses. "You already bailed on Violet's test today. I'm not letting you—"

Olivia started upright, the book falling off her lap. "Violet, the water test! I'm so sorry, I completely forgot! How did it go?"

The trip to Stonehaven had not revealed Violet's talent, and upon their return, Dean Ravine had declared that Violet had no aptitude for Gemming. As Forging had been ruled out and she'd spent all her life among Tillers, only one possible guild remained: Spinner.

Olivia had promised to tutor her, but there had always been another book to read. And now she'd faced Garmont's Splash Pad by herself. For the last few days, all of the Spinner apprentices had cobbled footwear that would—or should—allow them to walk across water. Everyone so far had passed, except, it seemed, for . . .

"Wetly," Violet said, and Olivia heard a squelch as she shifted. "I don't think my boots will ever be dry again."

"Here," Olivia said, tugging out her own bootlaces. "Switch with me. Mine are *extra* absorbent. Put them in and your boots will be dry in no time."

"Thanks." Violet plopped onto a cushion and began to thread them through while Olivia wound Violet's into her own shoes. Her footwear had been cobbled to always keep her feet perfectly dry, no matter the circumstance.

"Please just come," Kessa said, speaking for the first time. "We miss you, and if you don't, Tourmaline will be insufferable."

"I will be," Tourmaline agreed. "If you hate it that much, you can always sneak into Aunt Rubi's study and read some of her books."

Olivia bit her lip. "Does she have any on unicorns?"

"Several."

Olivia sighed. It looked like she was going to a party after all.

Ten minutes later and with the help of her Dresser, Olivia was ready. Her chiffon gown of yellow pleats rippled around her, while a transparent cloak attached to her shoulders floated prettily in her wake. To complete the look, the Dresser had presented her with a shell-pink wig, and when Olivia slipped it on, she looked exactly like the tapestry of Honoria Sash, down to the gold necklace Kessa lent her for the night.

The others cheered when she exited her dorm room, and together the four of them made their way up the spiraling staircase and into the astronomy tower. Olivia had never been before, even to visit Tourmaline, and was surprised to realize that unlike the rest of the academy, its walls were made entirely of diamond-paned glass, giving an uninterrupted view of Lumin City's distant lights. The only stone in the room was the column in the center that held the door to the stairs, and the stone arches that held up the ceiling. Olivia thought it was strange that the astronomy tower had an opaque roof, but she supposed the wrought iron balcony that encircled the outside provided enough of a view.

Apprentices in costumes drifted between ice sculptures and tables piled with fruits and cheeses while a violin played a tinkling melody. A girl in a wide gown stepped to the side, and Olivia could finally read the banner that had been artfully draped on the head table: Protect Our Unicorns Fraternity.

"It's a *P.O.U.F.* party!" Olivia said, whirling to face Tourmaline. "If you'd told me that, I wouldn't have come!"

"I know," Tourmaline said. "That's why I didn't tell you."

Olivia bristled. "Let's get out of—"

"What's *she* doing here?" Paisley stood in front of them in a silver gown, the overskirt cut away to display moon-pink silk beneath. Bright white ribbons weaved in and out of her dark hair, creating a frothy mane that spilled down her back. A delicate chain circled her head, upon which a small, spiraling glass horn had been attached. Of course. *Of course* Paisley's chosen costume was the Rider's unicorn.

"I invited her," Tourmaline said, grabbing a small plate of finger sandwiches and passing them to Olivia. "If there's an issue, I'm sure Aunt Rubi would be very curious to know why, seeing as it's an academy policy that clubs are open to all guilds at all times."

Paisley's mouth thinned. "Just make sure she doesn't get any ideas. *Unicorn hunting* ideas," she added, as though her intent wasn't clear in the first place. She stalked away, her shoes clip-clopping against the flagstones.

Olivia whirled on Tourmaline. "You're a member of P.O.U.F.?!"

"I joined before I knew you." Tourmaline shrugged as she picked up an iced pastry. "Aunt Rubi wanted me to at least try making friends, and I stayed because Paisley's uncle sends *the* best minicakes." She took a bite and sighed contentedly.

Kessa disappeared to sit with the musicians, and soon her flute sang out above the chatter, calling everyone to dance. A moment later, Tourmaline pulled Violet to the center of the room and demanded she sing. Olivia hadn't even known Violet *could* sing, but Violet's sweet voice blended perfectly with Kessa's silver flute as she sang a twist on "Sparkle, Sparkle, Youngest Star," replacing *sparkle* with *twinkle*, along with a few more changes that made the ancient song feel brand-new.

When Violet finished, everyone burst into applause and Olivia clapped until her palms were red. Someone in the crowd called for her to sing again. Cheeks flushed, Violet obliged.

Olivia, meanwhile, remained on the edge, feeling awkward, looking awkward, being awkward. Not knowing what else to do or where the dean's suite of unicorn books could be found, she picked up a minicake and took a bite. It *was* obnoxiously delicious.

Balancing several onto a clay saucer and pouring herself a goblet of raspberry cordial, she retreated to the balcony. The iron railing stood waist-high, and at every few feet a Gemglow had been carefully balanced. Although, as Olivia set her plate on the rail and looked more closely, she realized they weren't Gemglows at all. Gemglows made their own light, while these large crystals seemed to reflect the ambient light of the night sky.

Peering into the orb, she saw crystalline filaments twine and twist through the ball like miniature comets. As she stared, she thought she saw one of the strands shift, or perhaps brighten.

Suddenly, Olivia could make out the reflection of the night sky above her—the seven stars of the Rider's constellation—winking at her in the depths of the crystal. Their lights merged, becoming haloed and fuzzy, before snapping into a scene:

A unicorn gallops.

A young woman on his back clutches his neck, her cheek to his mane. Her cascade of ebony braids whips in the wind and her stola bunches around her knees as she holds on tight to a scrap of cloth.

The image shifted.

No unicorn this time, but an older woman wearing a scarlet physician's coat. Crouching over a cradle, she dips a washcloth into a bowl of shimmering gold liquid and slowly drips it into the baby's mouth. The woman turns, wiping a stray curl off her forehead. Her face is familiar, though far younger than Olivia has ever seen it: Nan.

Another shift.

A girl with two red braids runs down a mountain toward a rock upon which three unicorn hairs gleam. And then—

No.

No no no no no no—

"Olivia!"

Olivia jerked back, her fingers still on the cold curve of the crystal ball.

"Are you all right?" Violet asked. "You look like you're going to be sick."

"Not on Aunt Rubi's crystal balls!" Tourmaline said,

throwing an arm around Olivia's shoulder and guiding her to an empty garden chair.

"Crystal balls?" Olivia whispered. She felt dizzy and parched, as though she'd been in the sun too long. "Don't they show Gemmers the future?"

If that was the future, she could stop it. But—

"It's a common misconception that crystal balls reflect the future," Tourmaline said, forcing Olivia to sit and handing her a small goblet of juice. "In a way, they do. They reflect and collect starlight, which travels years, sometimes a million years, to get to our eyes. The crystal distills the light so that we can see what the stars witnessed so many years ago."

"But that's the *past*."

Tourmaline shrugged. "What happened before is sure to happen again, and in that way, the past *is* our future. Just as unicorns were once, then gone, and now are again."

"So, what's in the crystal ball . . ." Olivia asked, fingers clenching the goblet's stem. "Is it always true?"

"Of course. Stars don't lie—Olivia!" Tourmaline's eyes narrowed. "Did you *see* something? I thought only Gemmers could read crystal balls!"

Surprising, and yet, not.

Not after what Olivia had seen.

Not after what she now knew.

"Actually, I do feel sick," Olivia said, passing the goblet back and standing up. "I'm going to go to bed."

Olivia practically floated down the stairs, through the

deserted hallways, and into the privacy of her empty suite. She felt like a ghost, except for the fact that her finger ached. Holding up her hand, Olivia sighed. The thimble had fully formed again, creating a tiny crown on her finger.

You are a very powerful Forger, Joust had said.

But she wasn't. She knew she wasn't.

Just like she knew she wasn't a Gemmer. And yet, she'd just read a crystal ball.

Holding the thimble up to her mouth, she whispered to it, asking it to come off. For the first time, it listened. The metal fell from her fingertip and into her waiting palm. It was still warm from her skin, and using the heat, Olivia gently pinched the steel and pulled, twisting, lengthening it, just as she would have done with a bit of fiber from a hank of sheep's wool. Soon she had a steel thread, which she bent into a silver circlet.

Never put strange metal on your head, Kessa had said. *Most Forgers can only manage Metal Telepathy with someone of close kin . . .*

Olivia tied the drapes shut and lay on her bed. Waiting, hoping it would work. Praying that it wouldn't. She closed her eyes.

If someone were to learn how to sever a living unicorn from its horn, the provost had said, *then they hold the core of the unicorn's power and face none of the consequences.*

When Olivia opened her eyes again, the dormitory was gone.

Instead of her bed, she lay in a dreamy jungle. Flowering

cacti, trumpet vines, palms, and pines bloomed, sprouted, and towered around her in a tangle of green that was both chaotic and serene. Water lilies as large as platters floated on a nearby pond while a million rosebuds decorated an arched gateway. Olivia walked under it, following a dirt path that led to—

Her breath caught.

In an ivy-covered clearing, an old maple grew. Lichen spotted its bark, and its roots were as gnarled as Nan's hand but just as strong. The branches reached out, offering a long rope swing. Olivia had almost no memory of her parents but one: sitting in her mother's arms while her father pushed them higher and higher.

She was in a dream, but not her own. However, only one other person in the world would be dreaming of this swing, this tree, and this garden that smelled like the treasured bottle of Rosemarie Hayes's perfume.

"Olivia?"

Olivia turned.

Her sister stood there, her bun a yellow bud upon her head and her green eyes sad. So very, very sad.

"You figured it out."

"Laurel." Olivia's throat tightened. Tears pricked her eyes. "Why didn't you tell me that *I* broke the unicorn's horn?"

PART IV

*Sparkle, sparkle, youngest star
How I wonder where you are.
Up above my world, so nigh?
Or a diamond in new skies?*

*'Tis your bright and tiny spark,
Lights the Rider in the dark,
Tho' I know not where you are,
sparkle, sparkle, youngest star.*

—Carat's Fables

CHAPTER TWENTY-NINE

"Olive Pit, how could I do that to you?"

Laurel's response, if nothing else, told Olivia that even though this was a dream, it was also real. Because if it had been just a dream, a made-up wish, Laurel would have said, "Don't be ridiculous, of course you didn't break the unicorn's horn! Everything is perfect! Let's go home!" But Laurel and the stars had seen what Olivia had done, and now Olivia knew too:

Storm clouds. Wind. A Dandiloon spins out of control.

Three gold flecks fly off the gondola. Two hit the ground and their gold spills onto the grass. The third, however, falls into the cleft of a lightning-struck tree, its impact softened by rot and ash.

A girl with two auburn braids runs down the mountain, focusing on the unicorn hairs gleaming on the boulder. The girl reaches. Her fingers grasp the strands. Then—

The girl's gone.

Blown out, like a candle.

Suddenly the girl sparks back into existence, and she's not alone.

Her arms wrap around a unicorn's neck as the unicorn pulls them out from the nothingness. As the unicorn's hooves find Arden again, the girl slips. With desperation, the girl reaches up—and her palm connects with the horn.

Light flares. The unicorn neighs. And the girl's body hits the ground.

The unicorn rears, and the stars moan in horror. The unicorn's horn—its compass, its purpose—is broken. Confused and terrified, the unicorn gallops away.

The girl remains on the ground. In her hand something shines like the point of a star.

The Dandiloon appears over the ledge and lands. A second girl with yellow hair jumps out shouting, "Olivia! Olivia!!!!" She reaches for the girl's pulse and sees what's in her hand.

Laurel falters. Then, she grabs the bit of unicorn ivory and puts it in her kit. Taking the Blastachio from Olivia's pocket, Laurel smashes it against the boulder.

Olivia's eyes flutter, then, "Yelck!" She jerks upright and slaps her hands over her nose. "What is that? It smells like rotten meat and burned hair and—is that damp celery?!"

Olivia looked down at her hands that had touched a unicorn's horn. *Broken* a unicorn's horn. "It's not my magic at all, is it? It's the unicorn's magic. I . . . I *stole* it."

Laurel hesitated, then nodded.

Heat flooded Olivia's eyes, and then she was sobbing, crying as she never had before—

—for the unicorn.

—for her friends who'd believed in her.

—for Nan, hiding in exile.

—for Laurel, wrongly accused.

—for herself, and the loss of who she thought she was.

Through it all, Laurel held tightly to her, arms solid even in a dream. "Stop, Olivia. It's not hopeless! It can be fixed."

Olivia pulled out of Laurel's hug. "You can heal the horn?"

"I think so," Laurel said. "We just need Ambrosia—"

"Ambrosia!" Olivia's voice cracked. "Laurel—how could you? How could *we*—?!!"

Laurel tucked a wisp of hair behind her ear. "How could we what?"

"I know our family secret," Olivia ground out. "And why it's secret! Our family has been dealing in unicorn magic, in *unicorn artifacts*." Her stomach clenched. "Is that why the mayor had the rib sliver on him? He was going to give it to Nan? Or—"

"Olivia, for all that's green, stop spinning tales and listen!" Laurel's voice cut through Olivia's machinations. "There *is* unicorn magic in Ambrosia, but nothing like you're thinking."

"*Tell. Me*," Olivia pleaded. "No more secrets!"

Laurel bit her lip. "All right." She paused, thinking, then asked, "What do you know about unicorns?"

Infuriatingly, very little, but Olivia tried. "Unicorns are pure magic. They can open any door. Snowdrops bloom in their steps and their magic changes things—"

Laurel held up a hand, stopping her. "Good. And what is Nan famous for? Aside from Ambrosia."

"Nan's known for having a bark worse than her bite," Olivia said, thinking out loud. "She's known for Bumblebee Apothecary, being our grandmother, and . . ." She trailed off.

"And?" Laurel prompted.

"And . . ." Olivia closed her eyes, remembering Buddle. Remembering home. Nan's gardens, the friendly willow, the fishpond, the prize beehives . . .

A thought settled on Olivia so softly, she almost missed it, except, when she opened her eyes, she saw Laurel's dreamscape had shifted. The varied jungle had transformed into a meadow of small white flowers with petals that curved like a bell.

Snowdrops.

"Bees," Olivia breathed out as Laurel let the swing sway to a stop. "Ambrosia isn't a botanical at all, is it? It's honey from the snowdrops that grow in a unicorn's steps!"

Laurel tucked her head, nodding. "Yes.

"Then," Olivia said, looking at the spread of flowers, "that means—"

"We are *not* a family of trappers or hunters. Just the opposite, in fact," Laurel said, sliding off and standing up. "The Hayeses have always been both gardeners and guardians of unicorns and their magic. Three hundred years ago, our ancestor Arbutus Hayes saved the last snowdrop flower from the hoofprint of the last unicorn. From that time on, generations of Hayes physicians have tended that blossom. Keeping it—the very last drop of unicorn magic—alive for centuries. Sharing its blessings as best we could while at the same time knowing we must protect it at all costs."

"Sharing its blessings . . ." Olivia repeated, ". . . by pouring it in soil?"

Laurel rolled her eyes. "I knew you weren't paying attention in the Dandiloon! Yes. I *told* you. I've been tracking the potential, the *magic*, in soil. Early on, I came across these"— she waved her hand in the air, searching for the word—"bare spots I guess, places where the dirt had been drained of all its potential, making it *impossible* to grow anything. You could call it a blight, perhaps. I haven't figured out what is causing them, but I've gotten much better at predicting places where it might strike."

"So," Olivia said, slowing teasing out how her sister had managed to look so guilty to everyone, even to her own sister. "You've been sprinkling Ambrosia on the blight spots, trying to heal the earth."

Laurel nodded. "Just a drop seems to help, but now . . ."

Bending down, she kissed a bloom. It opened, revealing delicate gold pistils. "Our snowdrop is very old and unable to produce much nectar. The three vials I lost were all that Nan was able to cultivate in the last five years."

"But unicorns have returned," Olivia said, looking around the meadow and remembering the sway of petals around the sleeping unicorn. "Shouldn't there be whole fields of snowdrops in Constellation Range?"

"You would think." Laurel shook her head. "Nan and I have been looking for the unicorns' hidden valley, but so far, we've haven't had much luck. We've found some flowers, but at our current rate and the early winter, Nan estimates the hives won't be able to produce a vial's worth of ambrosia until next summer." Laurel frowned. "Why are you grinning like that?"

Olivia was grinning like that because, for once in her life, her big sister was wrong. They *wouldn't* need to wait until then to heal the unicorn. The stars had shown Olivia where the third and final vial of Ambrosia could be found, and so Olivia now told Laurel.

Laurel gasped. "I think I know *exactly* which tree you're talking about! Olivia"—Laurel gave her a quick hug—"you can fix everything!"

"You mean *you* can fix everything." Olivia smiled. "You're the physician."

But Laurel was shaking her head. "I don't think I can. *You* broke the unicorn's horn." She reached for Olivia's hands. "I didn't even know it was possible for unicorn ivory to break.

It shouldn't *be* possible. Which is why I think you, Olivia, are the only one who can heal the horn, which is why you must be *extremely* careful. If anyone finds out—"

"—I'll go to prison."

"If you're lucky," Laurel said, and let go. "You are now a girl with a unicorn's capabilities. Olivia—you could be *hunted*."

Acid rose in Olivia's throat. "Laurel, the jar of soil with my name on it. What was it?"

"Dirt from where you said the sinkhole was," Laurel replied, and Olivia realized with a jolt that her sister had believed her all along. Laurel began to pace, the dreamscape moving flowers out of her way. Even in her sleep, Laurel was kind.

"What you described to me, what the sinkhole felt like, it was similar to how the blighted soil feels to me. Empty. *Thin*. I wanted to see if it contained a clue to *what* is hurting the crops that try to grow there. There's really only ever four options." Holding up a finger, she listed each one. "Weather, fungus, mold, or parasite."

"The weather has been consistent," Laurel said, dismissing it, "and if it's a fungus or a mold attacking a plant, you can *see* them on the leaf, the little colonies they build. But with a parasite, you spot the hole in the leaf before you see the caterpillar."

But they weren't talking about leaves.

They were talking about Arden. They were talking about an entire *world*.

Olivia stilled. "Not a *caterpillar's* bite. It's—" *SLAM!*

Olivia's eyes opened to the curtains of her four-poster bed. She was awake, and by the sound of Cami's loud giggle and Gabi's snort of laughter, the party was over. Olivia reached for the circlet around her head, but all she could feel was skin. The steel had vanished along with the dream—not that she would be able to go back to sleep.

Not now that she knew that the future of the unicorn, and maybe all of Arden's unicorns, depended on her.

Olivia rubbed her metal-less fingernail, missing the thimble's comfort, but she still held tight to its reminder: she wasn't alone, so long as she had stories.

And she had so many stories now.

Arbutus Hayes's. Laurel's. Dean Barry's. Kessa's. Tourmaline's.

But there was someone's story she didn't know—yet. She needed to learn it, and soon.

The fate of the world depended on it.

CHAPTER THIRTY

"Olivia?" Violet's voice floated into the drying chamber, her words muffled by the rows of freshly dyed fabric hanging from clotheslines. "Where are you?"

Olivia paused in her pacing and stood on her tiptoes. "Here!" she called, raising her hand to wave over the fabric. "Don't touch anything!"

Yesterday, the Spinner apprentices had worked alongside the Tillers to carefully dip linen into barrels of Sigh Dye, brewed from shade plants. Once dry, the fabric would flutter ever so slightly, creating a tiny breeze that would keep the wearer cool. However, until the cloth was completely dry, the dye would have the opposite effect and paralyze anyone who brushed up against it. So, until Dean Barry deemed it dry and safe, the chamber was off-limits, making it the perfect place to meet.

Olivia heard Violet's footsteps pattering toward her, then a gasp as Violet stepped around a sheet and saw Olivia.

"You look *terrible*," Violet said, voice hushed. "What *happened* last night?"

What happened, of course, was that Olivia had attended a terrible P.O.U.F. party, discovered she'd broken a unicorn's horn, learned it was *her* fault her family was in hiding, and realized that no one was tracking down the *actual* trapper. The little of the night that had been left to her, she'd spent awake, gathering things and waiting for her friends to wake up, read her note, and meet her in the drying chamber.

Before Olivia could even try to explain, Kessa appeared.

"Wow," said Kessa, eyebrows lifting slightly as she took in Olivia's state. "You know, it's called beauty sleep for a reason."

Olivia ignored the remark. "Tourmaline, are you here?"

"We're here," Tourmaline called, and Olivia noticed her friend standing next to her, Ghost perched on her shoulder. The fossil's talons gripped Tourmaline's collar as she leaned to get a better look at the objects Olivia had lined up on the table. "What's all this stuff? Why did you want to see us so early?"

Olivia spread her fingers on the table and took a deep breath. "I know who the trapper is."

Violet stiffened. "How?"

"Who?" Kessa asked.

"What?" Tourmaline snapped.

Olivia could answer all their questions with the same answer.

"*It began to gnaw on the dark edges of forests,*" Olivia recited, "*slurp molten gold from the mines, munch mountaintops, and even chew through the seams of the world.*"

Her friends stared at her, quiet, but their expressions were loud enough. Tourmaline broke the silence. "To be crystal clear, you're trying to tell us that the unicorn hunter is actually—"

"Yes." Olivia nodded. "The Devourer has returned."

Kessa let out a strangled laugh, but Violet shushed her. "Go on," she said, looking at Olivia intently. "Why do you think that?"

"Ghost," Olivia said, reaching out to rub the creature's skull.

Tourmaline pushed her hand away. "Ghost isn't the Devourer!"

"'Course he's not," Olivia said, taking a step away but keeping her gaze on the bony creature. "Ghost, er, *came back* after the unicorns started disappearing, but that doesn't mean he can't help us." She took a deep breath. "Tourmaline, when I met Ghost, you said he might be an Original, a creature *born* of magic, not made of magic. Pure magic."

"And?" Tourmaline's eyes glittered dangerously behind her quartz frames.

"I think the Devourer is an Original, too," Olivia said. "A creature of pure magic. A creature that could rival a unicorn in strength and magic because only—"

"Only pure magic can trap a unicorn," Kessa finished. She

drummed her fingers against the table, and Olivia could see the musician making sense of what was both said and unsaid.

Olivia nodded. "If Ghost can come back, if unicorns can come back, then why can't the Devourer, too?"

"Because," Tourmaline snapped, "the Devourer burned up in the sun—drowning in sun's fire, remember?"

"Maybe," Olivia agreed. "But we don't know that there was only *one* Devourer. We don't know what kind of creature it is—if it has feathers or scales or fur."

"We know it had many heads," Kessa cut in, her fingers tapping a quiet rhythm on the flute she'd pulled from her toolbelt. "Like Coda the Curious sang, *'Many heads with one heart, claws and feet and worlds apart.'*"

"Exactly," Olivia said. "Though even that description is vague. But Ghost"—she looked at the fossil, who stared back blankly, as he always did—"Ghost was *there* when Arden was young. Ghost might remember a creature so hungry it could eat mountains. Eat *magic*. Eat—" She stopped, not willing to say the next gruesome truth aloud.

Eat unicorns.

"Ghost doesn't remember anything," Tourmaline said, then sighed. "I guess this is when you tell me you have a plan?"

Olivia's plan was simple, really. It only needed an apprentice each of Spinning, Gemming, and Forging, and Nan's amber beads.

Olivia had always loved her grandmother's beads. Loved fingering their shiny smoothness and studying the bits of flora and fauna and air bubbles that both marred the jewels and enhanced their beauty. She was counting on these imperfections to save them now.

Olivia watched as Tourmaline dropped the necklace into a crucible and coaxed heat into its clay walls. Beside her, Kessa played her flute, the breath from the instrument helping to keep the crucible's temperature steady. Soon, the amber beads glistened, softened, then melted, letting loose the ephemera that had been trapped in the resin.

"All right," Tourmaline said, sweat glistening on her neck as she stepped away from the liquefied amber. "Your turn."

Olivia moved forward and carefully dipped into the melted amber a string the exact auburn shade of her hair. Because it was. Using strands from her brush, Olivia had spun her hairs into a fisherman's twist, a string traditionally used to make deep-sea nets. Though they weren't catching any krakens today, they were trying to dredge up something equally evasive. Her hair wasn't unicorn mane, of course, but magic was in the material. And the unicorn's magic was within her. She hoped it would be enough.

Olivia hoped *she* would be enough.

With each dip of the string, the coat of resin thickened, slowly transforming into an amber candle.

"You think this will work?" Kessa asked as Olivia trimmed the wick.

"Nan says that the nose holds more memory than the brain," Olivia said. She set the stone candle into the iron holder. "Once, I saw her brew a perfume after a journeyman carpenter's head got clunked by a log. He couldn't remember his name, but after one whiff, he could remember everything, even where he'd put his lost keys. Are you ready?"

Olivia watched as Tourmaline hammered flint and flicked a spark onto a twig. She handed it to Olivia, who turned to Violet.

"*Me?*" Violet asked.

"You're just as much a part of this discovery as the rest of us," Olivia said, and she meant it.

Without Violet, it was possible none of them would have become friends. It was Violet, after all, who was the first apprentice in the school who believed Olivia when she said Laurel was innocent. It was Violet who had made her think to reach out to Tourmaline. It was Violet who told Olivia that Kessa was trapped in the caves. She was the spark to their kindled friendship, and together, the four of them would light the way to the unicorns' future.

"If you're sure . . ." Taking the twig, Violet touched flame to wick, and the candle glowed.

Now they just had to see if Olivia's plan would work: If the wick she'd woven would be able to snag the scent of the ancient flowers and air. If the fragrance would help Ghost remember what he was and the world he'd come from. If he could remember Arden's greatest enemy.

A dusky gold scent seeped into the chamber. Tendrils of smoke spiraled into Ghost's nasal cavities, and the ancient creature stirred. Despite his usual skittishness around fire, he leaned over the candle, vertebrae swaying.

Olivia closed her eyes and focused on her nose. She smelled smoke and vanilla and then something sweet, like the first spring day. Or maybe, *the* First Spring Day. Olivia's heart leaped. Was this the smell of a young world, brimming with magic and potential, with drakons in the air and melusines in the streams? She inhaled deeply, and then—

She began to cough. Sputter. *Choke.*

Olivia's eyes flew open.

Smoke obscured everything except for the conflagration in front of her.

Fire. The table was on fire!

Olivia-sized flames roared from the table, growing taller and more ferocious with each second. Heat smacked her face and she took a step back just as Tourmaline rushed by, screaming.

"GHOST!GHOST!GHOST!"

Olivia looked again at the inferno, and this time she saw a creature in the fire's heart. Flames flicked along Ghost, outlining his metacarpus, radius, and humerus before flaring off into orange-and-crimson plumes.

Wind whipped around Olivia, clearing the smoke just enough that she could see Kessa a few feet away. Her flute was at her lips, and her breath, amplified by the silver, pushed the flames back away from the girls, the highly flammable fabric, and the castle's wood rafters. But how long could she protect them? The flute already looked pink with heat.

"GET BACK!" Olivia yelled, grabbing Tourmaline's shoulder as a wall of hot air slammed into them. The diamond panes shattered and twinkled in the firelight as Ghost exploded out the window and into the sky. His wings stretched out like sunrise, filling the horizon with fire. Below, people began to shout.

Olivia saw two Forger apprentices lean out from the floor below, staring up at the burning bones. Bells clanged on either side of the river. Horns blared from the boats as everyone in Lumin City looked at the sky.

Ghost, whatever he was, was a secret no more.

CHAPTER THIRTY-ONE

Tourmaline stumbled back from the window. "He needs help! Whatever he remembered, he's scared—he's so scared!" She sprinted toward the door.

"Did you see what happened?" Olivia asked the others as they ran to follow.

Violet nodded. "Everything seemed fine, and then Ghost—he started *shaking*. He lunged at the candle and swallowed—actually *swallowed*—the flame! It disappeared for a moment and then he just *burned*."

Panicked apprentices crowded the halls, congesting the stairs.

"Smoke! I smell smoke!"

"Is the academy on fire?"

"Put your earbuds in!" The last shout was Kessa's, and Olivia had just enough time to stick her willow buds in before Kessa sounded the Luring Horn.

Though Olivia could not hear the horn, she could see its effect as the students and scholars around them slowed, dazed, and drifted to the sides of the staircase while the girls sped down the now-clear center and out the great double doors. Tourmaline, legs strong from mountain climbing and rock lifting, pulled ahead, running to the center of the lawn, where high above, Ghost burned like a second sun.

He flew higher and higher and higher until Olivia could no longer see him, an ember extinguished in an ocean of sky. Except—

Something was falling.

Not a skeleton. It was too small for that.

Tourmaline held her skirt wide, and whatever it was dropped into the fabric. Though Olivia couldn't hear Tourmaline or see her face, she saw her friend crumple to the ground. Olivia pumped her legs harder, and then she was at Tourmaline's side.

Olivia yanked the willow buds out of her ears and flung her arms around her friend's shaking shoulders. Tourmaline sobbed.

"Where is he?" Olivia asked. "Where's Ghost?"

Tourmaline didn't answer, but Olivia followed her gaze to where a ruby the size of a coin nestled in the scorched folds of her skirt.

Ghost.

Or what was left of him.

"He's gone," Tourmaline whispered. "Ghost is *gone*."

Olivia knew loss. It'd been written into her own story at a young age, and she'd seen others grapple with it the few times Nan's botanicals had been unable to help. Olivia knew there were no words that could lessen grief. So, instead of trying to say anything, she wrapped her arms around her friend's shaking shoulders. There could be novels of comfort in a hug.

She waited for Violet to join, but Violet hung back, staring at the jewel. Her brows furrowed beneath her bangs, and then suddenly her expression cleared.

Violet dropped to her knees beside them. "I know what Ghost is!"

"*Violet!*" Olivia gaped at her friend, who was usually so kind and understanding. "I don't think this is the best time now that, you know . . ."

"He's *not* dead," Violet said, not bothering to whisper. "Tourmaline, I think Ghost is a phoenix—and phoenixes *don't die*. I mean, they do, but then they rise from the ashes! They're *reborn*." She shook her head as though trying to shake sense into her words. "What I'm trying to say is that's not a jewel; that's an *egg*."

Tourmaline shrugged out of Olivia's hug. "What? What's a phoenix?"

For the first time since Olivia had known her, Violet looked confident. "Ghost never *really* died," Violet went on. "He just didn't have a chance to complete the phoenix cycle—birth, death by fire, then rebirth." She put a hand on Tourmaline's knee. "I bet he's a young phoenix. I bet this was his first time burning, and that's why he's always been so scared of fire. But with you by his side, Tourmaline, he was finally able to face the flame. Go on, take a look."

Tourmaline's face scrunched. She pressed a finger to the ruby. Immediately, her expression changed.

"There's a heartbeat," she breathed. She shook her head and looked up at Violet, her cheeks still tearstained but her eyes now luminous. "How did you know?"

Olivia, too, wanted to know where Violet had read about phoenixes. In all the stories Olivia had ever collected, she'd never heard of that tale. At the moment, however, there were more pressing matters than a book she'd missed.

"You need to hide him," Olivia instructed Tourmaline as they all scrambled to their feet. "Everyone saw Ghost. The Watch will come and take him away."

"Too late," Violet said, and Olivia whirled around just in time to see a giant man in platinum chain mail and a broadsword step off the stairs and onto the lawn. A handful of people wearing the white of Lumin City's Watch followed close behind him, forming a barrier between Grandmaster Toll and the scholars running to keep up. "They're already here."

The Watch had demanded to speak with Tourmaline, while Provost Malchain ordered Violet and Olivia to her study. Kessa, meanwhile, was outside, sitting in her father's narrowboat with Watchmen on either side making sure she did not leave.

Grandmaster Toll had been incensed when he arrived. "NECROMANCY!" he'd shouted as he reached the girls on the lawn. "MIND CONTROL! *THIS* IS WHAT YOU TEACH YOUR STUDENTS, AQUILA? *THIS* IS THE GREAT UNIFYING ACADEMY?"

"Collect yourself, Donte," Provost Malchain had said as she arrived. "All is well."

"WELL?!" Toll's rage seemed to momentarily render him speechless, but he quickly found his breath. "YOUR APPRENTICES ALMOST BURNED DOWN A HISTORICAL LANDMARK!"

"But we didn't, Daddy," Kessa had protested, slipping past the Watch to stand next to her father. Though she was the tallest of all the apprentices, she only reached her father's elbow. "I played the Luring Horn to stop—"

"Enough." The look on the man's face was one that would haunt Olivia for a long time. "We will be discussing your future, young lady, right after the provost and I discuss the future of the academy."

The future of the academy. Olivia's future. If the academy shuttered, the Watch would take Olivia. Her belongings would be confiscated, and maybe this time the Watch *would* find the secret hidden in *The Account of Olivia the Observant*. Laurel and Nan would be exiles forever. And the actual trapper, whoever—whatever—they may be, would still be out there, consuming magic.

Consuming unicorns.

Now, Olivia sat outside Malchain's office, her hands cold yet sweaty. Violet was in there currently being interrogated by the provost, but Olivia hoped it wouldn't be for much longer. After all, none of this was Violet's fault. She didn't have magic.

The halls of the academy were eerily quiet. Usually at noon, they teemed with hungry apprentices making their way to the Banquet Hall, but once the scholars had been sure it was safe to reenter the still-smoking castle, they had directed everyone to the throne room. Everyone, that is, except for Olivia, Violet, Tourmaline, and Kessa.

"Olivia!"

Olivia started and looked at the study, expecting to see Violet exiting and the provost beckoning her inside. But the door was still closed and the hall remained empty.

"Tourmaline?" Olivia asked the air.

"I need to show you something," her friend whispered. Olivia felt a hand slide into hers, and then the unnoticeable Gemmer pulled her in the direction of the astronomy tower.

"Hang on," Olivia protested. "Malchain said I needed to—"

"There's no time," Tourmaline said, and tugged harder. "Toll is petitioning the Prime Minister to shut down the academy as soon as possible. Like, as in *today*."

"What?" Olivia almost tripped on the steps. "But the trial! We're supposed to have a chance to prove ourselves!"

"Well," Tourmaline said, voice dry as twigs, "Toll seems to think that recent events negate the need of a trial. They're interrogating Aunt Rubi right now."

"Did you tell him that Ghost was never really dead?" Olivia asked. "That you're *not* a resurrectionist?"

"Obviously," Tourmaline said, "but Kessa's father has only ever studied how to make a sword pointier. He doesn't know the first thing about Gemming! So how *in* earth, *under* earth, and *below* earth could he even begin to understand fossils?" Her voice cracked with frustration. "Aunt Rubi tried to explain, but when he realized that Aunt Rubi already knew about Ghost and hadn't reported his existence to the Grand Council, he flew into an inferno. Even if the academy does stay open, I don't think Aunt Rubi or I will be allowed to stay. Which is why I wanted to show you this now."

They had reached the landing, and just like last night, Tourmaline opened the door and Olivia stepped out of the marble pillar and into the middle of the tower room. All remnants of the P.O.U.F. party had been cleared away, and the room was empty except for Ravine's crystal balls, which circled the perimeter like numbers on a clock.

The grip around Olivia's hand lessened, and Olivia noticed Tourmaline standing next to her. A new ruby pendant had been added to the collection around her neck, and unlike the other jeweled necklaces, this one didn't sparkle. It glowed, a spark waiting to be kindled again. Tourmaline fiddled with it as she hurried to the south-facing windows.

"Olivia," she said. "The candle—*it worked*."

Olivia's breath caught. "Ghost remembered the Devourer?"

Tourmaline stopped in front of the wide windows overlooking the east bank. "I think so. Right before Ghost swallowed the flame, he, I don't know"—she waved her hand, as though looking to pluck the right word—"*pressed* a memory into me."

"Pressed?"

She nodded. "Like a footprint in sand. The outline is clear, but the details are fuzzy. But I remembered flying—the sun in my eyes, hot air beneath my wings—and below was a river valley. *This* river valley, except it looked different." Tourmaline swept her hand toward the east bank, where the buildings and houses of Alloy Alley and Jewel Way hugged the river's edge. "There was no Lumin City and"—Tourmaline paused, taking a deep breath—"there was no island. Where we are standing now was a huge, giant pit."

Olivia's heart skipped. "A pit, you mean, like a sinkhole?"

"Yes." Tourmaline nodded. "Right in the middle of the river. I flew closer—I mean, Ghost flew closer—and as he did, he saw humans charge the water, brandishing swords, shovels, and needles, and on the banks, hidden by trees, were people in togas and stolas manning catapults filled with molten rock."

"And then?"

"Then the memory ended," Tourmaline said. She frowned. "Wait. Before Ghost swallowed the candle's flame, there was fear. So much fear, it erased everything else."

Half thoughts swarmed Olivia, each one stinging, demanding to be noticed.

Bottomless pits in the middle of rivers. Holes in mountains. A thousand years ago.

She shivered. It sounded like a story. One she knew by heart.

Time before memory, something hungry stalked the land . . . it began to gnaw on the dark edges of forests, slurp molten gold . . .

Olivia leaned out the window of the tower and stared over the hedge at the gray waters rushing by the academy. She wondered what lay beneath the river, what had been in that pit, and if it was still there. But that was ridiculous, of course, because she knew what lay under the castle. She and Violet and Tourmaline and Kessa had all seen the catacombs for themselves. Seen the intricately carved pillars, the archways, and the sealed door—

The sealed door.

The sealed door with a snake eating its own tail.

If Anders stands there; gates beware.

Olivia gripped her friend's arm. "Tourmaline," her friend's

name rasped against her suddenly dry mouth. "The sealed door in the catacombs, the one with the serpent on it, where is it?"

"Oh, um . . ." Tourmaline paused, calculating angles and soil depth. "There," she said finally, pointing east, "where sun first hits the river in the morning."

At last, the missing thread. The tapestry was complete.

Olivia whirled around. "Tourmaline, this *isn't* an astronomy tower. It's a *watch* tower! The Devourer is sealed in the ground below us!"

"What?" Tourmaline shook her head so hard her bushy ponytail flicked her nose. "No, the Devourer followed the Rider into the sun."

"*'And drowned in sun's fire,'*" Olivia quoted, gesturing at the river, where late afternoon light played across its surface. "*Drowned*. They didn't gallop into the sky, they crossed the blue expanse of the Rhona and dove into the sun's reflection. Anders and his court must have sealed the Devourer into its own den so it could not escape. They even placed the weight of an entire island on its door! Then King Anders built his first castle here so that Arden could always stand guard!"

"But the door is still sealed," Tourmaline said. "If it *is* the Devourer, it can't get out. It can't be what's hunting the unicorns *now*."

Olivia shook her head. "No—the carving tells us everything we need to know. The Devourer is a kind of serpent, and snakes lay eggs. Its eggs could be all over Arden—*waking now that unicorns have returned.*" She whirled away from the window. "We have to tell the provost!"

But as Olivia stepped toward the door, blue light lit the room as a lightning bolt struck the tower. The atmosphere sizzled, and then a polished accent boomed across the island:

PRIME MINISTER NADIA MARTINSON, SPEAKING FROM THE SEASHELL PALACE ON THE SUNRISE ISLES:

I, IN CONJUNCTION WITH THE GRAND COUNCIL OF ARDEN AND IN LIGHT OF RECENT EVENTS, HAVE AGREED TO THE FOLLOWING REVISION IN THE ACADEMY'S CHARTER.

HENCEFORTH, THE SENTENCE THAT ONCE READ, "THE UNICORN ACADEMY SHALL UNDERGO A TRIAL ONE YEAR FROM THE DAY ON WHICH IT BEGAN," SHALL NOW SAY, "THE UNICORN ACADEMY SHALL UNDERGO A TRIAL SIX WEEKS AND ONE NIGHT FROM THE DAY ON WHICH IT BEGAN."

Olivia's heart compressed like a fan. Six weeks and one night meant—

THE TRIAL BEGINS TOMORROW AT DAWN. THE NAME OF THE APPRENTICE HAS BEEN DRAWN. YOUR CHAMPION IS . . .

In the same way Olivia knew the Spinner princess would open the door for the jealous queen after the seven Tillers warned her not to—

In the same way she knew a youngest sister's promise to her older sister would never be kept—

Olivia knew what would happen next. Still, her heart crumpled when the name echoed through the halls.

. . . VIOLET LEE.

CHAPTER THIRTY-TWO

Violet, however, was nowhere to be found.

In the few minutes it took for Olivia and Tourmaline to run down the tower stairs, chaos had uprooted the school. Tillers hurried to the cellars to gather their jars of pickled vegetables while Forgers marched to the smithy to collect their tools. A group of Spinners that included Paisley walked by with traveling looms in their arms. Sam followed, his pockets suspiciously lumpy.

Olivia grabbed his arm. "Have you seen Violet?"

"Nope," Sam said, shrugging off her hold. "The scholars are looking for her, but she wasn't in the throne room."

"She was with the provost," Olivia said, just as the provost hurried down the hall, head bowed in conversation with Dean Hatchett. Olivia wondered if she shouldn't follow and tell the provost what she and Tourmaline had pieced together, but she was pulled from her thoughts as Sam said something.

"What was that?"

"I said, you don't want your Messaging Threads, do you?" Sam asked. "Dean Garmont said we should take our work from the classroom, and since you didn't take yours . . ."

"Why would he want us to pack up?" Olivia demanded. "Violet will pass the test!"

"Sure," Sam said, already walking toward a group of Tillers who looked eager to trade pots of dye for whatever Spinnery Sam might have up his sleeves.

Anguished, Olivia turned to Tourmaline. "No one believes in Violet!"

Tourmaline looked uncomfortable, but before she could say anything, Dean Ravine appeared. "Follow me, Tourmaline. Now." Ravine whisked Tourmaline away, leaving Olivia alone in the commotion.

Olivia tapped thumb and forefinger together, missing the comfort of her thimble. If she were still a lackie and had become the champion of the academy with only hours left until the trial, she knew *she* would be in the library. But Violet was more practical than that.

Olivia headed for the kitchens.

Cupboard drawers slammed as Olivia entered the first of the academy's many cellars. There, on the ladder, with a bulging pack on her back and pulling down a clay jar, stood Violet.

"Running away?" Olivia asked.

Startled, Violet dropped the jar, and it hit the ground with a dull *clank*. "Oh, it's just you," she said when she saw Olivia. "Would you believe me if I said no?"

"Nope," Olivia said, scooping down to pick up the jar. A thin crack spidered down its side. "But how could you leave us?"

"It's for the best," Violet said, stepping off the ladder. "If I drop out, then I'm no longer a student! They can find someone else to be the champion."

Olivia shook her head. "I don't think it works that way. If you leave now, then the academy fails. And if the academy fails, what will fail next? Remember what Provost Malchain said the first day? If we can't figure out a way to more than just coexist, then we risk more misunderstanding, more fighting. And Arden can't afford that, not now that the Devourer is back!"

"Or so you think," Violet said. "You don't have proof, and I don't have magic! I can't do anything! And I can't go home without m—" She broke off as Olivia ran her thumb over the clay jar. And as she did, Olivia prodded the clay to remember what it had been like to be damp and malleable. The fracture closed.

"There," Olivia said, handing the jar to her.

"Olivia." Violet looked suddenly pale. "Did you just—but you're not a—?" Her eyes widened. "The thimble! I thought *Kessa* cursed it, but it was you, wasn't it? You're Spinning and

Forging and Gemming—oh." She looked at Olivia, horrified. "*You're* the unicorn trapper. *You have the unicorn's horn.*"

"I have the horn," Olivia said, "but I'm not the trapper. I promise! But you see—I do have proof the Devourer is back. And Tourmaline and I figured out—"

"Show me," Violet interrupted. "If you have the horn, show me."

Olivia hesitated, but then, didn't Violet deserve her trust? Violet had always trusted her, and look what Olivia had done with that. "If you promise to stay and try to pass the test," Olivia said slowly, "I will."

Violet nodded. Olivia opened her coin purse and tugged out *The Account of Olivia the Observant: Apprentice to Tiller Master Laurel Hayes*. With her bronze pen, Olivia sketched in the missing apostrophe. The pages fused, and then the hollow formed. Just as before, the unicorn ivory gleamed.

Carefully, Olivia handed the book to Violet and studied her friend's expression. But it was impossible to tell what Violet was thinking. Guilt squirmed through Olivia as she suddenly saw how it must all look to her friend. Olivia, also lacking magic, had stolen magic and excelled in class, all while letting her friend flounder.

"You've had this," Violet said slowly. "You've had it the entire time."

"Yes." Olivia nodded, needing to explain. "So you see—I *can't* be the trapper! I've been here, in the academy, even as more unicorns have disappeared. I swear to you, Violet, I am not the trapper! And I'm so sorry for not telling you sooner. But"—Olivia's words gathered speed as she raced toward the end of her apology—"we have the rest of tonight *and* the unicorn's horn to wake your magic before dawn. We can do this, Violet! *You* can do it!"

"And then?" Violet's lip quivered.

Before Olivia could answer her question—could explain how they would heal the unicorn as soon as Laurel and Nan had cultivated enough Ambrosia—a paper bird darted through the cellar and zoomed toward them. Olivia expected it to swoop toward Violet, but instead the provost's message pecked Olivia's cheek, unfolded itself, and floated down into Olivia's outstretched palm.

Report to my office upon receipt.
(That means now.)

"We need to go," Olivia said, taking the closed book back from Violet and slipping it into her kit. "Come on—we can go to the provost together."

"No thanks," Violet said, stepping up to place the mended jar back on the shelf. "I've spent enough time with her today, and I need every minute between now and dawn. I'll meet you in the library?"

Olivia smiled, relieved. Violet had forgiven her. Violet would stay.

"The Unicorn Wing," she agreed. "There's no books, so

no one is ever in there." Then she sprinted out of the cellar, leaving Violet behind. But it was the last time, she vowed to herself, that she would.

Apprentices still milled in the corridors, though fewer than before, and she guessed most were in their rooms, packing their trunks. She ran through the empty grand foyer, nodding her head in the direction of King Anders's statue, a quiet thanks for guarding them all this time. She wondered if Tourmaline had managed to convince Ravine of their theory. She passed under the jeweled chandelier, which had begun to glow now that night had fallen, and up the stairs.

As Olivia passed the mirror on the first landing, she thought she heard someone whisper her name. But when she turned, no one was behind her. She climbed on until she reached the third floor and then took a left at the suit of armor.

"*Olivia!*"

Olivia stopped. This time, there was no questioning it. She had heard her name—and she recognized the voice.

"Laurel?" Olivia looked around, but all she could see in the hall was a grandfather's clock a few yards away and the suit of armor next to her. She eyed the armor suspiciously, wondering if she should check in the visor, but then she noticed something off with her reflection in the breastplate. The face was similar to her own, but the hair was different. Instead of braids, her hair was pulled into a bun, and the color was off—a murky brown. But even with her blonde hair dipped in walnut juice, Olivia recognized her sister.

"Laurel!" Olivia whispered. "How are you doing this?"

"Kessa," Laurel said, her voice tinny and metallic. Olivia peered closer. Sure enough, behind Laurel's shoulder, she could make out Kessa's face in the blue ripple of steel. "She calls it Reflection Hopping. The Watch has a bunch of spycraft on board."

Olivia stared. "How are you with Kessa?"

"The Watch caught her last night," Kessa said, her features coming into focus as she leaned forward and Laurel shifted to the side. "They were already on the way to the school when they saw Ghost. Laurel's on the boat with me. The Watchmen got tired of babysitting and left me in charge for a few minutes while they stretch. And now she's asking me to let her go."

"But"—the Forger frowned—"Olivia, is this really your sister? The guards said they found her in the mountains because they sensed Metal Telepathy nearby, but—your sister is a Tiller. And you're a Spinner, so . . ." Her frown deepened. "How can you two have performed Metal Telepathy?"

"Laurel," Olivia said, "did you find *it*?" From the stairs below, she could hear students climbing toward them.

Laurel's reflection nodded. "Exactly where you said the Ambrosia would be—in the lightning-struck oak."

Olivia grinned. "It's her!" she confirmed to Kessa. "Get her out of there and meet me by the holly bush!"

The apprentices rounded the corner, and Olivia quickly stepped forward, hiding the armor from view. The group of

Tillers looked curiously at her as Olivia breathed on the breastplate and pretended to polish it with her sleeve, but they didn't stop to ask. By the time they were gone, the reflections of Kessa and Laurel had vanished.

Olivia whirled around, ready to go back the way she came. The provost would forgive her lateness. Because when Olivia returned, it would be with the unicorn, her horn whole, her memory mended, and the Hayes family name cleared.

Then the unicorn could help Violet find her guild, and in the morning, when every grandmaster in Arden had gathered in the throne room, they could prove once and for all why the Unicorn Academy of Artistical and Magical Learning should still stand.

Then they could all—apprentice, journeyman, master, grandmaster, and unicorn, turn their attention to other matters. Matters like the holes perforating the Mender's map, making Arden look like a sieve. A chewed crust. A world on the verge of crumbling.

And then, it did.

The earth heaved.

Olivia's stomach dropped as the ground threw her—and the grandfather clock, suits of armor, and sconces—into the air. Wood cracked. Tapestries ripped. Walls split.

Earthquake.

Olivia sprawled onto the floorboards, hitting her chin and mashing her teeth together. A plaster wyvern broke loose from the molding and smashed next to her ear, coating the floor in a thousand sharp pieces.

Half crawling, half running, Olivia made her way to the stairway, where she saw other apprentices. A Forger boy held a shield over a Tiller girl, protecting her from debris as she shoved splinters back into support beams. The chandeliers that remained on their hooks swung wildly, mixing color and shadow into the confusion.

Olivia breathed in and almost gagged as a stench permeated the stairs—the smell of decay, of rot, of death. As she staggered down the steps, she wondered how much longer till she reached the great double doors and the safety of the lawn.

She would never know.

Because as Olivia reached the last step, she saw stars glittering above her. She gripped the banister, holding fast as she heard other apprentices stop behind her and scream.

The roof of Unicorn Academy was gone.

And not just the roof.

The grand foyer of Unicorn Academy no longer existed. Where there had once been a checkerboard floor and a statue of King Anders now lay a great pit.

"Go up!" Olivia croaked. "Go back!"

She heard her call repeated as the news spread across the

apprentices. She pressed back, angling her body away from the pit, where a gurgling wheeze emanated from the dark, a sound not unlike the wind playing between mountain peaks. But now Olivia recognized the sound for what it truly was: an inhalation.

In the fractured light, Olivia glimpsed something pink in the belly of the school.

She'd always thought of pink as a happy color, the color of sunsets, petals, and beribboned slippers. But this pink was the color of the inside of a cheek, and just as wet and glistening.

As Olivia watched, the pinkness undulated and the Devourer surfaced.

CHAPTER THIRTY-THREE

Olivia had been wrong.

The Devourer wasn't a snake.

It was a worm.

A worm as long as the Rhona, with the girth of a tower and a mouth instead of a face. A mouth completely encircled by rows of gnashing teeth. It was appetite made flesh, and nothing would ever fill it. But that didn't mean it wouldn't try.

The Devourer surged upward, its trench-sized grooves compressing and expanding as it slid along its own trail of mucus and toward Olivia.

"GET AWAY FROM MY STUDENTS!"

Arms shoved Olivia back, and she stumbled into the apprentice behind her, a Forger with ash-blond hair. He gripped Olivia and tugged her to the steps as Dean Garmont sailed by, gripping a diamond-shaped kite. He lay stomach flat against the fabric, his hands holding on to ribbon reins that pulled the kite into loops above the worm's head. As he did, Olivia saw the thinnest thread of silver spiraling from his sleeve, his embroidered spider trying to weave a web to catch the beast.

But cobwebs don't catch worms.

The Devourer inhaled, and the kite spun downward into its waiting mouth. Before Olivia could scream, the embroidered spider threw one last thread at a remaining pillar. It caught, yanking Dean Garmont off the kite and swinging him to the mezzanine.

"SIDE DOORS," he bellowed, even as he pulled out a cord from a curtain and began to whirl it around his head. "GET TO THE DOCK!"

Olivia ran, her feet pounding the stairs as she heard the whistle of spears arcing toward the worm and a rattle of metal. Dean Hatchett appeared on the other side of the twin stairs, directing the suits of armor toward the pit. Olivia glanced back and saw a spear sink into the worm's skin, but then it clattered away, its steel tip suddenly corroded.

Olivia almost vomited. The slime didn't just help the Devourer move. It was acidic—it began to digest whatever it touched before the Devourer's mouth had even approached.

She did not look back again.

Instead, Olivia followed the stampede of apprentices up the stairs, through the hall, and back down again, racing for the side door that would dump them out of the east wing. The floors continued to jump and shake, mirroring the undulations of the Devourer as it squirmed from its burrow.

But *how* had it escaped?

Who had unsealed the door?

Tourmaline couldn't have, even if she'd wanted to, or she would have opened the door that first night in the catacombs. Had it been Ravine, then? Had the talented academic with little regard for rules listened to Tourmaline and gone to look herself?

Ahead, a student screamed as a sconce fell off the wall. A column shuddered, and Olivia saw two figures near the exit, their hands splayed across the walls to make sure the doorway held as the apprentices streamed through.

Tourmaline and Ravine.

Their faces shone with effort, and though both were shorter than most of the apprentices running by, Olivia thought they had never looked so tall. If they were *here*, then neither Tourmaline nor Ravine could be responsible for releasing the Devourer. But then—

"Hurry," Ravine grunted. "We can't hold the castle forever!"

Olivia pounded across the threshold and crunched down onto the gravel path. Ahead of her, apprentices ran toward the dock, where boats from Lumin City were already speeding toward them.

For the second time that day, the capital's bells rang in warning.

If Olivia had gone directly to the provost instead of conversing with Kessa's and Laurel's reflections, could she have prevented the Devourer's release? All her questions and their answers did not matter now, though. Because either way, Olivia knew what she had to do next.

While the rest of the apprentices and scholars ran for the dock, Olivia turned in the direction that would bring her past the marble steps and toward the woods. She'd just left the steps as a great boom echoed and the front wall crumbled.

With a sickening *slurp*, the Devourer slid, segment by rippling segment, out of the academy, its pitlike mouth never closing as it sucked in stone and brick and pillars even while its skin burned away the marble of the academy staircase.

Pinpricks of fire exploded across Olivia's skin as acid flicked off the worm's body. Still, she kept running, darting out of the way of the topiaries that now charged the invader. The leafy guardians attacked with all their might, all their roots, and all their thorns. Rosario's claws punctured pink flesh, but they were nothing to the vastness of the maggot. They did nothing to slow the Devourer as it continued to spill out of the walls and writhe toward the Unkempt Woods.

Toward the holly bush.

Toward the sleeping unicorn.

Olivia ran faster. Behind her, she could hear the shout of the scholars still giving chase to the worm. Spears and arrows and axes whistled, but weapons were useless against a tornado.

The worm stretched, covering fifty of Olivia's strides in a single undulation. Before Olivia had even passed the pavilion that marked the beginning of the wild meadow, the Devourer had reached the holly bush—and the two girls standing bravely before it.

The first stood facing the burning berries, her hands rustling the leaves as she pleaded with the bush to reveal the entrance. The second stood tall and straight, but before the monster, Kessa looked as tall as a toothpick. With her flutes taken away, she had only a thin rapier to defend them.

The Devourer bore down, insatiable. Unstoppable.

Nothing *could* stop it, except . . .

"Laurel!" Olivia shouted as she yanked Tourmaline's prism earring from her pocket and with her other hand unhooked her sling. She loaded the crystal, then swung, sending the earring soaring across the meadow and into Laurel's waiting hand.

Holding the prism to her eye, Laurel ran forward and disappeared into the berry's glow.

One long second passed. Then another. Then—

The unicorn burst out of the holly. She reared, broken

horn outlined by the rising moon, hooves reaching for the stars.

Nothing was impossible for a unicorn.

But.

The unicorn's bray as it lashed out into the night sounded as jagged as her horn. She was as erratic as lightning and willing to strike tree or man or mountain, not caring which one.

The unicorn was lost unto herself.

Betwixt.

When her hooves slammed on the ground, the unicorn bucked and twisted, more beast than star.

Olivia needed the horn.

It was time to mend what she had rent.

Fumbling in her kit, her fingers touched the *Account* just as the worm exhaled again. Its rancid breath misted the island. The stench made Olivia's eyes water, and her vision blurred. She wiped tears away. She needed to see.

Horn and unicorn *must* be reunited. With the dirt coating her finger, Olivia smudged an apostrophe onto the page. The hollow appeared . . .

. . . and only the hollow.

The unicorn's horn was gone.

The last time Olivia had seen the horn's radiance, it had been in the pages of the book she'd handed to Violet. Then the provost's messenger had tapped her on the cheek. Olivia hadn't seen the horn again, because Violet had returned the book closed . . . and empty.

Now Olivia had the answers to the *who* and the *how*: somehow, Violet had manipulated the shard of unicorn ivory to unseal the door.

But Olivia didn't know the *why*.

She only knew her heart was broken—and when Grandmaster Toll's howl pierced the night, she knew hers wasn't the only heart about to break.

Kessa threw herself in front of the wild unicorn, startling the mare into a frantic gallop. The unicorn disappeared into the Unkempt Woods—safe, for now. But now Kessa stood directly in the worm's path.

The Devourer sucked in.

And Kessa, rapier still held high, vanished into its great maw.

CHAPTER THIRTY-FOUR

"Kessa!"

Donte Toll—Forger Grandmaster of Lumin City, Commander of the Watch, Secretary of Education, and Father of Kessa—streaked past Olivia and attacked the worm.

His broadsword swung. As the blade arced across the night, it glowed red as though it had just been pulled from a forge. It thinned, lengthening until it was no longer sword-shaped, but a long, thin cord of molten metal that whipped toward the worm and struck—

       setae

            epidermis

      vessels

            intestines

          —cleaving the Devourer

                in

                  two.

Green blood sprayed, but the grandmaster charged forward

and reached into the cavity of the nearest half, pulling his daughter free.

Even from yards away, Olivia could see Kessa was too still.

She lay in her father's arms while Donte Toll curved over her like a question mark. Before despair could drag Olivia to her knees, she saw Laurel limp toward the grandmaster. Her sister gently pulled Kessa's head toward her and lifted the vial of Ambrosia to her lips.

As Olivia drew near, Kessa groaned.

A strangled cry burst from Grandmaster Toll, and his shoulders heaved as he hugged his daughter tight.

"She'll be fine," Laurel told the grandmaster. "But she still needs to go to Healer Hall and have others examine her." Grandmaster Toll did not need to be told twice. Without ever putting Kessa down, he jumped to his feet and ran toward the dock.

"Laurel," Olivia said, staring down at her sister, "what about you?" Though it was hard to make out in the low light of the holly's embers, she could see a dark stain spreading out from under Laurel's leg. "Is there any Ambrosia left?"

Laurel grimaced. "No, but you're a Spinner—stitch me up."

"I can't." The admission almost made Olivia choke. "The horn, Laurel—I don't have it! And without the horn . . . I don't have any magic."

She was lacking, again.

In the dark, Olivia could hear the nearing shouts of the scholars as they finally reached the worm. Olivia began to shout, "HERE! OVER HERE! WE NEED HELP—!"

"No," Laurel wheezed out. "They'll arrest me!"

"But if you don't get help," Olivia said, "it won't matter if you're free. You'll be dead." Olivia knelt beside her sister on the slick grass, and her hand found Laurel's. She grasped her sister tight. "I promise, I won't leave you again."

Laurel didn't say anything, but Olivia felt her fingers squeeze back and press the prism earring back into her palm.

Olivia shouted again, "HELP!"

But the scholars did not stop. Instead, they kept running, their weapons up as they advanced on the worm's halves.

In the glowing light, she saw Dean Barry streak by.

"MOVE!" Barry shouted, whirling an ebony staff above her head as though she were about to strike—but strike what? The Devourer had been defeated.

Then, in Olivia's periphery, something twitched.

The worm stirred.

Both halves.

"Worms," Laurel said, voice faint, "they regenerate!" Even before Laurel finished speaking, a squishy *pop* sounded as one half of the worm began to grow teeth in its newly formed mouth. But before it could fully form, the other half swayed, opened its mouth, and inhaled.

Olivia looked away from the gruesome sight. It was just as

the carved archway had tried to warn them: the Devourer, eating itself.

The scholars of the Unicorn Academy moved as one upon the gorging annelid.

"We have to get you out of here!" Olivia said, trying to tug Laurel up, but Laurel sagged back onto the ground. Sliding off a hair ribbon, Olivia wrapped it around Laurel's gash in a makeshift tourniquet. Then she stood, half of her hair whipping into her eyes as she faced the worm, sling at the ready. The worm, however, didn't pay attention to her—nor did it pay attention to the scholars and their attack.

Every spear Dean Hatchett threw rusted as soon as it brushed the worm's slime.

The ropes Dean Garmont tossed at the creature did not rust, but they lacked grip, and the worm simply slid out.

The ivy Dean Barry directed hooked tiny roots into its skin, but the plant lacked weight. The Devourer surged forward, unbothered.

The rocks Dean Ravine hurled at its flank held weight, but they were rigid, and shattered into pebbles as the worm's segments squeezed tight.

There was no end to the cycle. No victory.

There was only hunger.

The Devourer continued toward the Unkempt Woods, its entire body a giant tongue anticipating its first true meal in a thousand years.

Unicorn blood. Unicorn magic.

It would not be stopped.

It *could* not be stopped, unless . . .

"Olivia," Laurel croaked. *"Pure magic."*

Tears streamed down Olivia's cheeks and she shook her head. "I don't have the horn," she repeated. At last, Olivia had made a mess even Laurel could not fix.

Her sister jabbed her in the ribs. "I'm not talking about the horn. I'm talking about you. You said only pure magic can break pure magic. Olivia . . . *you* broke the unicorn's horn. That magic, it isn't the unicorn's—it's yours. And it *always* has been!"

Olivia shook her head. "That's not possible. Anders's First Principle of—"

"I don't care," Laurel said. "You've *always* been impossible! You've *never* followed the rules. *Don't start following them now.*"

Screams. Cracking wood. Despair scraped through Olivia, hollowing her out until she felt as empty as the void the unicorn had rescued her from. Olivia pressed her hand to her heart, where she could feel the raised threads of the embroidered unicorn push against her palm. The academy still stood, which meant she was still its student—and still a unicorn guardian.

"I'll try," Olivia whispered, but Laurel didn't answer; she'd passed out. Olivia was on her own.

With a hard yank, she snapped the gold-chain necklace

Kessa had given her the night before. The seashell charm tumbled into the grass, but Olivia let it fall, focusing instead on the links in her hand. Each gold link was independent, whole unto itself but they preferred to be connected to each other. Gold was a soft metal, and Olivia could feel that it didn't mind if she wanted to add something to it.

Olivia Forged.

Taking Tourmaline's prism earring, she placed it beside the warmed and welcoming gold. Lightly, she began to wrap the chain around the prism, to remind the rock that stone and metal were siblings, each born in the core of the earth. Once, perhaps, they had even swum next to each other, no definition between them.

The crystal grew hot but it fought the gold, wanting to hang on to its rainbows, loving how its current form caught the light. Olivia promised it could still catch things, and so the crystal relented.

Olivia Gemmed.

Next, she yanked out her remaining hair ribbon and let her hair spill across her back. The ribbon in her hand needed no persuasion. It did exactly as it was meant to do: hold tight to wayward things. The silk wrapped around the crystal and metal, gathering it into a long single thread of gold light.

Olivia Spun.

Trees fell, splitting against the earth, and Olivia fought to focus. There was one material left, but she had never Tilled—and she had tried and failed so many times before.

The thread sensed her doubt. It began to unravel.

"No," Olivia said, and lunged for a piece of ivy that had been flung from the tower. She wrapped the ivy around the thread, imploring it to speak to her.

Don't you want to protect your home? Olivia prodded.

Silence.

Her hands shook. She couldn't do it!

Whatever Laurel thought, without the horn, Olivia was nothing. *She was just a lackie.*

But even as Olivia thought the words, they didn't ring true. Olivia was telling herself an old story, and she had so many new stories to tell. When she'd last tried to Till, she'd stood in Constellation Range and asked the grass to speak to her. But maybe, the green was waiting for *her* to speak to *them*.

She'd collected so many stories, but she'd never shared her own.

Taking a deep breath, Olivia closed her eyes and let everything fall away. Holding the ivy to her lips, she whispered to it the tale of a girl who loved her family, but needed to find her own sunlight. And so, the girl left and built a home among stone and metal and thread, but she never forgot the green that had first nourished her roots. Her roots were strong, and it was only because they were so strong that she could wander and spread and grow until, maybe, one day, the whole world became her home.

Beneath her fingertips, she felt the waxy smoothness of the ivy's leaves and the tiny tickling of its root hairs. The ivy liked that story. It, too, liked to wander. It, too, liked to grow.

Olivia Tilled.

The thread of pure magic—the thread of stone's and metal's and green's and silk's potential—grew longer and longer as Olivia shaped it the same way a trellis guides a stem. Soon, it was no longer a *thread* of pure magic, but a *net* of pure magic. A net that was both hefty and strong, adhesive and flexible. A net that could trap the Devourer, except—

Olivia's fingers faltered.

The Devourer had been trapped before.

And it had escaped.

A net wasn't the answer. Trapping wasn't the answer.

The thread began to unspool, reverting back into what it had once been.

But Olivia wouldn't let it.

You are now a girl with a unicorn's capabilities, Laurel had told Olivia in her lush dreamscape. And Olivia knew unicorns changed things.

Olivia had changed . . .

. . . . so why couldn't the Devourer?

Olivia's fingers twisted and she changed the pattern.

Not a net, but a blanket.

Not a cage, but a cocoon.

Holding one end tight, Olivia cast the thread out into the

night. It glowed as it soared over the sweaty, battered scholars, and touched the worm.

The thread grew, spreading like ivy, protective as metal, strong as rock, and as gentle as silk. And woven through it all, the unicorn's quiet call to dream and to change. So that one day, one year, one century from now, the cocoon might open, and from it slip wetly folded wings and a new kind of creature, one that did not chew the seams of the world. A creature that would instead flutter from snowdrop to snowdrop, cultivating magic instead of consuming it.

The scholars stilled their desperate battle, and stood, awed, watching as with each wrap, the thread of pure magic compressed the worm, making it infinitesimally smaller, until—the same way an acorn holds a towering oak—the cocoon was no bigger than a coin. Bending down, Olivia picked up the shimmering jewel and set it in the center of a newly bloomed snowdrop. The petals arched together, sealing the worm away until it was ready to emerge, something whole and new.

Exhausted, Olivia sank onto the ground beside Laurel, whose breath was steady even if her face remained pale. Around them, Olivia was aware of people running—of shouts and exclamations, copper chimera wings clanging in the night sky, of alchemists and scholars and townspeople and grandmasters alike flooding the island—but Olivia sat still, holding her sister close.

A lion chimera spiraled downward. It landed a few feet away from the girls, then knelt. The woman seated astride his shoulders slid off. She wore a wreath of feathers, and a gold-embroidered unicorn shone from her left breast pocket. Pulling off indigo riding gloves, the woman held out her hand.

"Olivia Hayes," said Prime Minister Nadia Martinson of Arden, "it's about time we met."

CHAPTER THIRTY-FIVE

Olivia sat, rib cage tight, as she waited for the Prime Minister to speak.

For the last hour, Prime Minister Martinson had been silent, letting Olivia unspool all of the many secrets, questions, and worries she'd collected since the moment she'd confused a vial of *Cap of Curls* for *Cap of Mushroom*.

With her eyes focused on the maps pinned to the Prime Minister's silk pavilion and ignoring Provost Malchain's piercing stare as she stood behind the parliamentarian's chair, Olivia had carefully relayed how she'd come to find herself in a strange sinkhole in the wilds of Constellation Range. How then she'd enrolled in Unicorn Academy only to discover she could understand not just thread, but metal and stone and green. She shared the terrible realization of *how* she'd come by these abilities and how Laurel had helped her piece together the true cause behind the missing unicorns. She'd flushed as she relayed her hunch that had almost burned down the school and then faltered, barely able to breathe, as she spoke of Violet's betrayal and the release of the Devourer.

She shared everything, except the secret ingredient to Nan's Ambrosia. She was still a Hayes after all, and she would keep her family's secret safe. The Prime Minister might be able to protect her from the Grand Council, but she wouldn't be able to shield against Nan's disappointment. *Nan*. What would Nan—

"I believe you."

Olivia's head snapped up to look at the Prime Minister. She was the same age as Nan, with wrinkles and white hair that fluffed out from under a wreath of copper chimera feathers. Gemglows hanging in macrame illuminated the large tent filled with patterned rugs, stacks of documents, and the Prime Minister's blue eyes.

Olivia's ribs remained tight. "You do?"

"Yes." The Prime Minister plucked a copper feather from her wreath and set it on a blank piece of paper on her desk. Immediately, the quill began to scratch across the surface, writing out words like *urgent* and *send squadron* and *destroy Wyrm clutch*. "Even if I hadn't seen you Spin pure magic with my own eyes, I would still believe you. There have been many anomalies in recent days, and I would be a poor leader if I chose to look away."

Anomalies like a living unicorn separated from her horn.

"My unicorn," Olivia said. "Has anyone found her?"

"Not yet," Malchain said, and it was the first time she'd spoken. Usually so prim, her bun was now a tangle of white hair and leaves. Even her beloved axes were still covered in grime. "I'll go ask," she said, already walking toward the pavilion's flap. "I need to know if they've found . . ." She trailed off, then cleared her throat. "Nadia, we'll talk soon, yes?"

The Prime Minister nodded, and Provost Malchain blew the woman a kiss before disappearing outside.

Olivia slumped in her chair. "What does it all mean?" she whispered. "How can I still manipulate magic without the unicorn's horn?"

And when, she wondered, but did not ask out loud, *would she ever fit in?*

"It means," the Prime Minister said, reaching across her desk and picking up the quill's most recent sheet, "that we need to learn more." Shaking it once to dry the ink, she handed it to Olivia. A quick glance told Olivia it was a permission slip asking Olivia's legal guardian to allow the Prime Minister to escort Olivia Gladiola Hayes to Prophecy's Keep.

"Prophecy's Keep?" Olivia asked.

The Prime Minister nodded. "The Keepers have sent word they are down to the last snarl of your yarn. It's time, I think, we know exactly why your fate is so tangled—for your sake as well as Arden's." She stood and gestured toward the exit. "Laurel is sixteen, yes? When she wakes, have her sign it, then please send her to me. I need to hear more about these so-called *thin* spots."

Dean Barry stood outside the pavilion waiting to escort Olivia across the lawn now dotted with purple and green tents. Calls still echoed through the dark as grown-ups lifted rubble and turned over rocks. With the exception of Olivia (and perhaps Violet) all of the other apprentices had made it safely to Lumin City. Olivia wondered when they would be able to return to the school. The academy itself looked as though someone had taken a giant bite from its center. The wings, however, still stood, more or less unmarred. It was still beautiful, even in this state, and Olivia hoped the Gemmer masons would be able to repair it to its full glory.

Dean Barry led her to a tent made of quilted leaves. Inside, Olivia found Laurel curled up like a fiddlehead fern. Someone had combed out her hair and woven it into two yellow braids, making her look more like the young girl Olivia remembered from their childhood on the edge of the Endless.

"She'll be fine," Dean Barry assured as she tucked a blanket under Laurel's toes. "When the holly hedge opened, a few bits of the soporific plants we used to keep the unicorn asleep got into her wound. I'm not sure when she'll wake. It could be in ten minutes; it could be ten days. Pillow?"

Olivia nodded and took the pillow the dean offered. But

even when Holly left, Olivia remained standing, unable to relax.

"Laurel, please wake up," she said. "I need to tell you something. I need to know what you think."

Laurel remained asleep.

Sitting on the edge of Laurel's pallet, Olivia rested her head in her hands, trying to sort through her thoughts. Trying to make sense of the last few hours. But the only thing she could concentrate on was an unwanted story that had slithered into her mind as she'd spoken to the Prime Minister.

A story that said Olivia was missing something.

A story that said Olivia was wrong.

"Laurel," she said, speaking to the quiet of her sister's tent. "Anders sealed the Devourer away under the island, behind the underground door. But the carving on the door wasn't of a worm. It was a snake."

She rested her chin in her hand, and looked at her sister, knowing the words Laurel would have said if she were awake. *How many world-eating monsters could Arden possibly hold? Of course the worm is the Devourer.*

"But," Olivia said to the air. "In the legends, there's only ever *one* Devourer mentioned. I know I said eggs, but what if I'm wrong? And a worm doesn't *exactly* fit the vague description all the historians agree on. You know, 'One heart, many heads.' Technically, worms had *many* hearts and only *one* head."

Olivia's own head hurt. If only there had been *time* to sort through it all, to *think*. But Violet had gone and stolen the unicorn's horn. She'd opened the stone door, looking for a place she could hide away from the pressure of being the academy's champion. She'd released the worm. And then—

Tears spilled down Olivia's cheeks.

No matter what had happened, the Violet she'd known was no more. It wasn't impossible for Violet to have escaped the worm. After all, she had the unicorn's horn, and where there were unicorns, there was always hope. But the Violet Olivia had thought she'd known, the one she'd believed was her best friend, never would have stolen the unicorn's horn in the first place.

Giving in to her grief, Olivia curled next to Laurel. Kicking off one boot, she let it fall to the ground. She tried to do the same with the other, but the lace was knotted too tightly. Stretching in the dark, Olivia reached for the bootlace. She paused.

The material beneath her fingers was strange. The fibers of the bootlace didn't feel like plant or hair, but something else entirely. She hadn't noticed before, but then again, she'd never spun four magics before, either, until just this night. Curious, she rubbed the bootlace between her fingers. She sensed the lace's dissatisfaction. It did not like the new boot it held. It did not like that the other lace did not match. It did not like this world.

This. World.

Olivia jerked back, almost rolling off the pallet. Her heart thudded. This lace—it was *Violet's* lace! The one she'd exchanged to help Violet dry out her boots.

But what did it mean?

Fingers shaking, Olivia tugged at the bootlace again. *The magic is in the material,* the Mender had told her mere weeks and hundreds of magic lessons ago. *Listen.*

So, Olivia did.

Violet's shoes pounded against hot pavement as she sprinted up the hill to the castle. Its single redbrick tower soared above gardens, casting much needed shade on the nearby picnickers sprawled on the grass. Violet bounded up the stone steps and pulled the ivy-covered door open. As she slipped inside, her lace snagged on the wood sill, undoing its bow.

The lace dragged behind Violet, bumping over flagstones, as she hurried by large groups of sneakers huddled around a pair of polished leather shoes. Violet's feet knew this place well, and they did not hesitate as they navigated treasure-filled antechambers and uneven stairs. They only slowed as they left the stone floors of the castle proper and stepped onto the worn wood floors of Gallery 17.

The gallery was crowded today, people milling about as

they took in the tapestries—seven in all. Grand, ancient things, stretching up to the ceiling and wrapping the room in silk, gold, and blood.

So. Much. Blood.

Blood dripped from a unicorn's flank while soldiers in a river attacked it with spears and dogs.

Blood coated the muzzle of a dog as a unicorn bucked, trying to defend itself from hunters carrying spears, swords, axes, knives and horns.

Blood stained the hide of a unicorn, caught and collared in a garden.

But today, Violet did not study the Unicorn Tapestries. Instead, her feet shuffled to a side door marked with a small brass plate that proclaimed:

DR. AURORE LEE
CURATOR OF MYTHICAL ANTIQUITIES
THE CLOISTERS
NEW YORK CITY'S METROPOLITAN MUSEUM OF ART

Violet pushed the door open.

No one was inside. Walking in, she plopped into a chair in front of a large wooden desk with several heavy drawers. She sighed and leaned back, pulling her feet up to rest on the single clear spot. The rest of the desktop was covered in a variety of knives and scissors, a gold key with no teeth, a carved alabaster goblet with a Post-it note that said *Windemere Box #4*, and a map . . . a map of mountains, forests, tiny castles and even tinier villages, and at the top, a unicorn's horn pointing north. Black triangles spangled the map, creating a shape that looked like an upside-down teacup or perhaps, to some, slightly like a whale. The legend above read WAYS BETWEEN WORLDS.

Off to the side sat a stack of stapled papers. At the top of each, in black ink, screamed the words:

THE MOST ANCIENT ORDER OF THE OUROBOROS

Beneath, impressed upon the center of the page, shone a glossy snake eating its tail, the order's motto marching around its curve: *Many Heads, One Heart.*

"Feet off my desk."

"Sorry, Mom." Violet's legs swung down as a woman with black hair and high heels strode into the office. Her shoes tapped across the floor, a counterpoint to the jangling bridle hanging from her arm. A bridle with a five-pointed star on it. A golden bridle.

The Golden Bridle.

The shoelace slid to the tent floor.

Violet's shoelace. Violet, who knew nothing about chimera

but knew *everything* about phoenixes. Violet who knew strange lyrics to familiar songs. Violet who had no magic—because she wasn't a Tiller, or a Forger, or a Gemmer, or a Spinner.

She was from another world.

A world that—judging by those bloody tapestries—had hunted their own unicorns to extinction. A world that was now looking for unicorns. *Hunting* unicorns.

Olivia's stomach heaved. And somehow, the hunters had possession of the Golden Bridle, and by now, perhaps they even had the horn of a living unicorn.

A horn that could open any door . . . or any *Way*.

The map of the Ways Between—it almost exactly matched the map above Olivia's bunk, where she'd so carefully traced Laurel's travels. It almost exactly matched the Mender's map of the unicorns' last known locations.

Almost matched, but not quite.

Because the map of the Ways Between held *more* marks than either of the other two.

Olivia pushed to her feet and fled out of the leafy tent. Night dew seeped through her socks as she raced back toward the Prime Minister's pavilion. But when she reached the tent, she saw the flap was open, the interior empty, and the lion chimera that had been lounging by its side, gone.

Olivia ran toward a group of grown-ups picking shattered glass from the ground.

"Excuse me," she said, voice hoarse. "Do you know where I can find Provost Malchain?"

A man paused in his cleaning. "Not sure, but she might be with the Tiller dean." He nodded in the direction of Barry's cottage. Olivia took off, but before she could make it more than a meter or two, something silver flashed in her periphery.

Battle-axes!

Turning, Olivia sprinted into the Unkempt Woods.

"Provost!" Olivia yelled as twigs slapped at her ankles. "Provost Malchain! I found something!" In the dark, it was hard to follow the woman's trail.

She heard a snap to her left and there, just beyond, silver flashed again. Darting under a branch, Olivia squeezed through a thicket to find a clearing.

And in the clearing, softly filtered moonlight fell onto the unicorn with a lightning-shaped horn.

Olivia stood still.

The last time Olivia had seen the unicorn, she'd been screaming fury, teeth bared and eyes clouded by immeasurable loss.

This time, however, as Olivia looked into the unicorn's sapphire eyes, she saw that they were clear and bright. And in them, Olivia saw herself reflected.

This time, the unicorn did not run away.

She simply waited.

Olivia, holding out her hands, bowed her head. "I'm sorry," she whispered. "I'm so, so sorry. I no longer have your horn. But," Olivia raised her head, "I promise—I *vow*—to do everything I can to restore it to you."

Olivia took a shuddery breath, trying to give definition to the emotions welling within. "I'm not sure what I am—a Spinner, Tiller, Gemmer, Forger, or Iackie—but I do know I would choose to be your guardian, if you let me."

The unicorn—with mane woven of moonlight and hooves hewed from diamond—turned her head and walked deeper into the forest.

A cry caught in Olivia's throat. The unicorn—she was leaving! But then the unicorn paused . . . and looked back at her.

An invitation. A guiding star.

A billowing hope, a bone-warming joy swept through Olivia. She took a step forward, then another, now certain of where she belonged.

Olivia followed the unicorn.

ACKNOWLEDGMENTS

Stories are wild, mysterious creatures and it takes a skilled expert to coax them onto the page, in this case, editor extraordinaire Sarah Shumway. Sarah, thank you so much for maintaining a steadfast belief in unicorns (and in me). Thank you, too, to the rest of the book wranglers at Bloomsbury: Ariana Abad, Erica Chan, Nicholas Church, Alona Fryman, Alexa Higbee, Oona Patrick, Laura Phillips, Hannah Rivera, and Lily Yengle. In particular, my deepest gratitude to Donna Mark and John Candell for the gorgeous designs and to the extremely talented Maxine Vee whose exquisite illustrations have brought Arden to life.

Thank you, too, to my agent Stephen Barbara for his patience and endless encouragement, as well as to the rest of the incredible Inkwell team: Sidney Boker, Lyndsey Blessing, Hannah Lehmkuhl, and Jessie Thorsted. I also need to thank Carmen Lewis for her dauntless enthusiasm for Arden.

To my herd—Sarah Jane Abott, Rhoda Belleza, Tara Sonin, Angela Velez, Catherine Waters, and Alexa Wejko. A huge hug to Melissa Albert, for reading several drafts of this book and loving them all. To the kids of Brookstone Park, past and present, it's been fun chatting with you about books and I hope you keep reading all your life. I am indebted to Alice Spector for reading quickly and for the best review I've ever received. Thank you, too, to everyone who has sent an illustration or written me about your love for Arden. I'm terrible at responding, but your words have sometimes been the only reason I can write mine.

Thank you to Gabriella and Matthias for still talking to me, and to my parents, Marguerite and Zoltan, for their listening ears and helping hands. Papa, I'd probably still be writing this book if not for you. Gratitude goes to Jelena, for igniting my imagination and doing her best to sleep through the night, and from the bottom of my heart, thank you to Andrej. This book wouldn't exist without you.